LOON POINT

LOON POINT

A Novel

CARRIE CLASSON

LAKE UNION
PUBLISHING

This is a work of fiction. Names, characters, organizations, places, events, and incidents are either products of the author's imagination or are used fictitiously. Otherwise, any resemblance to actual persons, living or dead, is purely coincidental.

Published by Lake Union Publishing, Seattle
www.apub.com

EU product safety contact:
Amazon Media EU S. à r.l.
38, avenue John F. Kennedy, L-1855 Luxembourg
amazonpublishing-gpsr@amazon.com

ISBN-13: 9781662530449 (paperback)
ISBN-13: 9781662530432 (digital)

Cover design by Ploy Siripant
Cover image: © Emily Anderson

Printed in the United States of America

This book is dedicated to my parents, Wayne and Jone Classon, who taught me to love the Northwoods and planted the crazy idea that I could do pretty much anything I set my mind to.

Chapter One

It was as quiet as it got at the Last Resort.

In the early spring, Norry would feel the silence and listen for the sound of her heart beating—briefly worried it was as frozen as the lake outside her door. After a decade in the city, Norry had assumed she needed to be surrounded by people. But now, in her mid-forties, she spent much of her time alone. Beneath the enormous Norway pines that shaded her log cabin, Norry's only neighbors were the white-tailed deer and the red squirrels and the occasional bear rousing from its intermittent slumbers to look for an early-spring snack.

Sometimes, as the temperatures changed, she would hear the ice creak and groan as it shifted uneasily beneath the heavy snow. Solitude would weigh heavily on her this time of year, and she would turn on Minnesota Public Radio just to hear a human voice.

"Winter storm warning!" the announcer said. Minnesota weather forecasters always tended toward the histrionic, but Norry had learned never to underestimate Minnesota weather. March was often the snowiest month of the year. If the storm tomorrow was as severe as they were predicting, there was no telling how long it would take Bud Gustafson to get her plowed out.

She jotted down a list on a Last Resort notepad, one of the old ones that only listed a seven-digit phone number. Then she grabbed her keys and her parka off the hook, threw the parka over her sweatshirt, slid into her SORELs, and jumped into the old Jeep with The Last Resort written on the side. Driving down the gravel road toward town, she saw a small figure headed her way. It was a young girl, walking in the center of the road, paying no attention. Norry slowed the Jeep to a stop.

"You headed somewhere?"

"Um . . . I'm going home. I live up ahead."

Norry knew there were no houses along this road but remembered there was a lone trailer off to the side that had been sitting empty for years. She had noticed a car parked there a few days ago. That must be where this little thing was headed. *Heck of a place to live,* Norry thought.

She looked at the girl. Her jacket was several sizes too big, and her jeans were filthy. She had her hands stuffed in her pockets, and her black, curly hair was sticking out in every direction. She was looking with interest at Norry's Jeep.

"What's the Last Resort?"

"It's my resort."

"Isn't that a bad thing?"

"The resort?"

"No, isn't it a bad thing—when you have no choice?"

"No. Well . . . yes, it can be. But not in this case. It's a nice resort. A lot of people choose it every year."

The girl didn't look as if she believed Norry.

"You should come by and see it sometime. It's just down the road."

The little girl seemed to be thinking this over.

"My name is Norry."

"I'm Lizzie."

"Do you need a ride?"

"No, I'm almost home."

"Okay, Lizzie."

Norry felt she should say something more. She couldn't think of anything. "You take care," she said.

Norry drove on. The girl seemed even smaller in the rearview mirror.

"People live in all kinds of ways." That's what her father would have said.

Norry's father had followed his seemingly predestined calling in the mid-1980s and bought the remote resort in northern Minnesota—eight log cabins built in the 1930s, including the family home. Recently widowed and still grieving, Ned Last had moved with his only child, Norry, to the unincorporated town of Loon Point. He'd planted a hand-painted wooden sign at the turnoff from County Road 6 when Norry was a child, and other than the once-a-decade repainting it was subjected to, the sign remained exactly as it was.

The Last Resort

"It's a ridiculous name," Norry had complained to her father as a teenager.

He'd looked at her, genuinely perplexed. "What else would we call it? That's our name."

When Norry's father had first bought the resort, there'd been several folks living up there in the woods—before the roads were plowed in the winter, before the mail delivery made it out that far. Most of them were older guys, although there was one woman who lived on her own. They went fishing, they dried and canned food, and somehow, they got by. Some folks went for the better part of a year without seeing a soul. Her dad had gotten to know most of them, stopping by from time to time to see that they were okay. He'd bring a jar of wild raspberry jam or some cookies and spend an hour chatting.

"People live in all kinds of ways, Norry," he'd say when he got home, and Norry had understood that people got to choose how they lived, by and large, and that these folks would never be happy living in town. But those people hadn't been kids. This was a lonely place for a kid. She took one last look behind her. The little girl was gone.

Norry shook her head. That old trailer was a piece of junk. It had been a piece of junk when her father was still alive and hadn't improved with age. Norry made a mental note to bake some cookies and drop them off at the trailer. That Lizzie looked like she could use a few cookies, and there wasn't much else to do this time of year. Every year, from early March until late spring, the resort was empty, except for Norry. By the time the first guests showed up, the lake would be open and the first spring flowers pushing through last autumn's leaves. Norry would watch the wildflowers bloom and fade. She would hear the loons call as they mated and guarded their nests, as they swam with chicks on their backs, and finally, as they flew away in the fall, leaving their adolescent offspring to fend for themselves on the long migration south. There would be a brief break in late autumn, before the ice was hard; then ice fishing would begin. It wasn't as busy in the winter, but there was usually someone in the little cabins until the ice got too thin to drive on. Then, for a time, she would have the place to herself again.

The seasonal pattern was comforting and routine, and Norry watched it all, wearing the same jeans and Last Resort sweatshirt, abiding by the seasons, year after year—only occasionally pausing to contemplate this life she never imagined she would have.

She had left the Last Resort in her twenties and moved to the city, certain she would never return for more than a visit. No one was more surprised than Norry when, after her father died, she decided to stay and run the resort.

The first thing she had planned to do was change the name to "the Loon Point Resort" until she discovered there already was a Loon Point Resort in Minnesota, and she couldn't deal with that kind of confusion. She briefly considered changing her own surname, just to avoid the embarrassment of being forever associated with a bad pun. But she had been Norry Last all her life—even through her brief and painful marriage—and she couldn't see changing it now.

Ultimately, she decided she didn't need to tell anyone her surname. Locals knew it, of course, but the joke was now nearly forty years old, and everyone had long ago run out of humorous variations—except for Bud Gustafson. Bud plowed the snow on the single-lane road that led to the Last Resort, and he never ran out of bad jokes.

"Hey! You're my Last customer today!"

"Give it a rest, Bud."

But he was the only one. And there was no reason for anyone to call her anything other than Norry. For days at a time, no one said her name at all. So that was how she thought of herself: "Norry No Last Name."

She didn't need anything more. She was fine, just as she was. Norry listened to the radio and sometimes felt that nothing—nothing but the music—connected her to another living soul.

~

Wendell had problems.

He sucked on his inhaler as he looked around his house, and what he saw wasn't good. Wendell had never imagined he'd still be living in the house he grew up in. He'd had big plans. He was going out west to Hollywood, and he was going to become a big-time screenwriter. Except he hadn't. He'd taken that job at the tool-and-die shop for a few years, and after that closed, he'd worked as a handyman at the mobile home court, and before he knew it, Wendell realized he wasn't going anywhere. When his mother got sick, he'd moved in to help her for a few years, and by the time she died, he was stuck in the little rambler in Loon Point that he swore he'd be out of by the time he was eighteen. Wendell was now seventy-two.

Wendell still thought about the movies. He still thought about hanging out with the starlets and seeing his name on the big screen. He would have been great; he knew that. If he'd done it, he would have been the best. He'd just never made the move. The time had never been right. Hollywood had beckoned, but Wendell never made it out to California. He stayed in northern Minnesota, and the farthest west he'd ever got was to Wyoming on a summer vacation with his mother.

Wendell spent a lot of time imagining what might have been, if things had worked out differently. He had more talent than ten of those so-called genius writers working in Hollywood, that was for sure. The dreck they churned out! They had no artistry, no style, no class. They were just trying to appeal to the lowest common denominator. Wendell shook his head. Thinking about those bums in Hollywood always got him worked up. He needed his inhaler.

But today, he had something other than the dire state of Hollywood to distract him. Today, Wendell had bigger concerns. The guest bedroom ceiling had a leak.

He called it the "guest bedroom" because that's what his mother had called it. But that was a long time ago. He had no idea how long it had been leaking, because he couldn't remember when he'd last looked in there. He tried to think what was in that room. There were a lot of books. And boxes of his mother's craft supplies. A bunch of recyclables he had meant to take to the Eco Station. A busted microwave. Some patio furniture and garden tools. The guest bed might still be in there—he wasn't entirely sure. It wasn't possible to get far into the room anymore. There was too much stuff.

What he knew for sure was that he heard water dripping. This was a bad situation. Wendell could not have his stuff ruined by water. He wasn't sure what was being destroyed right now, but he knew it wasn't anything he wanted to lose. His screenplays were there, for sure. He hadn't seen them in a while, but they were there, in a box somewhere, and that box might be getting wet. The idea made Wendell very anxious.

Wendell sucked his teeth. He was missing a tooth. Well, he was missing a couple, but the one in front bothered him. He'd always thought he had a great smile. He'd had a Hollywood smile. That missing tooth bothered him. And now this.

Wendell leaned into the guest bedroom and listened. He heard more dripping. Then he closed the door.

~

It didn't seem like things were getting better with Mom.

Every day, when Lizzie got home from school, she'd hold her breath when she walked into the trailer, hoping Mom was still there, hoping she wasn't dead, hoping maybe she was better. But Mom didn't seem to be getting any better. Since they'd moved, almost a month ago, the bus had let Lizzie off in Loon Point, near a bright-colored sign that said **The Last Resort**. A single-lane road led to their little trailer, sitting alone in the woods. She hadn't known the Last Resort was a real place until she saw the woman in the Jeep.

Lizzie walked down the gravel road, making a deal with God.

"Here's the deal, God," Lizzie began, hitching up her backpack. "If you'll make Mom better, I'll never leave my clothes on the floor. And I'll do the dishes right away after supper—before they get sticky. And I'll be nice to Jodie Johansson—even when she says horrible things."

The last bit, about Jodie Johansson, was asking a lot. Lizzie waited a moment for God to realize what a major concession she had made.

Jodie was in the fifth grade, two years older than Lizzie, and today she'd called Lizzie "Last Resort Loony Lezbo Lizzie," which was a lot to ignore and made all the kids on the bus laugh. Lizzie didn't know why Jodie had to pick on her when there were plenty of kids her own age she could torment. But Jodie had a captive audience on the bus and was upping her game every day. The bus driver had told Jodie to stop. But he was hard of hearing, and Jodie sat in the way back of the bus. When he heard all the kids laughing, Lizzie caught his face in the rearview mirror, and she realized he thought everyone was having a good time, and he was happy. Lizzie hated to make him unhappy. So she sat as far up in the front of the bus as she could and thought of mean things she could do to Jodie—if she ever got the chance. So far, all she'd managed to do was sneak some chewed-up gum into Jodie's long blond hair and put a dead frog she'd found flattened on the road into the pocket of Jodie's new backpack. Lizzie had heard Jodie scream when she went looking for her phone. It had been hard not to smile. But Lizzie would give it up if Mom got better.

"I need some help here, God," Lizzie finished. Then she remembered to say "Amen." Amen was like hitting the Send button to make sure a request made it to its destination.

Lizzie could see the trailer down the road, her mom's rusted car parked beside it. She hitched her backpack to a more comfortable position. She'd checked out all the school library books that would fit in her pack. There were three big books, covered in shiny plastic, and she was thinking about those books now, the next three in the series she'd just started. She was doing everything she could to stop worrying about Mom—and so she didn't notice she was being followed.

Lizzie knew there were bear in the woods. They were hungry in the spring, and they had cubs. Last year her second-grade teacher, Mr. Benson, taught them all about the animals in northern Minnesota. He told the kids in her class they should keep their eyes open for black bear and give them lots of space if they saw one—especially in the early spring.

"They're unpredictable with cubs. Don't take any chances!" Mr. Benson had said.

Mr. Benson said people had been attacked by black bear. It didn't happen often, he said, but it did happen. Since they'd moved to the little trailer in the woods, Lizzie had been on the lookout for bears. So far, she'd only seen deer. But right after the Jeep from the Last Resort drove off, Lizzie heard something.

She whipped around. It wasn't a bear.

It was a dog. It was just about the ugliest dog Lizzie had ever seen.

Its fur was the same color as the gravel road. It was super skinny, and it had scabby things on its face and sides. One ear was almost straight up, but the other ear was bent over, and the dog had eyes the color of butterscotch candy. When she stopped to look back, it stopped and looked straight into her eyes.

"Who are you?"

The dog tipped its head to the side.

"What do you want?"

The dog looked off to the side as if considering this, then looked back at Lizzie.

"I've got nothing. I'm not even sure I've got a mom right now. I sure don't have any dog treats, if that's what you're looking for."

At the word *treats*, the dog sat, waiting for a treat.

"No. You don't get it, do you? I live in a trailer, and my mom is . . . well, she's not great right now, and you can't follow me home. I don't have anything to give you."

Lizzie squatted so she could look more closely at the dog. It had no collar. Its teeth looked like baby teeth. Right now, it was smiling at her as if they shared a secret.

Lizzie stood. "Go away!"

The dog cocked its head again.

"You heard me—go! Get! Go home!"

The dog stood and backed up a few steps.

"Go!" Lizzie said with more force. The dog lowered its head. It started down the road. Then it turned back to look at Lizzie. Lizzie felt her chest tighten up.

"Go! Go away!"

The dog turned away and headed down the gravel road. Lizzie could see its hip bones were sticking out in back and its tail was filled with burs.

Lizzie bit her lip. She watched as the dog kept walking.

Then she turned and headed down the road toward the trailer. When she got to the metal steps, she felt her heart beating a little harder. She opened the door.

"Mom?"

Silence.

"Mom?"

Lizzie saw the dishes from last night's dinner in the sink. She saw the laundry basket was still full of dirty clothes and was sitting in the living room. She carefully pushed open her mom's bedroom door. There was a mom-shaped lump in the bed.

"Mom?"

Lizzie glanced at the table next to the bed. There was a small baggie of pills on the table. She went to the side of the bed. When she saw her mom's chest rise and fall, Lizzie exhaled. She realized she'd been holding her breath since she'd walked in the door.

She walked back into the living room, which was also the dining room and her bedroom. Mom said the trailer was temporary. They were only staying here because they'd had to leave their old house, and Mom said the only place she could find was this trailer in Loon Point.

Lizzie was hungry. She looked in the cupboard. Mom hadn't been to the store in a while. There were crackers. There was some cheese in the fridge, but it had green on it. Lizzie cut the green off and sat on the couch, which doubled as her bed, and ate crackers and cheese. It was getting dark. Maybe Mom would wake up and they would get a pizza.

She opened her new library book. It wasn't new, Lizzie saw. It had been checked out a lot. The pages had rough edges, and the paper felt soft. She spent a moment just feeling the edges of the paper and the shiny plastic cover. Sometimes she thought this was the best part of reading. The worst was when she turned the page and saw there weren't any more.

She glanced at the laundry basket. Mom hadn't been to the laundromat, so Lizzie would have to wear something stupid tomorrow, something that looked dorky or didn't fit. That would give Jodie something new to talk about. There was nothing else clean left in her closet, which was also the coat closet. She turned on the little light that was built into the wall over her bed. She opened her library book. *Chapter One.* Lizzie heard a noise coming from her mom's bedroom.

"Mom?"

Mom went into the bathroom. Lizzie heard her coughing. She heard the toilet flush. She came out of the bathroom.

"Mom? I got a new book. And I saw a dog on the way home."

Mom didn't say anything. She was walking funny. Finally she said, "I gotta sleep now, okay? I'm not feeling great."

"Okay. Will we have dinner?"

"Just . . . Can you just get yourself a snack?"

They used to have snacks after school. They used to sit at the green wooden table in their old house, and Mom would want to know all about how school was and what the teacher said, and she'd take Lizzie's art or her test, if she'd gotten a nice comment on it, and put it on the fridge. Lizzie looked at the fridge. There was nothing on it except the number for the only pizza place that would deliver all the way to Loon Point.

"Okay."

Mom went back to bed. Lizzie bit her lip. Everything was okay. Everything was going to be okay.

Chapter Two

Wendell noticed the problem had spread.

The living room ceiling now had a big black stain. He hadn't seen any actual water dripping, but it looked as if the ceiling had a substantial sag in it. He peered into the dark space. He couldn't get real close, because there were a lot of cardboard boxes stacked over there. And some computer equipment he needed to repair. A rear-taillight assembly. A lot of books. Some clothing of his mother's. A bunch of Christmas decorations and a Christmas tree. There had been a lamp over in the corner—maybe there still was. Wendell wasn't sure. Anyway, it was hard to see what was going on, but it appeared the ceiling was several inches lower in the corner than it should be. Wendell was becoming alarmed.

He walked from the living room to the bathroom. He turned on the light.

Shit.

Wendell spent as little time looking at the bathroom as possible. He ought to clean it, but nobody came into the bathroom but him, so what did it matter? He couldn't remember the last time he looked up at the ceiling, but now that he did, he saw the problem was worse than he had feared. The bathroom ceiling was dark. Okay, it was mostly black. And fuzzy. That couldn't be good.

Wendell realized it was possible the house was falling in around him.

"Well, let it!" he said aloud.

His voice sounded strange. Wendell went for days without talking to anyone, and sometimes, when he talked to himself, his voice sounded like a stranger's. He'd always thought he had a good voice. He had a voice for radio. It was one of the things that had always held him back. He had this magnificent voice, and he also had all these terrific story ideas. Which should he pursue? Should he offer up his vocal talents to one of the networks? Or should he send one of his scripts to a big studio? If he did one thing, he might not be able to do the other. Wendell used to spend entire afternoons agonizing over his options while pumping out the septic tank at the mobile home park.

If he'd worked for radio, he'd have ended up hawking worthless products and shilling for pharmaceutical companies, and his talents would have been wasted. Then, as he'd seen the bilge being produced by the movie companies, he'd had a premonition that his script would fall into the wrong hands and he would lose all artistic control. They would cast the wrong leading lady, for sure. They would mess with the ending and try to create a clichéd Hollywood story out of his utterly original and unique work. The thought of it had made him mad. Screw them.

Time passed, and Wendell got older. His asthma had gotten worse. Some tenants at the mobile home park had lodged complaints. They said he wasn't doing his job. The management figured they could do better by hiring some Mexican who couldn't even speak English. Fine. Screw them. He'd showed them. He'd quit and started on social security the day he turned sixty-two.

His monthly check wasn't a lot of money. And his mom's account had been pretty well cleaned out by the time she was buried. Those robbers at the funeral home had wanted a fortune for the funeral. Then he owed taxes. Minnesota property taxes were over the moon. Crazy was what it was. He was already a little behind on the bills. And now this—whatever it was—going on with the roof.

Wendell sucked his teeth. Nothing to be done. Nothing to be done about this today. This was just the sort of thing that always happened to him. Wendell had the worst luck of anyone he knew. He always had.

~

The morning came, the sky was dark, and Mom was still asleep.

Lizzie surveyed the contents of her closet and realized, no matter what she picked, she was just serving herself up to Jodie on a platter. There was a plaid skirt that looked like something out of an ancient television show Mom might have watched as a kid. There was a red dress she had worn the last time they went to church at Christmas. There were what she thought of as her good jeans, which had a big rip in the back, and she couldn't wear until Mom fixed them, because her underwear would show. And there were her bad jeans, which she'd worn until they were way too dirty. The melting snow was muddy, and the walk to and from the bus every day had stained them almost to her knees.

Finally, Lizzie found a pair of brown corduroys that looked clean. She put them on. She found a sweater she hadn't worn all winter because it was like a little kid's sweater, with Raggedy Ann on the front—which was bad enough—but one of Ann's eyes had gone missing sometime in November, and now she looked like she needed an eye patch. Mom had said she was going to find two matching buttons and fix it. Mom said a lot of things like that.

Lizzie pulled up the brown corduroys. They still fit on top. Lizzie was pretty skinny. But they were way too short. She tried to pull them down a little so the cuffs wouldn't be way above the top of her feet. She only managed to move them an inch or so, and it was hard to walk with them pulled down, but she thought she'd try, at least while she was getting on and off the bus. The sweater was clean. Raggedy Ann still looked like she'd had her eye shot out, but other than that it was okay. Lizzie put on her shoes and noticed they were getting tight. But they were okay. She was okay for another day. She left the library books on the couch that was her bed.

"Mom?"

"What is it?"

"It's time to catch the bus. I don't have many clean clothes."

There was silence behind Mom's door.

"I mean, I'm okay. I'm wearing my brown cords, but they're kinda short, and the Raggedy Ann sweater, but she's missing an eye."

"I'm going to fix that."

"Yeah. I know. But I couldn't find anything else to wear today."

There was a sigh on the other side of the door. Lizzie felt bad. She knew her mom was upset. "Fine. Wear it. It just looks a little funny, that's all."

"I know, but . . ." Lizzie didn't want to push it. Mom was awake and talking. Lizzie ate the last of the Cheerios. The milk tasted funny. "I gotta go now, Mom!"

"Have a good day, kiddo. I might run some errands today."

Lizzie thought that sounded promising. "The dirty clothes are all in the basket."

"Okay." Mom didn't sound excited about going to the laundromat.

"And we're out of Cheerios."

Silence.

"And I'll need more money for lunch tickets pretty soon."

"Fine."

Lizzie poured the last of the milk from her bowl down the drain. Mom would say that was wasteful, but the milk tasted weird. Lizzie remembered she was supposed to brush her teeth. She went into the bathroom and saw herself in the mirror. She'd forgotten to comb her hair again. Her dark hair was always curly, but today it was sticking out in all directions. Lizzie took a brush to it and got the front to look better, but she discovered there were knots in the back the brush wouldn't go through.

Too late. Gotta go.

Lizzie had a perfect attendance record. She got a special award last spring for not missing a single day of second grade, and she had only two months to go before she'd get it again this year. A couple of days last November—about the time Raggedy Ann lost her eye—Lizzie had been kind of sick. But Mom had been acting scary then. She'd stayed in bed for two whole days, and when she'd talked to Lizzie, she hadn't made sense. So Lizzie had gone to school even though she hadn't felt good. She liked school. It was the bus ride that was trouble.

She put on her down coat, her mittens still stuffed in the pockets. At the last minute, she grabbed a stocking cap. It might cover up whatever was going on in the back of her hair.

"Love you, Mom!"

Lizzie's mom used to say "Love you to the moon and back!" every day when she went to school. But that was back when they lived in town. Before Mom got so bad.

Lizzie stood with the door open, waiting to hear if her mom would say anything. There was no sound. She closed the door and headed down the gravel road toward County Road 6.

Late March was not a great time in northern Minnesota. They got a lot of snow, and then it would melt, and everything was muddy. The skies were gray most days. All the sparkle from the snow and ice was gone, and it would be a long time before the last of the snow disappeared and anything would grow again.

This year they'd gotten more snow than usual. There were still a couple of feet on top of the trailer roof. Yesterday it had gotten all warm and slushy, but today the slush had frozen, and it looked like more snow was coming. It was not a cheerful time of year, Lizzie thought, as she saw the yellow bus rounding the corner. She braced herself as she climbed the school bus steps.

"Oh, my God! Lezbo Lizzie's gone gangsta on us!" Jodie Johansson said the moment Lizzie got on the bus.

Lizzie figured it was the addition of the stocking cap.

"No, wait, it's a gangsta in high-waters!" Jodie crowed, pointing at Lizzie's ankles. "Loony Lizzie, are those supposed to be jeans or shorts? Or is that just what all the lesbos are wearing now?"

Jodie's two friends laughed, and all the boys looked at her ankles. Lizzie tucked her chin under her coat collar. It could have been worse. At least they couldn't see Raggedy Ann. Then, thankfully, Jodie got distracted laughing with her friends about somebody else, and Lizzie looked out the window, trying to be as small as she could.

The bus picked up speed, heading into town. Lizzie wondered if her mom was really going to run some errands. That would be good. Maybe they'd have a real dinner tonight, and she'd have less embarrassing clothes to wear to school on Monday.

And Lizzie wondered if her mom was ever going to get better. She was better, sometimes. Sometimes she seemed like her old self. She'd invite Lizzie to watch a movie with her, and they'd make popcorn. Mom would ask about school. Lizzie had always been good at school, and Mom called her a "beautiful brainiac," whatever that was. But things were not getting better. Lizzie could see that.

Mom would take pills, and she would get really spacy and either watch TV all night long or sleep. She'd forget Lizzie had school. She'd forget what day of the week it was. Lizzie knew she wasn't going to her job at the supermarket anymore. That had ended for good at least two weeks ago and was part of the reason they didn't have a lot of food around. There was only one big supermarket in town, and Mom said she didn't want to see those "assholes." *Asshole* was a bad word. Mom didn't used to say bad words. But Lizzie's mom didn't used to do a lot of things.

Lizzie was afraid her mom was in trouble. She bit her lip. She was glad she was going to school. They were learning about the Anishinaabe people, who had lived right where the town of Big Pine was now, hundreds of years ago. Lizzie was giving a report about them, and she was also writing a poem for extra credit. The poem was about all the animals that were around hundreds of years ago and what they meant to the people long ago. It was turning into a long poem, and Lizzie knew her teacher was going to like it. The poem was about the bear and the loons and the wolves and the deer. Thinking back about that time gave Lizzie a nice feeling. It was like reading her big books from the library. It took her somewhere else, to a different time, where things were better.

The bus pulled up to Big Pine Elementary School, a small brick building just off Main Street.

"Have a fabulous day, Loony Lesbo Lizzie!" Jodie said with a grand gesture.

Lizzie remembered her promise to God. God didn't seem to be paying much attention, but Lizzie thought she'd keep trying. Maybe God was impressed with people who didn't give up.

"Thanks, Jodie," she said.

After school, Lizzie felt the familiar tightening in her gut.

The bus ride home had been as bad as usual. Someone had reported to Jodie about the sweater Lizzie was wearing, and Jodie thought the one-eyed Raggedy Ann was hysterical. Lizzie stayed hunched up in the front row of the bus, trying not to listen as they got closer to the bright-colored sign where she could get off.

Now she was walking down the gravel road again. It was snowing, and she could see Mom's car was gone.

Mom had said she was going to run errands. Maybe she'd gone to get dinner or do some laundry. The trailer looked dark. Lizzie opened the front door. The laundry basket was still sitting in the living room. There was a twenty-dollar bill lying on a piece of paper on the table. *LUNCH MONEY* the paper said.

Lizzie turned on the light over her bed, which was also the couch. She read her book until it was almost dark. She was hungry.

Lizzie looked around the kitchen. She'd finished off the Cheerios this morning and the crackers last night. She looked up in the cupboards. There was a carton of oatmeal. Lizzie took it down, got out a pot from below the sink, and read the instructions on the oatmeal carton.

Boil water or milk and salt. Milk sounded good. There was still some milk, but by now it smelled really bad. She looked in the cupboard and found a box of powdered milk, but it only told how to make a quart. Lizzie poured a bunch of powdered milk into the water and stirred. Most of the powder had dissolved before the water started to bubble.

Stir in oats. They didn't have any measuring cups, but Lizzie measured out the oats in one of Mom's coffee cups.

Cook about 5 minutes over medium heat; stir occasionally. Lizzie stood over the pot and stirred. It was getting hard to stir because it was super thick and was sticking to the bottom, but she watched the clock over the sink until it had been "about five minutes." Then she turned the heat off. The mixture in the pot was very thick. As it cooled, it became solid. Lizzie tasted it. It needed sugar.

She was hunting through the cupboard, looking for sugar, when she heard a sound at the door.

"Mom?"

She was surprised how excited she was. Of course Mom was coming back. She was just late. Lizzie looked out the window. There was no car. No Mom.

She heard the sound again. Lizzie opened the door. Standing with its paws on the stoop was the dog. The same dog as yesterday. There was a small pile of snow on its head.

"What do you want?"

The dog looked up at Lizzie. She saw it was really thin.

"All I've got is oatmeal."

The dog tipped its head to the side, as if considering the menu.

"I don't know if dogs like oatmeal."

The dog leaned in closer. It nudged her leg. Lizzie felt her chest tighten again.

She'd always wanted a dog. Mom had said they could maybe get a puppy in the spring. "Then you'll have time to train it," Mom had said. But that was last fall, back when they still lived in town and things were better. Lizzie hadn't asked about a dog in a long time.

She saw the snow was coming down harder, and it was getting colder.

"Come on in."

The dog came into the trailer and immediately shook the wet snow off its back. It sniffed the house, as if making an inspection, walking from the living room to the bathroom to Lizzie's mom's room and back again. Then it looked up expectantly at Lizzie.

Lizzie got three bowls out of the dish drainer. She filled one with water and gave it to the dog. The dog drank and drank. She put oatmeal in the other two. She found a bag of brown sugar in the cabinet. It was hard, but she chopped off a piece and put it in one of the bowls. The dog watched intently.

"Dogs shouldn't eat sugar," Lizzie explained.

"Now we gotta wait till it's cool." The dog licked its lips and sat down.

As she waited for the oatmeal to cool, she noticed the trailer was getting colder too. She went to the thermostat. It was set to seventy degrees. Mom complained the trailer was not very well insulated. It was never as warm as the thermostat said. Lizzie turned it up to seventy-two. She waited for the familiar sound of the furnace kicking in. Nothing happened.

Lizzie wrapped herself in a blanket and ate her oatmeal. The oatmeal was solid, but it was good. The dog liked it, too, and ate it in one piece, then jumped up on the couch and nestled into the blankets.

"You're kind of dirty."

The dog heaved a sigh.

"Yeah, I'm kind of dirty too." Lizzie remembered she hadn't taken a shower in a while. She didn't remember exactly how long.

She finished her oatmeal, still waiting for the furnace to come on, but the trailer felt even colder now. She went over and turned it all the way up to eighty degrees. Nothing. Lizzie put her down coat on and sat next to the dog. It was getting darker, and the snow was coming down for real.

Lizzie took the two bowls and washed them before they got sticky—just like she'd promised God she would. Then she went back to the couch that was her bed, pulled the blanket around herself and the dog, and waited.

Chapter Three

"Well, this is shaping up to be worse than predicted," Norry said to the radio.

Norry was looking out over the lake from her kitchen window and listening to the worsening storm forecast. She could see nothing but the snow hitting her window and, beyond that, a sea of white. Bud Gustafson had called just as the snow started to come down hard.

"Can I get you anything?" he'd asked.

"Thanks, I'm good."

"You sure? I could make you my Last stop!" Bud laughed, as he always did.

Norry didn't respond. She'd known Bud most all her life, and he was never going to stop with the jokes.

She was putting in the last pan of oatmeal cookies and thinking about that little girl in the trailer. That trailer was a mess. Sad. The whole thing was sad, Norry thought as she pulled the pan out of the oven and rotated it 180 degrees. The oven was always a lot hotter in the back than the front.

She had a good mind to call her friend Virgie and tell her someone had moved in to that wreck of a trailer. Virgie would know the one she was talking about. But Virgie was in Mexico now, and she'd just give Norry an earful about how she needed to get on an airplane and come on down. Norry had no intention of going to Mexico.

"You need to come down and join me!" Virgie said every time Norry called.

"I've got business in the winter. I have a resort full of ice fishermen and snowmobilers."

Virgie owned the gift shop in Loon Point. She spent the winters in Mexico and made jewelry while she was down there. She'd show up in June with a tan and a pile of beaded bracelets and earrings and necklaces she'd made. Norry wasn't a jewelry person, but it was popular with the tourists.

"Well, come after the ice is soft. Come on down in late March or early April before anyone shows up at the resort. We'd have a blast."

Norry didn't have a good reason not to go. It was the time of year when Norry got the cabins spruced up. She'd get new towels, inventory all the kitchenettes to make sure they had a full set of dishes, inspect all the sheets for rips and blankets for stains, and put in an order for whatever was needed. But it didn't take her two months to get the cabins in shape for the summer. She just felt this odd reluctance to go anywhere. Even a trip into town was becoming a struggle. She found herself planning a week in advance and then buying enough in Big Pine to get her through several weeks, just to avoid leaving the resort. The idea of driving all the way to the airport, transferring planes in the Twin Cities, flying to Texas to change planes again, then flying to Mexico sounded awful.

Then, when she got there, she knew she'd be fretting every moment about the resort. Bear came out this time of year. They were hungry, and there was no telling what sort of mischief they'd get into. Sometimes the heavy snow caused big branches to fall in the spring, and Norry had to be on top of that. One spring, a couple of years ago, she'd had a good-sized birch tree land right on her house. She hadn't even thought it was completely dead, and it fell smack onto her cabin. She was glad she'd been around to deal with that.

No, there was no telling what could happen if she took off to Mexico. Virgie didn't have these kinds of concerns, with her little house and shop in Loon Point. She could drain the pipes, turn the key, and walk away. Norry took the last pan of cookies out of the oven and realized she was getting to be more and more like her dad.

Ned Last never left the resort toward the end of his life. "Don't you want to take a trip, Dad?" she had asked. "You never got away once, in all the years you ran this place. Isn't there someplace you'd like to go?" And Ned had looked at her as if she'd suggested he board a rocket headed to the moon.

"Norry! This is the place everyone wants to be. Folks spend all year waiting for the one week of the year they get to spend at the Last Resort."

"Well, yes, but they don't live here fifty-two weeks of the year."

"I know that, Norry. That is why I am so grateful. I will never take my good fortune for granted."

He couldn't even be talked into going to the doctor's office for his annual physical or the dentist for a cleaning. "My teeth are fine," he'd insist. "And what's a doctor going to tell me? That there's something wrong with me and I need to spend time in a hospital? A hospital would kill me in record time. No sirree. I'll stay right here and, when my time comes, I'll be right where I want to be."

And, as it turned out, her father was right. He'd had a heart attack in his sleep, and Norry found him in the morning with his hands folded on his chest and—she might have been imagining it, but she didn't think so—a trace of a smile on his face. It was the look he always gave her when he knew he'd been right all along.

She'd taken over the day-to-day operations of the resort by then. Her marriage had ended, and she'd come back to Loon Point, after swearing she could never live there again, and found herself stepping into the role her father thought she'd take on all along.

When she'd arrived to help her dad, she had assumed she would put the resort up for sale as soon as he passed. But by the time he died, she had settled into her life at the Last Resort. She was proud the business was doing better than ever. She found herself enjoying the brief, hectic summer and the slower snowmobiling season in the winter. She became keenly aware of the seasons in the way she had as a child, when the changing of the leaves and the ice forming on the lake were the most momentous occurrences in her life.

No, there had been no talking to her dad about leaving. And now she understood how he must have felt.

Norry slid the cookies off the pan and onto the paper grocery bag she'd cut open and laid flat on the counter. She had more than four dozen oatmeal cookies, and she was going to bring some to that trailer as soon as Bud Gustafson showed up in his big red truck and got her plowed out. She wanted to see what was going on down there.

"People live in all kinds of ways," her dad would have said.

"But some of them are better than others," Norry amended. And her dad wasn't there to correct her.

~

The good news was the dripping had stopped. Wendell stood in the doorway of the guest room and listened. He heard no more water, and he thought this was a good sign. He checked the thermometer. It was well below freezing and getting colder.

The bad news was that more snow was falling. The weather would warm again, and when it did, there would be more snow melting on top of his roof. But that was a problem for tomorrow. Wendell hadn't gotten where he was by wasting time worrying about tomorrow.

He was watching the news, and they were saying this storm could turn into something serious. Of course, the nearest town, Big Pine, was the only thing they reported on, and that was almost twenty miles away. A lot could happen in twenty miles, but the forecasters never seemed too worried about what would happen in Loon Point.

It just showed the indifference of the media. Every time he saw one of those phony-baloney weather guys on television, he was relieved he had not gone into broadcasting. Big Pine had the big bucks. It was a town of nearly five thousand people, so naturally the media would cater to them—folks who could pay for their news. Loon Point had fewer than one hundred full-time residents and nobody cared who lived or died in Loon Point. Wendell shook his head. They were a bunch of scoundrels, all of them.

Still, as he watched the ominous cloud of heavy snow working its way across the weather map, Wendell could see that Loon Point would be in the center of it, and he again had an uneasy feeling about his roof.

It shouldn't be letting in water, that was for damned sure. He wasn't sure when his mom had last replaced the roof, but it was now clear she had been ripped off. Wendell grew angry just thinking about it and reached for his inhaler. Bunch of stupid, overpaid contractors had cheated his mom—that's what he figured. What's an old woman gonna know about roofing, right? Although, as he thought about it now, he realized she might not have been all that old when the rambler was reroofed.

Still, she was a woman, and women were always getting taken advantage of by contractors. They had obviously done it on the cheap, and he was sure she'd paid top dollar for a new roof that was now—a few short decades later—leaking all over his valuable stuff. What would a contractor care about Wendell's scripts? Nothing, that's what.

Of course, if some "important" person lost their irreplaceable manuscripts, they'd have the FBI out investigating. But no one gave a good goddamn about him, because he was in Loon Point, not New York or Los Angeles. The whole thing made him so angry he had to sit down. Except he was already.

Wendell took another look out the window. The snow was coming down hard now. He wouldn't be able to get the car out for a while, by the looks of it. That was okay. He'd call up the grocery store in Big Pine and get them to deliver. Let some kid in his dad's overpriced SUV deal with the snow. Spoiled kids. Wendell had never had some hundred-thousand-dollar car to go zipping around in when he was a kid, that was for sure. Of course, he'd get hit with a big delivery charge. It was unfair, but life was unfair. What were you gonna do?

He figured he should probably go to bed.

Wendell headed off to his bedroom. He'd long ago given up the idea of changing into different clothes to sleep in. Who invented that stupid idea? Clothes were clothes. He also had stopped worrying about sheets and pillowcases and baloney like that. What were they for, anyway? Nothing, as far as he could see. People wanted to make money—that's what he figured. They made big bucks selling people on the idea they needed special clothes for sleeping in and fancy sheets on the bed, when all anybody needed was a couple of good blankets. Dumb. Wendell was glad he was able to see how dumb it was.

Besides, it would be hard to "make the bed," as his mother used to say, because there was a lot of stuff all around it. Some of it wasn't important stuff, but a lot of it was—books and magazines and newspapers and mail he hadn't opened yet. He couldn't walk around the bed if he had to. But he didn't have to—so there!

Wendell climbed over the stack of magazines on the accessible side of the bed. He should probably move those. One of these nights, he was going to trip on the way to the bathroom and bust his head open. That would be just great.

He knew if he busted his head open, no one would care. The thought quieted his anger for a moment. It was the truth. It was the simple goddamned truth. He could die tonight, on his way to the bathroom, and not one single person would give a shit.

Wendell lay awake for a long time after that.

~

Lizzie was not sleeping. It was too cold.

Instead, she talked to the dog. The dog was a boy, she determined. She knew about things like that. She decided the dog needed a name. She couldn't keep saying "Hey" every time she wanted to talk to him.

"What's your name?"

The dog gave the dog equivalent of a shrug. He was cold, Lizzie could tell. He had burrowed into the blanket and was pressed up next to her. Lizzie thought of all the dog names she knew. Most of them were named after characters in movies. She didn't think she should name the dog after a hero in a movie. They weren't real, and they weren't really heroes. Lizzie tried to think of who she admired.

"Mr. Benson."

Mr. Benson had been her second-grade teacher, and he taught all about the Northwoods. He taught the class about bear and white-tailed deer and loons. Lizzie especially liked learning about the loons—and that was before she even moved to Loon Point. That was when she was living in the house in Big Pine. Loons could dive 250 feet down into the water and stay below the surface for more than ten minutes. This was because they had solid bones. Most birds had hollow bones, Mr. Benson had told them. But loons could still fly, even with their solid bones.

Lizzie thought back on all the things Mr. Benson had taught her and decided Mr. Benson was her hero.

"I'm going to call you Mr. Benson. Okay?"

The dog lifted his head.

"Is that okay, Mr. Benson?"

Mr. Benson nuzzled her hand. It seemed to be okay.

Lizzie looked out the window. She could feel the cold air coming in at the edges, and she could see the snow had started to fall faster. No sign of Mom's car. No headlights coming. Lizzie was worried. She was worried about her mom, and she was worried about the cold.

"It could get really cold tonight."

Lizzie went to the closet. Her boots were too small, and they didn't keep her feet warm. She saw her mom's winter boots were there. That meant Mom didn't have her boots on when she left. Lizzie wondered where her mom was. She'd probably come home soon, but when? What if she couldn't get home in the snow? Mom wouldn't know the furnace was off. Lizzie thought about all this as she stared into the closet.

"I don't think we can stay here, Mr. Benson."

Lizzie tried on her mom's boots. They were way too big. She went over to the laundry basket and fished out three pairs of socks, and by the time she had the third pair on, the boots fit well enough. Lizzie put on a down vest, under her parka, and put on what Jodie called her "gangsta" hat. She went over to the table where the piece of paper that said *LUNCH MONEY* was still lying.

Lizzie bit the end of the pen as she thought. Where could she go? In Big Pine, it would be easy. She'd go across the street and tell the neighbor the heat had gone out. She'd tell them her mom's phone number, and they'd call, and then everything would be okay. Lizzie didn't have a phone, and she didn't have a neighbor. Or maybe she did.

Lizzie wrote *GONE TO THE LAST RESORT* at the bottom of the paper.

Then she and Mr. Benson headed out into the snow. There were already a few inches of snow on the road by the time they left the trailer, and it was coming down hard. Lizzie was cold, and there was a stiff wind. She wondered if Mr. Benson would stay with her. She didn't have a leash and Mr. Benson didn't have a collar, but the dog didn't seem interested in leaving her side. They marched down the road in the opposite direction from where Lizzie met the school bus. Lizzie didn't see any houses. She didn't see any lights. She hoped they were headed to the Last Resort.

It had to be getting late. There had been no sign of Mom, and Mom was always home by now. Well, not always, but usually. A couple of times, Mom had been gone all night when they still lived in town. She'd gotten home in the late morning, and her eyes were all glassy and she'd apologized and gone right to bed. Those were the first of the bad days, when Mom was still going to work but not as often. Since they'd been in the trailer, Mom hardly left except to get a few groceries. She was in bed most of the time. Back in town, she'd stay up all night watching television, but there was no signal in Loon Point, Mom said, so she just went to bed. She didn't read. Lizzie didn't know what she did.

Lizzie didn't like to think bad things about Mom, but she knew she was doing drugs. She'd heard about people doing drugs, and it had taken a while to connect that idea to her mom, but now she knew it was true. Only once had Lizzie asked, "Are you getting high?" Because that's what the kids on the bus said about the high school kids who hung out behind the grocery store. They were getting high.

Mom had gotten mad. "I've got serious pain, Lizzie! I threw out my back in that damned store, and they made me work anyway."

That was a long time ago. Lizzie had just started second grade when Mom threw out her back. But it still hurt, her mom said, and the doctors weren't going to do anything for her. Mom was mad at the doctors and mad at the grocery store, and Lizzie didn't want her mom to be mad at her, so she never asked her about the baggies by her bedside again.

"I'm getting better, kiddo," Mom said. But Mom didn't seem any better.

The wind hit Lizzie full in the face. As the snow got deeper, the walking got harder. Lizzie could no longer see the road, but she was following the space between the trees where the road must be. Mr. Benson was having trouble walking, too, and he was following in her footsteps now, hopping from one step to the next.

Lizzie was tired. On either side of the road, she could make out the shapes of trees, but there was no track, and the snow was almost to the top of her mom's boots. It was cold. Lizzie stopped. Her legs felt so heavy, and she didn't know where she was going. She thought the Last Resort would be just a little way ahead, but it felt like they'd been walking a long time, and there were still no lights and it seemed like the road went on and on. Lizzie looked back at the trailer, but she could no longer see the light she'd left on. And now it was really dark.

Lizzie sat down in the snow. She felt like going to sleep. She was sleepy and sad, and she now wondered if the Last Resort even existed. Now that she thought about it, the Last Resort sounded like a made-up place. It sounded like a fairy tale. Lizzie was staring into space, and she felt the cold creeping over her and her eyelids start to close.

That's when Mr. Benson barked.

Lizzie looked at him. He was looking straight at her with his butterscotch-colored eyes. His fur was matted with snow, and he was shaking. She hadn't heard him bark before. She'd never heard him make a sound.

He barked again, twice—louder this time.

"Okay. Okay, Mr. Benson. You're right. The trailer is cold, and it's a long way away. We gotta get to the Last Resort."

Lizzie got up from the snow with an effort. She pulled her cap down lower on her forehead. Then she and Mr. Benson headed down the road again.

Chapter Four

Wendell had just fallen asleep when he woke to a shrieking noise.

What the hell?

Wendell lay motionless in bed. He'd been having a dream. He was driving over the mountains to California. Except now his car was a semitruck, and he was hauling thousands of pounds of cargo and his brakes had gone out. The brakes were smoking and starting to burn, and he was hurtling down the mountain, out of control, careening down the winding highway at top speed.

He woke with a start and realized the squealing sound of his brakes was real. And it was right over his head.

What the hell?

The sound stopped. He was just about to dismiss it as a tree branch outside (although it was pretty damned loud for a tree branch) when the noise started again. This time, the squealing noise was accompanied by a cracking sound. It was not until that moment Wendell realized his roof was collapsing.

Then he saw it move. The ceiling slipped down closer to his face. There was a crunching sound, and a dusting of Sheetrock fell on his bed.

Holy shit. Holy shit. Holy shit.

Then he heard a mighty crash from the direction of the guest bedroom. His bed shook from the impact. The walls around him quaked. Something had fallen to the ground, and he knew without looking that the something was his roof. His house was falling down around him.

Wendell could feel his heart racing and a curious feeling rising within him.

Well, let it. That was what Wendell thought.

Let the goddamned roof fall if that's what it wants to do. Let it fall and bury me beneath it, and let them dig me out next month. What the hell do I care? I've got no reason to get out of this bed or out of this house, and I haven't had a reason for years. There's some goddamned poetic justice that I should be buried alive in my goddamned bed with all my work and all my dreams buried here with me! That was what Wendell thought.

He turned on the bedside lamp and was amazed only after the fact that the electricity was still working. In the dim light, he saw the ceiling on the far side of the room had dropped a good three feet. He saw rubble in the hallway to the bathroom, and he felt cold air wafting into his bedroom.

Wendell then realized that death might not come as quickly as he hoped, and he could very well freeze to death before the rest of the roof fell and finished him off.

He reached for his inhaler. Just his goddamned luck. He couldn't even get his death done right. He had to have the worst goddamned luck in the world.

He heard something crash at the far end of the house. He heard something settle and another crunch. Then he heard only the wind outside. Except now it was inside.

Wendell stared at the ceiling, which was now closer than it used to be. He sucked on his inhaler and wondered what was going to happen to him next.

~

It was a long way to the Last Resort—if that's where they were going.

Lizzie was walking as fast as she could through the snow, but it was higher than her boots now and so it was slow going, and she was worried about Mr. Benson. He was walking behind her with his head down, and he was shaking really hard.

"We're gonna get you someplace warm, Mr. Benson. We're gonna get there soon, I promise."

But Lizzie didn't know how soon it would be because there was still no sign of any house. There was almost no light left in the sky, but it looked like they might be coming to a clearing up ahead. Lizzie hoped she would be able to see farther when they got to the clearing. The snow was still coming down, but now the wind was really strong, and it was piling the snow up in big mounds in front of her that were hard to get through. She had snow blowing in her eyes, and she could see it had packed into Mr. Benson's fur. She wondered if Mom had gotten her note. She wondered if the snow was too deep for Mom's car.

Mostly, she wondered if that lady in the Jeep had been telling the truth and if the Last Resort was a real place, because if it wasn't, Lizzie was afraid that she and Mr. Benson were toast.

The clearing was getting closer, and Lizzie could see where the trees ended. With no trees, Lizzie would have no idea where the road was. This was bad. If she didn't know where the road went, she would never find the Last Resort. She kept walking, but the snow was piling up in drifts, and it was very slow going.

Then she saw something.

It was off to the left, at the edge of the clearing. She thought she saw a light. Then it disappeared. She strained to see it again. She figured she must have imagined it, and she remembered the story of the Little Match Girl and how she'd imagined all kinds of nice things right before she froze to death. Lizzie wondered if she was going to freeze to death, and she knew if she did, Mr. Benson would freeze, too, and it would be her fault. She had to keep walking.

As soon as she started walking again, she realized the light must have been behind a tree, because now she could see it again. It was a small yellowish light, and it was right where the trees ended up ahead. Lizzie turned to the left and started walking toward the light.

She came to the end of the trees and then saw something on a post. It was a wooden sign. It was too dark to read until Lizzie got close enough to touch it. She grabbed the edges of the sign and looked at the letters in the dark.

The Last Resort. Lizzie then saw the clearing up ahead was not a clearing at all. It was a big lake, covered in snow.

"Mr. Benson! We've almost made it!" Mr. Benson looked up for the first time in a long time. He leaned against Lizzie, and she could feel him tremble.

"Let's get you to the Last Resort, Mr. Benson," Lizzie said, and they headed straight for the light.

~

Norry was putting the oatmeal cookies in tins when she heard the knock.

She hoped it wasn't a branch knocking against the house, because if it was, it meant another tree might be on its way down. In weather like this, it could certainly happen. But then she heard it again, and the knocking wasn't against the side of the house. It was at the back door.

Who the hell would be knocking at her door on a night like this?

The only one who could even drive through this kind of snow would be Bud Gustafson with his snowplow, but he surely wasn't out plowing the road yet, and if he was, he wouldn't come to the back door.

Norry walked from the kitchen to the back. The door was hard to open, with a good foot of snow pressed up against it. Standing on the other side was a small person. No. It was a girl, and it looked like the same girl she'd seen the day before.

"I hope it's okay. You said I could stop by sometime. My dog, Mr. Benson, is really cold."

Norry didn't see the dog until then. It looked like a snowdrift.

"Lizzie! That's your name, isn't it? Get in here. Get inside right now. What on earth are you doing out in weather like this? How did you get here?"

"We walked. The trailer got cold. I don't think the furnace is working, and Mom . . ." The girl's voice trailed off.

"Where is your mom? Is she outside?"

"No. I mean, I don't think so. I don't know where she is, but I left a note on the table for her."

By now the girl and the dog were inside, dropping a wet pile of snow on the braided rug. The girl's hair was as matted with snow as the dog's fur, and as Norry looked at them closely, she saw they both had gone without a bath for a while.

"Do you have your mom's number?"

"Yes. I know it."

Norry grabbed one of her resort notepads with the loon logo and wrote down the number as the girl and dog continued to drip onto the braided rug.

"I'm going to give your mom a call, and I'll run a hot bath for you in the meantime. I'll get you a clean sweatshirt and towel off the dog. What did you say his name was?"

"Mr. Benson."

"I see." Mr. Benson, despite his formal moniker, was the sorriest-looking beast Norry had seen in a long time. He had to be a stray. Where had this sad little girl picked up this pitiful dog?

Norry started the bath running. She toweled off Mr. Benson, and the white towel was soon brown and soaking wet.

Lizzie went into the bathroom as Norry dialed the number. She got a voice message.

"Hello," Norry said at the beep. "My name is Norry, and your daughter and her dog are here at the Last Resort. It's about a mile down the road from your trailer. They are okay. Give me a call as soon as you get this."

Norry looked at the miserable wet dog, still shivering on her braided rug.

Now what?

~

It didn't seem like very long before Wendell saw the flashing of red and blue lights.

He stayed right where he was and watched the lights bouncing off what remained of the hallway wall. Soon he heard shouting, and there were more lights. Some sort of bright white light had been set up outside, and it was glaring through his bedroom window.

Wendell sighed. It looked as if he would not be allowed to die in peace.

He got out of bed and looked for his shoes. They were nowhere to be seen. He walked out of the bedroom in his socks—but not very far. The ceiling of the hallway was on the ground, and the hallway ended abruptly in a pile of rubble. Part of the bathroom was visible, but the ceiling was three feet off the floor.

"Wendell! Are you there? Oh, my God. Wendell!"

He recognized the voice. It was his pest of a neighbor, Lucille Munson. She lived in the house directly across the street. It would be just like her to call the fire department and get everybody riled up. Wendell looked through a gap in the ceiling at what was now the end of the hallway. He stuck a hand up through the hole and waved.

"I see someone!" A man yelled outside.

This was deeply embarrassing. Wendell had always hated attracting attention, and now he had some sort of crowd gathered outside his house, probably expecting to get in. They were not coming in. That was settled. He never had visitors. But then he realized he probably didn't have a front door anymore, anyway. And the back door couldn't be used because he used the area in front of it for storage. That door hadn't been opened in years.

He heard someone trying to force the back door open, followed by the sound of boxes falling.

"What the hell are you doing?" Wendell yelled.

"He's here!" the man outside yelled again. "Wendell! Is there anyone else in the house?"

That was the dumbest question ever. Where did they get these volunteer firemen, anyway? Everyone knew he lived alone. There had been no one in the house other than Wendell since that guy had been in to check the furnace ten years ago.

"Wendell! Can you wave again so we know exactly where you are?"

Obviously, he was going to have to do everything for everyone. As usual. Wendell stepped up closer to the opening where the ceiling in the hall used to be. He stuck his head out. A cheer rang out as several firefighters and Lucille saw him.

How embarrassing.

"Wendell! Don't move. We'll head over to you and pull you out!"

A few moments later, two firefighters had climbed up ladders outside his bedroom wall, and they had ropes they were throwing in his direction. Apparently, he was expected to pull himself out. He was not at all sure he was up to this.

"We'll come get you, Wendell. Stay where you are."

He could now see the firefighter with the loud voice was Bud Gustafson. Bud was the guy who ran the snowplow in town. Several times, Bud had piled way too much snow up on Wendell's side of the street and interfered with his view out the kitchen window. He had been wanting to take that up with Bud for years, but now did not seem like the right time.

In no time flat, Bud had shimmied down the roof, which was now slanted in the wrong direction. Bud got to what was left of the hallway, and before Wendell knew what was happening, Bud had hoisted him up through the hole in the roof. Bud was a strong guy, no question about it. Wendell was not an unsubstantial person.

Halfway to the edge of the roof, Wendell felt the roof suddenly drop a few more inches.

"We gotta get out of here quick!" Bud hollered, right in Wendell's ear. People did not realize that Wendell had very sensitive hearing.

The other firefighter, whom Wendell did not know and who looked like he was just a kid, was tugging on the rope, and Wendell realized Bud had attached it to him somehow, because he was now sliding up the remains of his snowy roof, headed to the edge where the ladders had been set against the side of the house.

When he finally reached the ladders, Wendell was able to see what had happened.

His roof had collapsed. He knew this, of course, but now he could see that only his bedroom corner, and a bit on the opposite side—over the kitchen and the back door—remained standing. The rest of the bungalow was crushed beneath the snow.

It was then the truth dawned on him. His stuff.

All his stuff—all the stuff in the guest room and the living room and the dining room and in front of the back door, all the manuscripts and newspaper clippings and trophies from high school sporting events and letters from the girl who dumped him just four months after graduation and the rejection letter he'd gotten from the manuscript competition that informed him he had not won but should keep on writing anyway and the recipe books that had been his mother's and the clothing he'd worn when he had been a few sizes smaller and his complete collection of the Encyclopedia Britannica, all the many, many things he had collected—that he needed for his life to be worth anything—all those things were under that pile of collapsed roof.

"Wait!" Wendell yelled as he reached the ladders. He could see they'd set up a stretcher below and were planning to haul him off in it. "Wait!"

"What is it?" Bud asked. He was helping to scoot Wendell to the edge of the roof. "You got an animal in there?"

"No. No, I . . ."

Wendell was ignored—as he usually was.

They piled him onto a stretcher and carried him over the snow and straight to a waiting ambulance. Only when he got to the ambulance did he get to explain what a huge blunder they were making.

"I gotta get my stuff. I can't just leave and . . ."

Bud, who was a big guy, pushed Wendell back down on the stretcher.

"Wendell, this entire structure is unstable, and no one—you hear me?—no one is going back into that house unless there are lives on the line. It's a miracle the whole house didn't go down at once. It's an even bigger miracle you happened to be in a part of the house that survived. You should be thanking your lucky stars, not worrying about losing your shit. You are one lucky man."

Wendell looked up at Bud and blinked. He had never thought much of Bud Gustafson, but he hadn't realized until that moment that Bud was a total idiot.

~

Lizzie climbed out of the bathtub and dressed in a long sweatshirt that Norry had left on the edge of the sink. It said **The Last Resort** on the front, with a picture of a loon swimming on the lake. She walked into the kitchen and saw Norry placing a cup of hot cocoa and a plate of cookies on the table. Lizzie took a seat at the table and helped herself to a cookie. Norry slipped one to Mr. Benson.

"Have you had dinner?" Norry asked.

"We had oatmeal. Mr. Benson loves oatmeal."

Norry looked very serious. "Lizzie, do you know where your mother is?"

Lizzie did not. She was worried Mom was at the trailer and mad at her for leaving.

"I called your mother, and I got her voicemail. I've tried two times since. There is no answer."

Lizzie looked down at her lap. She liked this loon sweatshirt a lot. She wondered if it was a loan, or if Norry was giving it to her.

"Is there anyone else I can call to get ahold of your mom? Is there anyone else who will be worrying about you now?"

"I don't think so." These were the best cookies Lizzie had ever tasted. She was sleepy again—but in a good way this time. She didn't want to talk about her mom. She didn't want to tell this nice Norry that Mom was probably getting high. But Norry was worried, she could tell. She was worried that her mom would be worried. Lizzie felt stuck.

"My mom is having some trouble."

"What kind of trouble?"

"I think her back hurts and she has to take a lot of medication and sometimes she takes too much and gets really sleepy."

"I see." Norry had her mouth pursed—like whatever it was she was seeing, she didn't like it very much.

"Thank you for the cookies."

"You're welcome, Lizzie. When did you last see your mom?"

"When I left for school. She was going to run some errands. When I got home, the furnace didn't work. It was getting cold, so we thought we would come over to the Last Resort. We didn't know it was so far."

"It's a long way in that kind of snow." Norry was still frowning, but she seemed nice.

Lizzie helped herself to another cookie.

"You'll stay here until we hear from your mom, okay?"

"And Mr. Benson?"

"Of course. He can stay with you, but I think he needs to dry off before you take him into bed."

Lizzie looked down at Mr. Benson. He was lying under the table, his chin on the floor. His butterscotch eyes flicked up to meet hers, and he sighed. He seemed happy to be out of the cold.

Norry gave Lizzie a brand-new toothbrush, still in the wrapper, and some toothpaste. She also had a brush and comb for her hair, but Lizzie didn't want to tackle that mess right now. She was tired.

After Lizzie brushed her teeth, Norry brought her into a little room. The walls were logs, like the whole house was, and there was one single bed in the corner. There was a little table by the bed with an old-fashioned clock with bells on the top, and there was a bookshelf filled with books on the wall facing the bed. Lizzie went to the bookshelf and saw the books were all for kids, and they were hardcovers, just like library books except without the shiny plastic covers.

"Those were my books when I was growing up."

"You grew up here?"

"I did. I grew up here with my dad. He ran this resort."

Lizzie pulled out a book. It was called *Little House in the Big Woods*, and it showed a girl with her family in a house that looked like the inside of Norry's house.

"You better get some sleep. You must be exhausted. Don't worry, I'll keep trying to reach your mother."

Lizzie climbed into bed. The sheets were crisp. There was a heavy red wool blanket on the bed.

"Will Mr. Benson be okay?"

"I'll let him come into your room as soon as he's dry."

"Okay."

"You get some rest."

"Okay."

The door closed. Lizzie could hear Norry talking to Mr. Benson. She could hear the wind outside. She pulled the crisp white sheet up to her nose and smelled it. It smelled like fresh air. Lizzie was okay. Mr. Benson was okay.

But where is Mom?

Chapter Five

Wendell woke up the next morning on an unfamiliar couch.

He wondered where he was. He suspected he was still asleep. He was lying on a large sofa with cupholders in the armrests, a sofa that looked nothing like the couch in his own house, which his mother had bought when she redecorated the place in the late seventies. He hadn't actually seen the living room couch in a few years because he had some stuff stored on it, but he vividly remembered it was a forest green wool, and this couch appeared to be leather. His mother would never have gotten anything as lavish as a leather couch. And she certainly wouldn't have gotten a couch with cupholders. Wendell wondered why he would be dreaming about a couch with cupholders when the crushing truth landed on him.

He had no home.

His home had been demolished. This was just the latest development in a life rife with misfortune and cruel twists of fate. Wendell dearly wished Bud Gustafson had not pulled him out of the wreckage. He felt like a fish pulled onshore. Bud was a sadist.

"You awake, Wendell?" Bud called from the kitchen.

Wendell blinked. He was awake. It all came back to him. Bud had taken him from the hospital to his house because there was no place to stay in Loon Point and most of the roads in Big Pine were still impassable. Bud asked him if he had any family in the area, and he did not. Obviously. His life would not be as riddled with hardships if he'd had a family to rely upon. No. Wendell was alone, and he had no shoes and he had lost all his earthly possessions and—now that he was fully awake—he wondered how he might kill himself, because clearly, there were few options left.

"You want some coffee?"

Killing himself at this moment was not practical, he realized. The coffee smelled good. It didn't smell like instant coffee, which was what Wendell usually had in the morning. It smelled like Bud had brewed this up himself. He probably had one of those fancy Keurig coffee makers, Wendell figured. A guy with cupholders in his couch was not going to be messing around with an old-fashioned coffeepot. A moment later, Bud emerged from his kitchen, a shiny metal percolator in hand.

"You take cream or sugar?"

"Both."

Bud returned from the kitchen with cream and sugar—real cream in a carton, Wendell noted—and took a seat on the leather recliner next to the couch.

"How you feeling this morning, Wendell?"

Of all the questions anyone could ask, that had to take the prize for the stupidest. But Bud drove a snowplow for a living. What did you expect? And last he checked, they didn't require an IQ test to join the volunteer fire department. How did he feel? Was that a serious question? His life's work was gone. His home was in ruins. The adversity that had dogged him all his life had taken its ultimate revenge, and only a perversely cruel fate had allowed him to live long enough to see it. How did he feel? What an asinine question. Wendell took a sip of his coffee. It was too hot. Of course.

"I made a few calls this morning," Bud continued.

This did not sound good. Wendell remembered Bud saying he was going to "make some arrangements," and he remembered he'd given Bud a lot of personal information he probably should not have. He was in shock. That's what the doctor said. He was in shock from having his perfectly fine roof collapse on top of him in the middle of the night.

"I got ahold of the insurance company this morning, Wendell. Your home policy hasn't been in effect for a few years. It looks like you let it expire about the time you paid off a home equity loan."

Wendell knew he needed his inhaler right then and there. He remembered it was still in his pocket from last night and started to suck on it.

"So, there's not going to be any money coming from that. I've contacted the county to see if there's any kind of assistance available, but we probably won't hear back for a day or two."

Wendell took a deep breath off his inhaler. Of course there was no insurance. Insurance was for suckers. He had never insured anything in his life if he could avoid it.

"So, we gotta figure out where you're going to go in the meantime. There's Sleepy Pines in Big Pine . . ."

"A nursing home?" Wendell gasped between breaths on his inhaler.

"Well, there's also some low-income apartments at Sleepy Pines for seniors who qualify, but there's a wait for those. The nursing care facility has beds available now, I guess."

A nursing home? His inhaler did not seem to be doing the job. They never lasted as long as they should. It was another example of Big Pharma ripping off the little guy.

"I know a nursing home is probably not what you had in mind," Bud continued, "but it would be just a temporary thing until something better came up."

Wendell took his inhaler out long enough to take a sip of coffee. He added more cream. The cream was good. He didn't usually have cream in his coffee because he didn't have cream. Then he looked up at Bud. Bud seemed to be waiting for some kind of response.

"I . . . I can't live in a nursing home."

Bud looked down at his hands. Bud had big hands, Wendell noticed. They were big and kind of red. Bud was a big guy all over. He wasn't exactly fat, but he had broad shoulders and was over six feet tall. That's how he'd managed to carry Wendell out of his house. If

Bud hadn't been such a big Neanderthal, he would have been left to die in peace.

"I hear you, Wendell," Bud said.

Wendell drank his coffee. He still had no shoes. He needed to bring that up with Bud. They should have at least provided him with shoes. It didn't seem like much to ask, but what did you expect from a volunteer fire department?

"Maybe I could make a couple more calls," Bud said. He was still looking at his big hands.

"I need shoes," Wendell pointed out.

"Oh, right. Lucille, your neighbor—she's let the Methodist church in Loon Point know what you'll need. She said she'd try to come by this morning with some clothes."

Great. It appeared Wendell was expected to wear the tatty castoffs of the Methodists. Perfect. He was now an official charity case.

"I've got to finish up plowing some driveways this morning. We ended up with more than a foot of snow last night. I'll make a few more phone calls while I'm driving, and we'll get you settled in somewhere later today. How does that sound?"

Wendell blinked. None of it sounded like anything he was interested in. He did not want somebody else's old clothing. He did not want Bud calling all over town, saying embarrassing things about him. Above all, he did not want to get "settled in somewhere" that Bud thought was appropriate. The whole thing had to be stopped in its tracks. Wendell had to let Bud know he would not stand for it—and he was just about to do so when Bud got up, put his cup in the kitchen, and headed out the door.

"I left some doughnuts in the kitchen, if you're hungry!" Bud said on his way out.

Doughnuts. This was Bud Gustafson's idea of how to deal with catastrophe. Eat doughnuts. This was the World According to Bud. Perfect.

Wendell watched Bud as he pulled his truck with the plow attachment out of the driveway and headed down the snowy street. Then he helped himself to a doughnut.

~

Norry hadn't gotten any sleep.

She kept trying that number and getting Lizzie's mom's voicemail. "Hi! This is Cat. Leave a message." There was no point in leaving seventeen messages, but she couldn't sleep, wondering if Cat was ever going to call.

Then there was the dog, the distinguished Mr. Benson. He was a mess.

Norry took a closer look at him and knew there was no way she was going to let him get in bed with that child. The dog was beyond filthy. He had left a pile of sand where he was lying under the table and a big brown spot where the snow had melted off him on the rug. And so, after Lizzie was asleep, Norry decided to give the dog a bath.

She filled the tub with a few inches of water, got out her raggediest old cabin towels, and herded the dog into the bathroom. Getting him into the tub was a challenge. The dog was nothing but bones and easy to lift, but when Benson caught sight of that water, he started paddling as if he was sure Norry planned to drown him.

"Come on, Benson," she coaxed as she slowly let the frantically squirming dog down into the water. But when Benson hit the warm water, he suddenly calmed. He sat down. Then he lay down.

"Okay, then. You see? This won't be so bad." Norry got out the shampoo.

It took three rounds of shampoo and four tubs of fresh water before Benson came clean. Norry washed his face with a towel. Then she tried to remove the burs from his tail, and Benson howled. She went into the kitchen and returned with a slice of lunch meat. Every time she pulled a bur out, she ripped off a bit of lunch meat and fed it to the agitated animal. By the time she was finished, Benson had eaten two full slices.

"You're a smart dog, aren't you, Benson?"

Then Norry rubbed him down with conditioner and rinsed him out a final time. He shook and sprayed water all over the bathroom, but at least the water was clean, which was more than she could say for her sweatshirt, which was covered with mud from lifting him into the bath. She toweled him off, dried his feet, and applied a little salve to the bare spots on his sides. Now that his fur was washed, they weren't nearly as visible. When she let him out of the bathroom, he looked like a new dog. She didn't have any dog food, but she had some leftover hotdish. Benson ate like there was no tomorrow. He loved wild rice.

By that time, Benson was nearly dry, and Norry had successfully distracted herself from her phone for more than an hour and a half. She checked her messages in case something had come in while she was busy feeding Benson baloney. Nothing.

Norry supposed she should be worried about Lizzie's mother, but she was not. She was angry. She was angry and getting angrier by the minute.

Norry led Benson to Lizzie's room. The girl was sound asleep. Norry looked at her hair and thought it looked like it might be as big a project as Benson's tail. How could that little girl and her dog be so badly neglected? Norry couldn't understand it and wasn't interested in trying.

The dog jumped up on the bed and lay beside Lizzie. Norry watched them for a few moments from the doorway. She didn't have a lot of guests, and this had been her bedroom growing up. It was funny to have a little girl staying here, a little girl just about the age she had been when she and her father had come to live at Loon Point. That had been after her mother had gotten so sick and finally died, after her dad said he couldn't stand to stay where they were, and what did Norry think about living up in the Northwoods?

Her father had bought her the complete set of Laura Ingalls Wilder books, and he'd read the first one, *Little House in the Big Woods*, aloud to her. Then Norry got impatient and read the rest herself. She wondered if this little girl liked to read. Probably not. Probably not with a mother who left her alone all night.

Norry knew she should call child protective services. The nearest office was in Big Pine. She decided she would call first thing in the morning.

Then Norry wondered if they would let Lizzie keep her dog. But she knew the answer to that. She bit her lip. She didn't expect she would sleep tonight. She took her phone with her to bed, set it on the bed stand, and noticed it was well past midnight. And then, surprisingly, Norry drifted off to sleep, dreaming about her father and the little house in the big woods.

She woke to the sound of her phone. She had not been asleep for long, and so she was not fully awake when she answered, but she snapped awake when she realized who it was.

"Hey, this is Cat Lundin, Lizzie's mom. I got your call."

Norry struggled to sit upright and clear her head.

"Who is this?"

"Cat, Lizzie's mom. What did you say your name was?"

Norry did not like the voice on the other end of the line. Then again, she had made up her mind she wouldn't long before the phone rang.

"My name is Norry."

"What's your last name?"

"Last."

"Yeah. What is it?"

"My last name is Last."

"I realize that. What is it?"

Norry tightened her grip on her phone. She was angry. She didn't get angry very often, but when she did, she stayed that way for a while. The last time she remembered being really angry was when those drunken nincompoop snowmobilers had removed the fire screen in front of the fireplace and let a log roll out and burn its way into the wooden floor before anyone had the wherewithal to put the damn thing out with a pot of water. Norry hated incompetence, and this Cat woman was making those snowmobiling doofuses look like a pack of Rhodes scholars.

"Your daughter is at my resort."

"Can I talk to her?"

"She's still sleeping, and honestly, I think she needs the sleep. She walked all the way from your trailer with your dog in that terrible storm last night. She had no choice because she tells me the furnace went out in the trailer."

"Dog? What dog?"

What dog? Norry closed her eyes. She'd heard it helped to count to ten, but she knew she'd never make it that far.

"My phone was left in the car," Cat explained.

Was left? Norry had not made it to six yet. "Was left?"

"Yeah, I didn't realize until just now."

"Well, your daughter 'was left' in a trailer with no heat."

"I didn't know that. I . . . I fell asleep. I appreciate you taking her in."

"My first call this morning was supposed to be to child protective services."

There was silence on the other end of the line.

"Hey. Don't do that."

"Give me one good reason why I shouldn't."

There was another silence.

Finally, Norry said, "Look, we're all here at the Last Resort. It's three-quarters of a mile past your trailer. You'll never make it until the road is plowed, but Bud Gustafson usually gets to us by midmorning. We'll be here when you get here."

"Oh. Okay. Okay, thanks."

"Also, the dog came here without a leash, so you might want to grab that."

"What dog?"

Norry closed her eyes again, but this time she didn't start counting. She hung up.

~

"Well, good morning, Wendell! How are you?"

Wendell saw that his neighbor, Lucille from across the street, had walked into Bud Gustafson's house, uninvited, and was now standing in the entryway with snow boots on her feet, two bags of clothing in one arm, a casserole dish in the other, and an enormous smile on her face. Wendell hadn't thought his morning could get any worse, but once again, he was wrong. He was just starting to formulate an answer that would begin to address Lucille's question but was not given the opportunity.

"Goodness' sake, Wendell, you must be just about the luckiest man alive!" Lucille exclaimed, gesturing wildly with the casserole dish.

"I heard that noise across the street and I said, 'What on earth is going on at Wendell's?' So I ran out on my porch right away and saw the whole center of your poor mother's house had just crumpled in. Just squashed in like a tin can! I thought for sure you would be buried alive, and I got on my phone right away and called 911 and those boys from the fire department in Big Pine were out here so fast I could hardly believe it. And then Bud, you know he brought his plow, and they were able to get those big lights set up. Was that ever something? I never saw the like."

He remembered the awful bright light in his bedroom. He could have done without the graphic imagery. He could have done without any of his eighty-year-old neighbor's blow-by-blow reenactment.

"And then, when they pulled you out of the wreckage! Oh, my. Everybody cheered, and I said a prayer to God, thanking him for his mercy, and I thought your mother, Eunice, must have been watching over you, Wendell, watching over you from heaven last night, because there is nothing left of that house this morning. I went out and looked as soon as the sun was up and only the one wall in the kitchen is still standing and the rest of the house is as flat as a pancake!"

Wendell's whole life was under that roof.

"So, anyway," Lucille continued, undeterred. "I've been to the Methodist church, and you know they keep a nice selection of clothing for folks who need it, and they're always short on kids' clothes, but they had a lot of things for men—you know, they get donations after there's been a death—and I picked up some nice things so you won't have to go wandering around in your pajamas."

Wendell was about to explain that he didn't believe in pajamas, but it was too late. Lucille had already made it out of her fur-trimmed snow boots and was heading into the living room with the bags of clothing.

"You've got sweaters here and some pants and shoes. I know you're a good-sized man, Wendell, and luckily that Earl Söderberg just passed late last year. His widow brought in all his clothes, and you know they used to live in Chicago before they retired on Elk Lake. So there's some lovely things here."

Lucille was now rummaging through the paper grocery sacks, pulling out clothes and laying them on the leather couch. Wendell could not imagine anything more humiliating.

"See? Some fancy sweaters, and some warm trousers, and a couple of jackets—one that looks like it was never worn—and shoes. He was a big guy and had big feet, and I figured you probably did too."

"I need shoes." This was the first statement Wendell had managed to get out since Lucille had arrived.

"Oh, you poor thing, of course you do! That's why I brought a whole bag of them."

Lucille dumped the shoes out on the couch.

Clown shoes. That's what came to mind. Wendell picked up a pair of light-brown wing tips. They looked like they'd never been worn, and the size was printed on the inside. Fourteen. Wendell wore a size nine.

Lucille smiled broadly. "Well! I feel so much better, knowing you'll have something to wear. I have to get to my circle meeting at church. I tell you, that snow will be gone in no time flat. Bud did such a good job on all the streets this morning, and now that the sun is out, things are almost back to normal."

Things were definitely not back to normal. Wendell silently fumed as he tried on a pair of Earl's athletic shoes.

Lucille was now getting her snow boots laced back up.

"Wendell, you let me know what else you need. This hamburger hotdish is ready to bake. Just stick it in the oven at three hundred and fifty degrees for an hour."

Lucille stopped talking for a moment and looked at him. He noticed she had tears in her eyes.

"Oh Wendell, I just can't tell you how happy I am that you made it out safe and sound. I'm going to tell all the ladies at circle that you are looking fine. Mary Söderberg will be there, and I'll let her know how much you appreciated poor Earl's clothing. Goodness! What a blessing you made it out. Wendell, you are the luckiest man alive."

With that, Lucille left Bud's house and almost skipped to her car, which was still running in the driveway. As she pulled away, Wendell looked down at his oversize shoes.

Here I am. The luckiest man alive.

Chapter Six

Wendell was still seated on the absurd leather sofa with cupholders. He had helped himself to another cup of coffee and another doughnut to go with it—because who knew when he'd eat again?

He was looking out on the street in front of Bud Gustafson's house and saw the sun beating down on last night's snow, making a mess of it. He imagined all this snow melting through what was left of his roof. He wondered when they were going to begin work rescuing his belongings. No one had said a word about it, and now, with these bags of ridiculous clothes, he had a sinking feeling that saving what was left of his life was not the priority of the Big Pine Volunteer Fire Department. But then, when had Wendell's life ever been a priority?

That was when Bud walked in the door.

"Okay, Wendell. I've got an idea."

Whatever this idea of Bud's was, Wendell wanted no part of it. Bud was the kind of guy who always had harebrained ideas. That was Wendell's guess, and this one probably was gonna be a doozy since he'd spent all morning hatching it. Wendell was going to ask about the search and rescue effort for his possessions, but Bud seemed to have other things in mind.

"Let's get going. I'm going to take you with me to Norry's."

"I need shoes."

"Didn't Lucille come by with a bag of clothes for you? She said they had a bunch of Earl Söderberg's clothes. He was a rich guy with a big cabin on Elk Lake. You'll probably be all set to go to the opera if you've got Earl's stuff."

Wendell wanted to point out that the loud argyle cardigan in the grocery sack was not exactly opera attire—not that he'd actually been to the opera, but he certainly knew more about it than a guy like Bud ever would. And that didn't solve the problem of the shoes.

Wendell now had three pairs of shoes. There were the wing tips, which were a size fourteen, and a pair of loafers, which would most certainly not stay on his feet, and a pair of what he had to suppose were walking shoes, but what an old guy like Earl would be doing with them, Wendell had no idea. They were bright red—shocking red, really—and they had white soles made of some kind of molded rubbery stuff. They were the most ludicrous shoes he had ever seen, but they were a size thirteen, and laced up tight, there was an off chance he might be able to keep them on his feet.

Wendell started lacing his feet into the giant red sneakers.

Earl Söderberg must have been going through a late-in-life identity crisis. That was Wendell's guess. No sensible man over the age of fifty would wear such a flashy pair of shoes just for walking around Loon Point. Maybe he thought he was going to start playing basketball again. Or maybe he had a skateboard to go with the shoes. More likely, Earl Söderberg was suffering from dementia when he bought them. Wendell looked at the red shoes on his feet with disapproval and saw Bud was waiting for him.

"Tie up your shoes, Wendell. We're going for a drive."

Wendell laced up the red shoes as tight as they would go, then added the garish argyle sweater to the ensemble. The sweater was big enough to button in the front, which was a relief. He had noticed that clothes were usually made much too tight in the middle these days. But the sleeves were preposterously long. They covered his fingers. Wendell was just about to tell Bud that he could not possibly leave the house in this sweater, wearing these shoes, when Bud scooped up the bags containing the remaining clothes in one hand, balanced the tinfoil-covered hotdish in the other, and headed out the door.

Wendell followed Bud out to his truck. Bud's truck was very tall and had a step you were supposed to use to get into it, but standing on that little step with shoes that stuck out three inches past the ends of his feet was not possible. Wendell tried taking the step backward, but then he didn't have anything to hang on to. It took him several long moments before he was able to heave himself into the passenger side.

Meanwhile, Bud raced the engine, ran the windshield wipers, adjusted the defrost, and did everything in his power to make Wendell feel foolish.

"You okay there, Wendell?" Bud asked when he finally made it into the truck. But Bud didn't wait for an answer. He had news.

"I'm taking you to the Last Resort."

That was it. Wendell could not take one more indignity.

"I'm not going to a nursing home!" he protested.

"No. Not yet. I don't want to get your hopes up. That may come. But first, we're gonna try the Last Resort."

~

Lizzie woke up and saw Mr. Benson was sleeping beside her.

She had gotten the book off the shelf, *Little House in the Big Woods*, and read the first few pages before she'd fallen asleep, and now, this morning, she felt like she'd woken up inside the little house. She felt like a totally new girl in a totally new place and—just to make the whole thing more real—Mr. Benson had miraculously turned into a different dog as well.

He had curls.

Mr. Benson was fluffy and curly, and he smelled like strawberries. Lizzie had no idea how this had happened, but she was starting to think this place was magical, like some places she'd read about in books.

Lizzie jumped out of bed. The floor was cold. She was still wearing the Last Resort sweatshirt with the loon on the front. She came out of the bedroom with *Little House in the Big Woods* in her hand and the newly curly Mr. Benson at her side.

"Well! Good morning to you!"

Norry was at the kitchen stove, and she was cooking something that smelled wonderful.

"I've made breakfast. Do you like blueberry pancakes?"

"Uh-huh. Yes, please. What happened to Mr. Benson?"

"He got a bath. When's the last time that dog was bathed?"

"I don't know. Probably never. I've only known him since yesterday."

"You mean Benson isn't your dog?"

Lizzie felt her stomach tighten. Mr. Benson was her dog, wasn't he?

"I saw him before, but he just came into the trailer yesterday and we had oatmeal together and then we both walked here. I guess I thought, after that . . ."

"No! I understand. After a thing like that, he would certainly be your dog. Sit down. The blueberries are some I froze last August."

"Last August?"

"Yes. I picked them in August. We had a bumper crop around the lakeshore."

"You picked them?" Lizzie never knew you could pick blueberries.

Norry gave her two big pancakes. They were the best pancakes ever.

"Your mom called."

Lizzie put her fork down. For a moment this morning, she had forgotten about her mom. Now she felt guilty.

"Is she okay?"

"She's fine. She said she left her phone in the car and that's why she didn't get my messages."

Lizzie knew that didn't explain where she was or why she hadn't come home, but Lizzie had a pretty good idea what the reason was, and she didn't feel like talking about it with Norry.

"Is she coming here?"

"As soon as the plow gets through. Bud should be getting us plowed out any minute. He's usually here by now. But I imagine he had a lot to do this morning."

"I started *Little House in the Big Woods*. It's just like here."

"Oh, no. I've got it much easier than they did. I can hop in the Jeep and be to Big Pine in twenty minutes if the roads are clear. And I've got company here most of the year. Right now, it's quiet, but it won't be quiet after Memorial Day, and it will stay busy all summer."

"Who comes here?"

"People from the Twin Cities, mostly. These cabins were built back in the 1930s, and my dad restored them when we moved up here in the eighties."

Lizzie looked around at the log walls and the wooden floor and the old-timey kitchen with a stove that had legs. She didn't care what Norry said. It looked exactly like *Little House in the Big Woods* to her.

Mr. Benson was eating a pancake and Lizzie was on her fourth one when they heard a vehicle outside. Lizzie's heart sank. She knew she should be excited to see her mom, but she was afraid her mother was going to look all spaced out like she did sometimes, and Lizzie didn't want Norry to see her that way.

The vehicle stopped outside. It didn't sound like Mom's car. It sounded bigger.

"Oh, there's Bud now," Norry said.

Norry opened the door, and a big man with a red face wearing a fur cap walked in.

"You took your time getting here!" Norry said.

"Well, you know you live in the Last house!" Bud laughed. "Seriously, I had a few things to get to this morning. The fire department got a call last night in Loon Point. A roof collapsed."

"Oh, no! Was anyone hurt?"

Lizzie leaned in. This sounded exciting.

"No, thankfully, no. But it was kind of amazing. That house is flat except for part of one wall right now. It looks as if the roof was in bad shape already, and that heavy snow was the final straw. Anyway, there was just one guy inside, and we got him out late last night."

Bud finally noticed Lizzie sitting at the table.

"Who is this?"

"This is Lizzie. She and her dog, Benson, showed up at my door last night."

Bud raised his eyebrows.

"Her mother will be coming by this morning, now that you've got the road cleared."

"Well, nice to meet you, Lizzie. What did you say your dog's name was?"

"Mr. Benson," Lizzie answered.

"Good to meet you, Mr. Benson. It looks like you could use a few more of Norry's pancakes."

"Let me get you a plate," Norry said to Bud. "You must have been up all night. I don't think folks realize half of what you guys at the fire department have to deal with."

Bud stayed where he was. He looked down at his hands.

"So, the fellow we got out of the house. His name is Wendell."

"Oh? Is that Eunice Eklund's son? I remember a Wendell who used to work at the Big Pine Trailer Park years ago."

"That would be him. He's in my truck right now."

"He's in your truck? Why don't you invite him in?"

"Well, I wanted to have a word with you first. He doesn't really have anywhere to go right now. He spent the night on my couch, and it doesn't look like he had any insurance on the house. The only real option for him is the Sleepy Pines senior facility in Big Pine. I gave them a call, but they don't have any apartments available for a while. They've got room in the care facility . . ."

"The nursing home."

"Right. And Wendell doesn't seem real excited about that."

"No. I suppose not."

"So I wondered if there was any chance you had a spot here while he waited for something better."

"Here at the resort?"

"Yeah."

Bud was looking at his hands again.

"I hate to ask you, Norry, but this fellow seems a little lost right now. I think he's still in shock. He hardly said a word all night, and all he could say this morning was that he had lost his shoes. I just thought a few days up here might help him before he got moved in to something permanent."

Lizzie couldn't see what kind of face Norry was making. She'd stopped eating pancakes while she waited to hear what would happen to this Mr. Wendell.

"Bring him in, Bud. We'll find a spot for him. I don't have the beds made up yet, and I'll have to turn the heat and water on, but I can get the Chickadee Cabin ready in an hour."

Bud looked up, and Lizzie saw he was smiling.

"You're the best, you know that, Norry?"

"I am a soft touch, and you know it, Bud. Otherwise, you would have called first and not dragged that poor guy all the way out here and left him waiting in the truck while you strong-armed me into giving him a cabin."

"Still, it worked, didn't it?"

Lizzie figured Bud and Norry must be friends. She wished she had a friend like Bud.

A moment later, Bud came back into Norry's house, carrying a casserole pan covered in tinfoil, followed by another man.

"Wendell, I'd like to introduce you to Norry, Lizzie, and Mr. Benson."

"Nice to meet you, Wendell. Let me get you some pancakes," Norry said.

The man stood in the doorway and blinked. He was carrying two brown paper bags and had thick glasses that were fogged up from the cold. He was kind of fat, and he was wearing a jazzy green-and-blue plaid sweater with very long sleeves that covered his hands. And it looked like he was wearing bright-red clown shoes. Lizzie liked him right away.

~

Norry had just served Bud and Wendell their pancakes when she heard another vehicle drive up.

She'd had to make another batch of batter and take another bag of blueberries out of the freezer. That poor Wendell fellow ate like he hadn't had a decent meal in ages. He didn't say a thing, but he rolled up the sleeves on that argyle sweater and dug into his plate of pancakes with gusto.

Norry wasn't entirely sure she wanted him in the Chickadee Cabin, but she wasn't going to turn him away now that he was here. It was a little annoying, having a single cabin to clean twice a week. She'd much prefer to have all seven cabins filled and work her way from cabin to cabin until the job was done. But now he was here, and he certainly looked like a fellow who could use a little help. Bud was right, it seemed like he might be in shock. That's when Norry heard the car.

It's her.

She reflexively looked over at Lizzie and saw her stiffen.

Between bites, Lizzie had been reading *Little House in the Big Woods*. Norry would normally have fussed about reading at the table and getting syrup and blueberries on the pages of her childhood book, but neither of those considerations seemed important right now.

That poor kid was not acting like someone pining for her mother. She was acting like she was afraid her mother was going to arrive. Norry had decided she was not going to like this mother of Lizzie's, no matter what kind of pathetic excuses she brought with her, and seeing Lizzie seize up like that just hardened her resolve.

Norry handed Wendell the pitcher of maple syrup and waited. Wendell could sure put away a lot of syrup. She'd had to open a new bottle of that as well, but Bud had given her a gallon last spring and was tapping the new year's syrup right now.

In addition to telling Lizzie how the blueberries she was eating had been picked here on the lakeshore, Norry had explained how maple syrup was tapped from sugar maples and then boiled down.

"It takes forty gallons to make one gallon of syrup."

"So it's real watery when it comes out of the tree?"

"Exactly." The kid was smart.

But she had never picked berries before, and that made Norry sad. How does a kid grow up here and never pick a blueberry? Norry was keeping tabs on her grudge against this mother of hers when she heard the knock at the door.

The room became silent.

"That's probably Lizzie's mother," Norry said and walked to the door.

Standing on the stoop was a slim woman with lank blond hair and circles under her eyes. She was dressed in something that looked like pajamas, right down to the slipper-like things on her feet. Norry pointedly looked at the woman's feet for a moment. They were soaked. What kind of person goes out in a snowstorm in slippers? Norry added one more point to her tally of offenses and poor judgment.

"Hi! I'm Cat, Lizzie's mom."

Norry stepped outside and closed the door behind her. They were now standing in close proximity on Norry's small stoop.

"Your daughter is inside, having breakfast. Do you know there is no heat in your trailer?"

"Yeah. I called about that. We're supposed to get more propane today."

"On Saturday?"

"I told them it was an emergency."

"There is a gauge on the propane tank."

"I know that—now."

"It's pretty obvious."

"Yeah, I know that."

There was an uncomfortable silence.

"Are you gonna let me in?"

Norry pursed her lips. She wondered if not letting this woman in was an option.

"You left your daughter and her dog alone when a winter storm was predicted in a house with no food or heat."

"I know it looks bad . . ."

"I have every right to call child protective services. This is a clear-cut case of neglect."

"I get that. I do. I've been having some issues lately . . ."

"You're on drugs."

"I've just had a lot of pain since my back went out! If that's never happened to you, you have no idea . . ."

"Spare me." Norry realized she could not keep this woman on her stoop forever. She couldn't send her away unless she wanted to get child protective services involved, and she didn't want to do that. She hadn't heard any real success stories from them. It was a rotten situation.

And this was not Norry's problem. She knew that. This was a kid who lived down the road, and Norry had her own life to live. No, this story probably did not end well. But this was not Norry's story. This was Cat's story.

And Lizzie's story.

Norry spoke before she thought. "Do you need some time?"

Cat looked up, confused.

"Would you like me to watch Lizzie while you get your shit together?"

Norry had expected Cat to get angry. She'd expected her to lash out and ask what the hell Norry meant, but Cat seemed to understand in an instant. Norry subtracted one point from her tally when she saw the look of relief on Cat's face.

"I do. I need just a little time. I need to get the house warmed up, and I need to get some groceries. I'd like things to be better—you know, better than they were."

"And dog food. You have a dog to care for."

"I do?" At that moment, Cat looked younger and far less capable than Lizzie.

"You do. His name is Benson."

"Where did she get a dog?" Then Cat dropped her head. Even she seemed to realize it was not a sign of great parenting when your child acquires a pet without your knowledge. "She's wanted a dog," Cat added quietly.

"Well, she's got one."

"I'll get some food."

"Okay."

There was another silence. This one was marginally less uncomfortable.

"Would you like some pancakes?"

"I don't think I can eat anything right now. Are you sure you can keep an eye on Lizzie for . . . maybe the rest of the weekend? I could pick her up tomorrow night after I've got more propane and some food and gotten some laundry done."

"I can do that."

"That would be great. Can I just . . . you know . . . say hello and goodbye?"

At that moment, Norry almost felt sorry for this young woman on her stoop.

"Of course."

Cat and Norry came into the house together. Lizzie looked closely at her mother when she walked into the house and seemed relieved. Norry wondered what she was expecting. Probably nothing good.

"Norry is going to let you stay here while I get more propane and get some laundry done. Would you like to spend another night?"

Lizzie nodded. She still had her hand in *Little House in the Big Woods*.

"Is that okay?" her mother asked again.

"Yeah. That's good," Lizzie said.

Benson walked over to Cat and started sniffing her wet slippers.

"You must be Benson," Cat said. "Aren't you a handsome dog?"

Norry saw a small smile form on Lizzie's face.

"Can we keep him?" she asked.

"Do we have a choice?" her mother replied.

One more small point in her favor, Norry noted.

Lizzie was now smiling. "He's a really good dog! He barked at me when I stopped walking in the snowstorm. I didn't know where we were, and the wind was so strong . . ." Lizzie's smile faded. Norry realized she didn't want to upset her mother.

"Anyway, we made it here, and Norry gave him a bath and now he's all curly!"

Cat shot a grateful look at Norry. Norry ignored it.

"Okay, then," Cat said. "Give me a hug, and I'll see you tomorrow."

Lizzie left the book face down on the table and went to hug her mother. Norry watched Cat's face. She looked like she was going to cry.

She should cry, Norry thought, *after what she did.*

But then Cat left, and the room felt very quiet. Bud stared down at his plate. Lizzie picked up her book. Norry watched the dilapidated car pull out of the driveway.

Wendell looked up from his pancakes.

"Who was that?"

Chapter Seven

It appeared that Wendell was headed for the Chickadee Cabin.

No one had asked him if any of this was okay. No one seemed to care one iota about what Wendell wanted. He had been hauled off to this resort—which he now realized was the Last Resort, not "the last resort," although there did not appear to be any significant difference in his case.

Bud had come out to the truck, where he'd left Wendell waiting, and told him that Norry had agreed to put him up in the Chickadee Cabin, and that was that. Wendell wondered what this "cabin" was like—was there running water or indoor plumbing? But Bud hadn't said another word. He'd grabbed the hotdish that Lucille Munson had brought over and told Wendell to follow him into this log cabin, where a woman named Norry was cooking pancakes for a strange little girl and a dog.

Wendell didn't have his car, as he pointed out to Bud, who seemed to have a poor grasp of details, and Bud said he'd take him to pick it up as soon as he was finished plowing Norry's place. And so, just like that, he found himself inside a strange house. If this was the headquarters of the Last Resort, he wondered what the Chickadee Cabin was like. But, under the circumstances (which appeared to resemble a kidnapping more than a rescue), Wendell didn't know what else to do. So he had a plate of pancakes, which, it must be said, were a bright spot in an otherwise disastrous day.

"What size are your feet, Wendell?" this Norry woman asked as soon as Bud left to do the plowing.

He should have known—now that he was a charity case, he could expect a loss of privacy and all sorts of personal questions.

"Size nine."

"I thought those shoes looked a little big."

Wendell's humiliation was complete. Now he had total strangers taking time off from cooking pancakes to comment on his ridiculous outfit.

"I think I might still have a pair of my dad's old shoes. He had a small foot."

A small foot! Apparently, in the new world of giants, anything smaller than the oversize appendages of Earl Söderberg was considered diminutive.

Norry emerged with a pair of ordinary shoes that appeared to be of an ordinary size. Wendell tried them on. They fit. This woman Norry might be domineering and presumptuous, but she had more sense than Bud and Lucille Munson put together. Although, Wendell had to admit, this was a low bar.

Meanwhile, the strange little girl at the table was watching him. It was unnerving. She was an odd little thing. Very thin, it seemed to him, with wild, curly black hair sticking out in all directions. She was reading a book, and he vaguely remembered it was one his mother had, so she couldn't be all bad.

She had a dog named Mr. Benson. He wasn't sure why this dog was addressed by his surname when nobody even bothered to ask Wendell his last name—which was Eklund, although no one seemed to care. No, in this crazy, upside-down world, a fluffy dog was fed pancakes and called Mr. Benson, while Wendell was fed the same fare and was plain old Wendell. The world was mad, that much was obvious.

A few minutes later, after Wendell had eaten a few more pancakes, Bud reappeared and told him they were going to fetch his car. Wendell had forgotten about his car while eating pancakes. He left the clothes

Lucille had given him in the house and followed Bud out to the truck. It was easier to get in the truck this time because he had shoes that fit.

"Nice shoes," Bud said. "Those must have been Norry's dad's."

Wendell looked down at the brown laced-up boots. He needed to ask Bud about the rescue efforts for his belongings. The sun was now beating down on last night's snow, and it was melting fast. He hated to imagine what was happening to his stuff right now. He felt his heart quicken as they turned the corner onto his street.

Bud pulled up in front of Wendell's house and parked. Or rather, he parked in front of where his house used to be. Wendell could not believe what he was seeing.

"It's . . . there's not even . . ."

"Yeah, the house really settled a lot since we got you out of it. Even the kitchen wall is caving in now, and the wall we set the ladders against last night is gone. We were damned lucky to get you out when we did."

This is Bud's idea of luck?

"I've got stuff in the house," Wendell began.

"Stuff?" Bud inquired. "You've got stuff of value in the house?"

Stuff of value! This had Wendell reaching for his inhaler—which was nearly worn out, another thing he had to deal with. He looked at the heap of rubble that was his house and felt a little faint, even with the inhaler. Gone. It was all gone.

"It's not gonna be possible to get to most of it," Bud said. "We could try to move part of the roof off with a Bobcat, but I don't think there's much chance you're gonna find what you're looking for."

Wendell was now sucking hard on his inhaler.

"But I'll tell you what. As soon as I finish the last of my plowing—I only have a couple more driveways in town—you tell me what it is you're looking for, and I'll bring the Bobcat over and try to get to it."

"What I'm looking for?"

"If you've got some family heirlooms or something," Bud continued, "I'll do whatever I can to get them out. I just don't want you to get your hopes up. I gotta tell you, I've never seen a house that collapsed so completely." Bud shook his head as if he was looking at some curious phenomenon—maybe a new tourist attraction.

Wendell stared straight ahead, seething in anger. This man was going to do nothing to help him, nothing to save his precious belongings, the accumulation of a life's work. This man was going to fish around for a trinket or two and seemed to think Wendell should be happy he was willing to do it. Wendell stared out of Bud's truck window and felt he might scream or explode or faint or some combination of the above.

"Sorry, buddy," Bud said, and patted Wendell's knee.

Wendell looked at the red hand patting him on the knee and, for the first time, felt his rage subside slightly. Bud was an idiot, that much was clear. But under the circumstances, perhaps an idiot was the best he could hope for.

"No," Wendell said. "I guess there's nothing I'm looking for."

Bud helped Wendell clean off his car and made sure he was able to get it started and pulled out of the snow. Then Wendell drove back to the Last Resort alone. He pulled in front of the cabin where he'd had the pancakes.

"Park over there!" Norry hollered at him.

He was going to have to get used to being bossed around, he figured, as Norry directed him to the far end of the resort. He parked and followed Norry to what was obviously the smallest and, he could only assume, least inviting cabin. The log cabin at the end looked to be no larger than a garage. Norry had keys in her hand attached to some kind of wooden fob—a slice of birchwood, as it turned out. She opened the door to the tiny cabin, and Wendell saw his future laid out before him.

The cabin had a stone fireplace across from the door, a single bed made up with a patchwork quilt, a small kitchen with an undersized refrigerator, a coffee maker, a tiny two-burner stove with an even smaller oven beneath, and a white enamel sink. There was a wooden table set against the window facing the lake, and at the back, a minuscule bathroom. The white curtains had chickadees embroidered on them, and there seemed to be a general chickadee theme throughout—although Wendell was no bird expert.

He saw that Lucille's castoffs had already been hung in the coat closet.

"I put that hotdish in the refrigerator, and there's coffee in the kitchen cabinet," Norry informed him.

No cream. No, there wouldn't be, Wendell thought.

"So, make yourself at home. Once you get things sorted out, we can discuss some sort of weekly payment, but I'll keep it reasonable. This is the low season, after all. Housekeeping is on Mondays and Thursdays. If you need extra towels or anything else, just let me know."

He turned to look at Norry as she headed out the door. He had no idea what to say.

"Don't worry, Wendell. You can stay here as long as you need to until you get back on your feet."

And with that, Norry closed the door behind her, and he was left alone in the Chickadee Cabin. Wendell looked around at his primitive new abode.

So. This is what it has come to.

~

"So? What did you say?" Virgie wanted to know.

Norry could picture Virgie, her hennaed hair pinned up in a messy bun, wearing at least three necklaces and two pairs of earrings, sitting out on her balcony.

Virgie had moved up to Loon Point just over ten years ago—after Norry had gotten divorced and returned, unsure of what she was going to do next, after her father had started slowing down and Norry was gradually taking over operations of the Last Resort. Virgie had left corporate life with some savings and turned a small house on the main street of Loon Point into her shop. First, she'd just sold books. Then she'd started making jewelry. Now she had a variety of artwork from local artists, as well as things she hauled back from Mexico.

Virgie was there when Norry's father died, and they'd grown close during that time. Norry liked having a friend she hadn't known since high school, someone who wasn't from Loon Point—or even northern Minnesota. Virgie accused Norry of being "a stick-in-the-mud," and maybe she was. Norry knew they were different. But they were both single women in their forties living in the tiny town of Loon Point, and their friendship seemed inevitable.

Norry had called Virgie to tell her the latest news from Loon Point. As predicted, Virgie invited her to come down to Mexico and spend the month. But Norry told her this was not possible, as she not only had a guest in a cabin but also a houseguest for the weekend. Lizzie and Benson were out exploring the resort, and Norry could see them walking along the shore. She watched them as she talked to make sure they didn't venture too close to the melting ice.

"I told her I'd keep an eye on her daughter while she got her shit together."

"Did she give you any idea how long that might be?"

"Yeah, I'm just watching Lizzie for the rest of today and tomorrow while she gets some shopping and laundry done. Although I'm not sure how much shopping she'll be doing. I get the idea she hasn't had a job in a while."

"Oh, Lord. That poor little girl."

"Yes. Well, she's here now with her dog, and this poor fellow, Wendell, is in the Chickadee Cabin, so I'm not going anywhere anytime soon."

"His roof totally collapsed?"

"Yes, it was bad, according to Bud. That last snowfall was heavy—but that wasn't the real issue. Bud said the roof was ready to go with or without a heavy snowfall. He was darned lucky he wasn't crushed."

"Wow. And it was lucky Lucille called the fire department." Lucille Munson was a regular customer of Virgie's.

"It was. I don't think he'd have made it out on his own. He's a quiet fellow, but he must still be in shock. I just showed him the Chickadee Cabin, and he seemed . . . overwhelmed. It was kind of touching."

"You've got a big heart, Norry."

"I don't know about that. But we have to take care of each other up here, you know. It's not as if there are a lot of resources to help a guy when his roof caves in."

"Well, good luck with your guests. Let me know how it all works out with Lizzie and—what did you say his name was?"

"Benson."

"Oh, him too! I meant the fellow in the Chickadee Cabin."

"Wendell."

"Yeah. Let me know how that goes."

"You miss a lot being in Mexico over the winter."

"I miss you! Take care—and give Bud a squeeze for me, will you?"

"Will do!" Norry hung up the phone. Then she wondered why on earth Virgie was asking her to squeeze Bud Gustafson—and why she'd agreed.

That evening, Lizzie and Norry and Benson had dinner. Norry brought out some frozen walleye Bud had caught that she'd been saving for a special occasion and made a cobbler with raspberries from the past summer. Over cobbler, Norry broached the subject of Lizzie's hair. Lizzie's hand flew to the back of her head.

"It's a mess," she admitted.

"What do you say we wash it and try to work out some of those tangles?"

Norry washed Lizzie's hair, and then she put in a lot of strawberry conditioner. Sitting on the edge of the tub, she slowly worked her way through the knots that had accumulated.

"Ow!"

Norry had come prepared. "Have a cookie," she said, handing Lizzie an oatmeal cookie in the bath. Norry was pleased to note that treats worked as well with Lizzie as they had with Benson.

Norry had a wide-toothed myrtlewood comb she'd been given years ago and seldom used. Norry's hair was fine and straight, and she had never had a hair challenge of this type to sort out. However, the comb was perfect for the job. She gently teased the strands of matted hair loose while Lizzie ate her cookie. She was so thin. Norry looked at the back of the young girl's narrow neck and her small ears, hidden in a forest of unruly hair, and she felt her heart constrict.

Watch it, Norry told herself. *This girl is not your problem.*

Maybe not. Maybe not.

But at that moment, Norry thought how good it was to smell the strawberry conditioner and watch Lizzie eating cookies and slowly work out the knots in her hair. Just for a moment, Norry told herself, it was okay to feel her heart hurt a little. Norry's heart had not felt this way in a long time, and it did no harm to feel it beating—to feel the ache of caring more than she knew she should.

Lizzie fell asleep for a second night in the room that used to be Norry's, with Benson at her side and *Little House in the Big Woods* open on her chest. Norry quietly removed the book, taking care to mark her place.

"You can take the book with you," she told Lizzie the next morning as they had waffles with the raspberries left over from the cobbler.

Lizzie suddenly looked troubled.

"Do you think maybe I could leave it here and read it later?"

Norry felt her heart squeeze again.

"I think that would be a good idea. Then you always have a reason to visit."

Lizzie smiled and went back outside with Benson. It was another sunny day, and the snow was disappearing fast. Norry watched Lizzie running along the lakeshore, her dark hair shiny in the sun, and she wondered how she had allowed this to happen. How had she allowed herself to care so deeply in such a short time?

Cat showed up just before sunset. She looked marginally better. She seemed to be wearing real shoes, and she said she'd had time to get some laundry done. She'd even remembered to bring a collar and leash for Benson. Norry was not handing out any extra points, but Cat did not get any further demerits this evening.

"She can keep the sweatshirt," Norry said. "And the comb."

Cat looked down at the floor. "Her hair was a mess. Thanks for helping her."

Norry watched this young woman as she talked to her daughter in the kitchen. Norry was still angry, but she also recognized Cat was not much more than a girl herself. Her bell-bottom jeans were wet from the melting snow, and her winter jacket had a rip in the side. Norry had to resist the urge to tell her she could stitch that up in a minute, if Cat would give her the chance.

This is not your life, she reminded herself. Again.

"Goodbye, Norry!" Lizzie said as she hustled out the door with Benson and her mother.

"Goodbye, Lizzie."

Cat's old car started up, and they drove down the driveway, and Lizzie was gone.

Norry closed the door and listened. She had forgotten how quiet her house was.

~

Things seemed to be better with Mom.

She had done the laundry, and Lizzie had clean clothes for school tomorrow. The furnace was working again, and there was new milk in the fridge and even some apples. Mom made spaghetti for dinner when they got home. Mr. Benson got real dog food, and he liked that as much as he liked everything else. But Mom seemed tired. She said her back hurt, and she needed to go to bed early.

"Okay. I got a new book."

Lizzie had forgotten where she was in her book from the library. It was a book about a wizard and elves, and Lizzie remembered she had liked it a lot. But right now, she was thinking about *Little House in the Big Woods* with Laura and Mary and Ma and Pa and Jack the dog.

She remembered how she'd woken up in the morning at Norry's and seen the sun on the log walls that were the color of maple syrup and how she'd learned where maple syrup came from. Norry had told her how the trees were being tapped a few miles away, in a forest of maple trees, and how Bud Gustafson would be staying in the "sugar shack" overnight while the syrup was boiling down. It was like there was a whole world right here—in Loon Point—that Lizzie never suspected. It was more surprising than elves and wizards.

Mom was already asleep in her room. Mr. Benson was sleeping beside Lizzie on the couch that was her bed. Mom had made the couch a little more like a bed, and she'd told Lizzie over dinner they wouldn't be living here forever.

"I'm going to start a new job on Monday," she told Lizzie. Mom was going to work in the potato plant outside of Big Pine. Lizzie thought that sounded funny—working in a potato plant—and Mom explained it was a potato-*processing* plant that made the potatoes into french fries. She said the money was better than at the grocery store, although it was a longer drive.

"We'll get out of this trailer this summer," Mom told Lizzie. "This is just temporary."

Lizzie was glad they wouldn't be in the trailer too long. But she liked the woods. She liked the woods more now that she'd spent the weekend with Norry. She knew the names of some of the trees—paper birch, Norway pine, bur oak. She didn't know the names of the birds, but she now noticed there were a lot of them.

"The loons will be back when the water is open," Norry had told her. "You'll hear them flying overhead." Lizzie wanted to hear the loons.

It was quiet tonight. It hadn't seemed this quiet at the Last Resort.

The next morning, her mom was already up when Lizzie was getting ready for school, and she made oatmeal for breakfast. Lizzie wore her sweatshirt from the Last Resort to school, and she didn't need to wear the stocking cap to hide her hair. She used Norry's comb, which was made of wood and came from the "Middle East," wherever that was. Probably New York. The comb was pretty. Her hair looked good too.

"I gotta go to the potato plant," Mom said. Lizzie still thought that sounded funny.

"Okay."

"You have a good day."

"Okay."

"I love you."

"I love you, Mom."

"I love you to the moon and back."

Chapter Eight

April was never a great month in Minnesota, and this April was no surprise to Wendell.

Everything was lost.

He woke every morning with the realization that everything in his life was lost and whatever good days he'd managed to have in the past were behind him. Living in this little hole-in-the-wall cabin on the outskirts of nowhere, Wendell now realized that it was more than his possessions that were buried beneath a ton of rubble. Wendell felt his soul had gonc missing among the detritus.

He had long harbored the suspicion he was different from other people. He saw most of humanity go about its business oblivious. People lived as if everything was great. Life was fine. They woke up stupid and happy and went to bed unchanged. He often thought how nice it would be to live in that kind of ignorant bliss.

Unfortunately, Wendell knew too much. He knew he was in the small minority of people who were only unhappy because they knew what the vast majority were too stupid to understand. People like Wendell knew there was no fairy-tale ending, no pot of gold at the end of the rainbow. Love did not prevail, and dreams did not come true—unless they were nightmares, and Wendell knew all too well how nightmares could invade our waking hours. His recent experience waking to the bright light in his window had confirmed this. None of it surprised Wendell. Although he did wonder, from time to time, why life had dished out such a disproportionate amount of suffering to him.

He considered this Norry woman. She'd apparently inherited this resort from her father—as rich people did—and now she simply coasted along, living off the wealth she had inherited at birth. He looked at Bud, a big bruiser of a guy without a thought in his head. He wouldn't know existential angst from an egg salad sandwich if his life depended on it. He lived his life with this sort of moronic mission of rescuing people from the inevitable emergencies that arose—little suspecting he was part of the problem. Bud just perpetuated grief and disappointment by allowing the victims to survive and endure yet more disappointment and grief.

It was an endless cycle, and it never ceased to amaze Wendell that no one—no one but Wendell—ever lifted their head up long enough to see the chain of suffering and senselessness and call it out for what it was. It was utter and complete futility. Wendell could not see how any thinking person did not realize this—he suspected that a great many actually did—but the majority of humans lived as blind beasts, and the remainder were in a conspiracy of silence, a transparent deception, in which they pretended to be satisfied with the deeply dissatisfying experience of being alive.

Wendell tried to think of a time when he had felt as these folks pretended to feel, and he came up empty. Oh, he'd had a reasonably happy childhood. That was the thing about childhood. You didn't yet know what a can of worms life would turn into. He'd grown up in Loon Point, and he'd enjoyed his time in school as much as anyone does. He'd been good at his classes, and he'd been good at sports, and he remembered thinking he was a big guy, going to Big Pine High, when he made a basket or scored a touchdown. The crowd cheered, and he had imagined what it would be like when he saw his name on the big screen someday, when instead of being idolized by the Big Pine cheerleading squad, he was adored by the starlets in Hollywood.

But life did not work out that way for Wendell. He had never gotten a single thing he'd wanted from life since the age of eighteen, and this—this final exile to the Chickadee Cabin—was fitting, he supposed, for a life that had been wasted, for a person who had never had a chance at happiness, for a man with the worst luck in the world.

Wendell looked out the window at the lake a few feet from the door of his cabin. The ice appeared to have nearly melted off the lake. Well, it was April. What did he expect? It was the month of mud and disappointment. It was the poster child month, the one month that best exemplified the rest of the months on the calendar. Illusions melt. Mud remains. Wendell saw the sun had clouded over. He saw the first raindrop hit the window in front of his little table, and he felt an unusual sensation rising up within himself.

He felt like he might cry.

Wendell had not cried in a long time. He'd cried when his girlfriend had left him after they graduated. He had cried at his mother's funeral. He had cried when he lost that screenwriting contest, the only contest he'd sent a manuscript to and the one he was sure he would win. But all those things were a long time ago, and they made sense. They all represented losses. Wendell couldn't imagine what he now had left to lose.

Another raindrop splashed against the window, and Wendell felt it rolling down his cheek.

Wendell had wanted to cry for a very long time. He put his glasses on the table, and he began to sob. Tears ran down his cheeks and his shoulders shook and he had trouble catching his breath, and he put his forehead down on the table and he cried like a baby.

~

April was a better month for Lizzie.

Mom was still working at the potato plant, and they now had regular meals together. Lizzie had gotten some new jeans that were the right length, and Mr. Benson had put on some weight so you could no longer feel his bones through his fur. Lizzie was still getting teased on the school bus, but now that her hair looked better and she had jeans that fit, Jodie got tired of thinking up new rude things to say and sometimes took a day off.

Mom checked with animal control to make sure no dogs matching Mr. Benson's description had gone missing, and Lizzie held her breath the whole time she was on the phone. But there were no lost dogs except for one chihuahua who had been missing since January, and everybody knew that dog had been dinner for a wolf or a coyote—or maybe even an eagle—a long time ago.

The paper birch around the trailer were covered in lime-green buds, and the first of the wildflowers were blooming. Lizzie didn't know what they were called, but they were white and pretty, and they filled the forest floor for a little while and then disappeared.

And the loons came back.

Lizzie heard them calling right over her head. They were returning to Loon Point, and they flew right over Lizzie's trailer, making that strange and wonderful sound that started out like the saddest song in the world and ended up like a wonderful joke they were all laughing about together. Lizzie knew they would be landing in the water right in front of the Last Resort.

Twice Lizzie went to visit Norry. The first time she went, Norry was pouring maple syrup from a big bucket into smaller bottles. "Bud must have had a bumper crop this year," Norry said. "What am I gonna do with three gallons of maple syrup?"

Norry poured the syrup through a funnel into smaller glass bottles and screwed the caps on tight. Then she gave one to Lizzie to take home. Lizzie stuck her finger in it, and it tasted exactly like she thought a flower must taste like to a bee.

The second time she was there, the ice on the lake was starting to melt, and it was all sparkly in the sun, with chunks floating in the water.

Norry was taking the barbecue grills out of storage, and she was putting a fresh coat of varnish on the wooden lawn chairs.

"Varnish is best for outdoors," Norry told her. "It doesn't dry and crack in the sun." Lizzie liked the smell.

But most days, Lizzie stayed at home after school and waited for her mom to get back from the potato plant. She and Mr. Benson would walk down the long road that led to Big Pine, and she would throw a ball. Mr. Benson was getting really good at catching the ball when Lizzie threw it straight up in the air. He'd watch the ball falling from the sky, move a little to the right, then a little to the left, then position himself to exactly where the ball was falling and catch it right in his mouth. Then he'd shake it, like he was celebrating, before running back to Lizzie and dropping it—all covered in dog spit—at her feet.

Then they'd go inside, and Lizzie would read until Mom got home. Mom was always tired, and some days she said her back hurt, which worried Lizzie. But she'd take a shower and make dinner, and all three of them would go to bed at about the same time, just as it was getting dark, just in time to hear the loons flying overhead, telling their sad jokes as they flew to the water.

Lizzie wished things could be like this forever.

Mom was saving money, and she said she hoped they could move into Big Pine before fall. She pulled a frozen pizza out of the oven and told Lizzie she'd been looking at apartments in town near the elementary school.

"Then you can walk to school instead of taking the bus every day."

Lizzie wouldn't miss the bus ride. She wouldn't miss Jodie or standing in the cold, waiting for the bus to arrive. But now that they were in Loon Point, Lizzie wished they could stay.

"Maybe we could live in Loon Point," Lizzie suggested, "but in a house."

"There's nowhere for us to live in Loon Point, Lizzie. There are less than a hundred people in the whole town. And we'd still have to drive to Big Pine every time we wanted anything. The only people living in

Loon Point are people with businesses that cater to rich tourists—or rich people with homes on the lake."

Lizzie figured this was true. The reason Jodie was on the bus was because her family had a big house on the lake that looked like it could be a hotel, but it was just for Jodie, her brother, and her mom and dad.

Of course, what Lizzie was thinking was that she'd like to live in a cabin like Norry's or (if she was honest) maybe one of Norry's cabins. That guy, Wendell, with the big red shoes, was now living full time in one of Norry's cabins. Lizzie thought he must be the luckiest person alive to get to live right on the edge of the lake in one of those log cabins the color of maple syrup, looking out at the loons as they hit the water, feet splashing, making that wonderful sound right up close.

Now that it was a little warmer, Lizzie would crank open the little window over her bed so she could hear what went on outside at night. She heard a great horned owl make its spooky noise, and she heard the white pine needles make a purring sound, and she heard sticks crack and guessed there were deer moving around close by. She heard red squirrels scold each other before they went to bed, and sometimes, usually just after sunset, she'd hear the loons on the lake, not too far away. The sound was distant and sorrowful, and it gave Lizzie goose bumps. Mr. Benson lifted his head up off the covers and tilted it a little, listening to the loons.

"Aren't they the funniest things, Mr. Benson?"

Lizzie wondered if the loons were making nests on the lake, and she wondered what would happen in the summer. She wondered where she and Mom would live and if she'd ever get to stay at Norry's again. Then Mr. Benson poked his nose under her arm and Lizzie buried her fingers in his curly fur, and she fell asleep to the noises in the woods.

~

"Hey," Bud said.

Bud had just driven up in that big red truck of his. The plow attachment was finally off for the summer, Norry noted.

In northern Minnesota, when people were looking for signs of spring, lots of folks took their cues from nature—perhaps the appearance of the first bloodroot or trillium. Many people considered the return of the loons the true start of spring. But Norry remembered years when the flowers had been buried in a foot of snow. And she remembered years when the loons had returned to a frozen lake.

Only when Bud took the plow off his pickup was Norry willing to concede that spring had arrived in earnest.

"Hey," Norry replied.

She was getting the last coat of varnish on the old lawn chairs. She'd sewn new covers for all the cushions. The chairs were going to look great this summer.

"You could do that once with polyurethane and be done with it for ten years," Bud said.

"And it would look like crap in two years. And covering it over with another coat would just make it look worse."

"Have it your way."

"I will."

"You'll always get the Last word!" Bud started laughing.

"What the heck are you doing here, anyway? Shouldn't you be fishing?"

"Since when have you known me to fish for crappie or perch?"

Bud was conscientious. Norry had to give that to him. A lot of locals would start fishing before the season, knowing the DNR would never catch them (and would look the other way if they did), but Bud always made a big deal out of the fishing opener for northerns and walleye and never pulled anything in early.

"So, what are you doing here?"

"I wanted to know what you were up to on Thursday."

"What I'm up to?"

"Yeah."

"I'm not up to anything. You know that. I never am. I spend this time of year getting things ready."

"Good. Then you can come with me to a concert."

"A concert?"

"Yeah."

Bud was looking slightly more red than usual, and Norry wondered what this was all about.

"What kind of concert?"

"I think it's . . . I dunno exactly. It's the kind of music you like. It's piano music, the kind of stuff they play on Minnesota Public Radio."

"Classical music?"

"Yeah." Bud was undeniably redder now.

"Why are you going to a classical music concert? I've never heard anything come out of your truck but country western."

"I got tickets, that's all. I thought you might like to go."

"You got tickets for me?"

"Yeah." By now Bud's complexion was closing in on the color of his red plaid shirt.

Norry stopped applying varnish for a moment and took a long look at him.

"Why? Was I your Last choice?"

Bud ducked his head and looked at his red hands.

"Was I Last but not least?"

She saw the edge of a smile forming on his now very red face.

"Were you hoping for a date before Last call?"

"Oh, Norry."

"What? You come here and ask me to go to a classical music concert when I know you hate classical music, and I'm supposed to think there isn't some kind of joke involved?"

"How long have you known me, Norry?"

Norry did the math. "About thirty years."

It didn't seem possible, but she'd known Bud Gustafson since high school, and in a couple of years, they'd be having their thirtieth class reunion.

She and Bud hadn't been friends in high school, of course. Norry was a nerd with places to go, and Bud was a jock who always knew he was going to stay around Loon Point, where he liked to fish in the summer and hunt in the fall and plow snow in the winter. Bud had always been here. Bud was the guy people counted on when they needed handyman stuff done for a fair price. He held the Big Pine Volunteer Fire Department together and had, for a while, served as a deputy sheriff until the schedule ate into his fishing time a little more than he liked.

Norry figured that by now, she knew everything there was to know about Bud Gustafson. She knew about his two marriages to women everyone knew were going to cause him heartbreak, and she knew about the death of the baby he'd had with his second wife—a loss that had gutted him.

Bud was a known quantity. He was like the lake or the loons or the changing of the seasons. He was reliable and annoying and kind. And he was not a guy who went out and bought tickets to a classical music concert.

Norry thought of all the things she might say to Bud. Instead, she only asked, "Why?"

"Geez, Norry. How dense are you?"

"Pretty dense. Remember, I'm always the Last to know."

"Oh, stop it."

Norry waited.

"I . . . I just wanted to ask you out. I've wanted to ask you out for a long time, and I heard about this concert, and it sounded like the kind of thing you'd listen to. So I bought a couple of tickets. That's why."

"So . . . this is like a date?"

"Yeah. Yeah, this is like a date."

"You dated Virgie, my best friend."

"So? That was ten years ago."

"I can't date someone Virgie dated."

"Virgie dated everyone!"

Bud made a good point. And now Norry remembered Virgie had told her to "give Bud a squeeze." Was it possible they were in this together? The thought was mortifying.

"You're overthinking this," Bud pointed out.

"This, coming from a man who forgets to clamp down a brand-new Evinrude and loses it in the middle of the lake!"

"Geez, Norry! That was thirty years ago. I was sixteen. And I was drunk. You've gotta let some things go."

"Where's the concert?"

"At the armory."

"What are they playing?"

"I don't know . . ." Bud fished the tickets out of his breast pocket.

"Choppin'," he said.

"You mean Chopin?"

"Yeah, whatever."

Norry smiled. "Okay."

"Okay, you'll go?"

"Yeah. That sounds like fun. I haven't been to a concert in forever."

Bud appeared to be at a loss for a moment. Then he smiled.

"That's great! That's really great. How about if I pick you up at five and we get some dinner in Big Pine first?"

"You mean like a Last Supper?"

"Norry!"

Norry smiled. "That would be great." She suspected she was now turning red.

Bud sprinted back to his pickup with much more speed than necessary and pulled out of the driveway. Norry picked up her paintbrush and continued varnishing the arm of a chair, but now she couldn't remember where she'd left off.

This was dumb. First-rate dumb. She'd had Bud as a friend for all this time, and now she was going to go screw things up and go with him on a "date."

Then she wondered what on earth she was going to wear.

Chapter Nine

Thursday came too soon, and Norry spent too much time worrying about it.

She hadn't been to anything remotely fancy in ages, she realized as she rummaged through the back of her closet, the place where clothes that were never worn slowly migrated until they were forgotten. Most of them, she discovered, were better off forgotten.

Why do I still have this? she kept asking, as she pulled out one disappointing dress and blazer after another.

Norry didn't have that many clothes, but it turned out she had considerably more than she remembered, since she wore the same uniform of jeans and a Last Resort T-shirt or sweatshirt 99.9 percent of the time.

Good Lord.

She pulled a floral monstrosity out from the depths of her closet and threw it up onto her bed, where it was exposed in all its hideous glory. It was clearly time for a trip to the used clothing store in Big Pine, which took donations. Norry yanked out a blouse in an unappetizing shade of pink.

Oh, yuck.

She wasn't getting any closer to finding anything to wear to the concert, but this inventory of her closet was long overdue. Now and then, she and Virgie would go out for a bite in Big Pine, but there was no restaurant in town where you couldn't wear jeans. In jeans paired with a newer Last Resort T-shirt, Norry never felt out of place. But now she was going to listen to Chopin, and she imagined folks with big lake homes would be there and . . . Norry's thoughts trailed off. She felt like a teenager, insecure about who she was and what she had or didn't have. Norry had passed that stage a long time ago, hadn't she?

She was a business owner and a mature adult, and she had no reason to give a moment's attention to what others thought of her—and honestly, she hadn't in a long time. This whole rummaging through the closet and working herself into a frenzy over what to wear to a concert at the armory was peculiar and uncharacteristic. Norry didn't like it. And it was all Bud's fault.

Why had she agreed to go to this damned concert with him? When he told her it was a date, she should have let him down gently, told him this was not going to work, maybe suggested someone else he could go with. Most of the suggestions that came to mind were quite a bit younger than Bud, but what difference did that make? Bud wouldn't mind taking some young thing to the concert. Bud would probably prefer it. No, Bud had asked her because it was Chopin and he knew she listened to Minnesota Public Radio, and he couldn't think of anyone else in Big Pine—and certainly no one in Loon Point—who would be interested in that, so he decided to ask poor old Norry Last. She really was his Last resort.

Norry sat on the bed next to the pile of rejects. She was going to get rid of all these clothes and she was not going to replace them with anything new. Norry was not a person who went out. She was not someone who needed fancy clothes. She was going to get rid of everything that was not a sweatshirt or T-shirt, and she was going to remember who she was—and who she was not. She was not a person who got all dolled up to go to the armory. And that was that.

She flipped through the clothes lying on the bed.

Okay. There was this blouse.

Norry pulled it out. It had stupid shoulder pads. How old must this be to still have shoulder pads? Wasn't that what they wore when she was in high school? Surely this blouse was not that old. No. It wasn't. It was just a simple blouse Norry had worn with a skirt or a pair of slacks a lifetime ago during her brief and terrible marriage. She was not going to think about that.

Norry grabbed the blouse, cut off the stupid shoulder pads, and tried it on. It was nice. It was a simple cream-colored blouse with pearl buttons. Tucked into a pair of black jeans and nice boots, it would do perfectly well for the concert. This was the armory, for God's sake. It wasn't as if she was flying off to Mexico.

And Norry realized part of the reason she never wanted to go to Mexico was that she didn't know what to wear. She didn't know who she was when she wasn't wearing her T-shirt with the loon on the front. She was one person all the time, and that person didn't go to concerts at the armory and certainly didn't fly off to Mexico.

But the cream shirt was nice. It wasn't silk, but it looked like it. And Norry still had a pretty good figure. She didn't own a scale, but she kept buying the same size of Levi's, so things hadn't gotten too out of hand. She liked the shiny black boots she'd put on. She'd always liked those boots and had worn them out with Virgie a few times. They had a little bit of a heel, and Virgie called them her "shit-kicking boots," so that's how Norry always thought of them.

Thinking of Virgie reminded Norry that Virgie had dated Bud, and that was not a pleasant thought. But then she also remembered that Virgie had given her a necklace that she'd worn exactly once—just to show she was appreciative. Norry never wore jewelry. She dug in her drawer until she found the necklace. It was made of sparkly beads in different colors. It looked like it would go with anything, so it certainly would go with a white blouse and jeans. *Great. I'm going on a date with Virgie's old boyfriend wearing Virgie's old necklace.*

Dumb. This whole thing was dumb.

Norry looked at herself in the mirror. The effect was not terrible. She would wear a little lipstick to the concert. That would surprise Bud—if he noticed. Did she want him to notice?

Norry sat back down on the bed with her pile of discards. Did she care what Bud thought about her? More to the point, did she care about Bud?

Of course she did. He was a great friend. He'd been her friend for years. He'd been a huge help after her dad died, when Norry discovered there was still a lot about running the resort she didn't know. Who pumped the septic? Who was the best person to check out the well? What should she do when the pontoon boat motor got wonky? She'd called him when she needed repairs, and he never charged her as much as she thought he should, so she'd gotten in the habit of cooking a meal for him from time to time. He'd come by for breakfast on the weekend and she'd offer him pancakes, or he'd bring over some walleye and she'd make a meal for them. It was very relaxed, and she liked his company. But it was never a date. It wasn't Chopin.

The radio was on in the kitchen, and as if on cue, Norry heard one of Chopin's nocturnes playing. She didn't know which one, but she knew it was Chopin. She felt wistful—and she felt something else. While she was content as Norry No Last Name at the Last Resort, she sometimes missed being something different as well. At that moment—sitting on her bed, wearing a cream-colored blouse that wasn't silk but felt like it, with a sparkly necklace around her neck, listening to Chopin—Norry realized she missed being someone who did different things, someone who wore different clothes, maybe someone who looked at people in a little different way.

Bud was a goofball and sometimes a pain in the ass, but nothing he did could hide his oversize heart. He had helped more people without payment than anyone Norry knew—and she knew she didn't know the half of what he did. Helping people was instinctual for Bud. It was why he was taken in by those two wives of his so easily. They both needed a lot of help that Bud was happy to provide. People joked about his bad taste in women, but Norry knew his heart had been hurt, being treated as poorly as he had been in the end. Bud never expected people to be mean. He always expected the best of everyone.

Norry looked down at her shiny black shitkickers, and she knew that whatever happened, she would not be mean to Bud. If nothing came of this date—and chances are, nothing would—it would not affect their friendship. She wasn't going to lose Bud as a friend.

As soon as she realized this, Norry felt herself relax. It was going to be okay. Chopin was still playing in the kitchen. She noticed she had a lot of varnish under her fingernails. Yet Norry looked back up at herself in the mirror and liked what she saw.

"I am allowed to do something different once in a while!" she declared.

The Chopin ended. The announcer on Minnesota Public Radio reminded listeners that the station relied upon listener contributions to make this programming possible. Norry hung up the cream blouse and stuffed all the dreadful castoffs into a grocery sack.

Then she went outside into the sunshine to finish varnishing her chairs.

~

"Mom!"

Silence. It was almost time for Lizzie to go to the bus. Mom was usually gone by now, off to the potato plant.

"Mom! It's late!"

Silence.

Lizzie pushed the door open to her mom's room. Mr. Benson poked his nose in and went over to the bed. He started licking Mom's hand.

"What?" she said.

"It's late. I have to go to school."

"Oh. Okay."

"Are you going to the potato plant?"

"What is this, the Inquisition?"

Lizzie didn't know what an inquisition was, but she didn't think she was one.

"No. I just thought you overslept."

"Maybe I did."

Lizzie waited for her to say more. Mr. Benson sat down and waited too.

"Look, I don't know what I'm going to do, okay? It's not ideal, slicing potatoes all day, you know? It's not exactly what I imagined I'd be doing with my life."

Lizzie didn't know what her mom had imagined she'd do with her life. Lizzie had never thought about this before.

"I might look for a new job."

"Instead of the potato plant?"

"Yes. I am sick to death of potatoes. I don't care if I never see another potato for the rest of my life. I've got a friend who just started work at a new bar in Big Pine. I might go apply there."

"Okay."

But it didn't feel okay to Lizzie. The last month had been good, and Lizzie had been giving the potato plant a lot of credit for Mom doing better. She knew it was really like a factory, but when she imagined the potato plant, she saw it as this giant, friendly green plant that held Mom in its branches and kept her safe in its leaves. Lizzie thought of the potato plant as a friend.

"I gotta go to school. I'm gonna get another perfect attendance award this year. I haven't been late or missed one day."

"That's terrific."

But Mom didn't sound like she thought it was terrific. She sounded like she thought it might be kind of dumb. Lizzie bit her lip.

"Bye, Mom."

"Bye, Lizzie."

"I love you."

But Mom was asleep.

~

Wendell had not gotten out of bed.

He did not see the point. He realized he had been getting up out of sheer habit for as long as he could remember, and he could just as easily break this habit as any other. So, instead of getting up in the morning and having a cup of coffee and staring out at the lake from his miserable little cabin, Wendell decided he would simply stay in bed. No one cared. Why not?

Wendell lay in bed and wondered what other useless habits he had acquired. Certainly, the habit of getting out of bed was overrated. He didn't exercise, so he didn't have to worry about breaking that habit. Nor did he eat particularly carefully. He'd noted he was eating a little less, living here in the Chickadee Cabin, simply because he was located in the furthest corner of godforsaken nowhere and there wasn't even a gas station nearby where he could pick up a bag of potato chips. Wendell liked potato chips.

Wendell realized that of all his habits, the one he held onto most stubbornly—and for the least compelling reasons—was his habit of living. He continued to live simply because he was too lazy to die. That was how he figured it.

He was staring at the log ceiling, imagining the spot where his house used to be, now scraped clean. Bud said it was all in the landfill. Everything that had been his life was gone. His whole life was in the dump. The one thing Wendell had hung on to was the most useless thing of all, and that was his living, breathing self. The only problem, as Wendell saw it, was that killing himself was a hell of a lot of work.

"Means, motive, and opportunity." Wasn't that what the cop shows always said?

Wendell had more than ample motive. That went without saying. And he had plenty of opportunity. Wendell had nothing more important than killing himself planned for the next two weeks, at least. At some point this summer, he was due to see his doctor, but that wouldn't be necessary if he was dead.

No, the problem was means. He needed an easy way to kill himself. He didn't like pain, and he didn't like uncertainty, and dying seemed to involve one or the other or both. He couldn't imagine going to all the trouble of finding a handgun. It wasn't as easy in Minnesota as it used to be. Then he'd have to learn how to operate the damned thing. He'd never shot a gun in his life, and he'd hate to get it wrong.

His other option was to get some super-powerful pills, but he wasn't sure how to do that. He could tell his doctor he was having terrible pain, maybe, or that he had insomnia. Then he'd get a prescription and take the whole bottle. But it was difficult these days, from what Wendell understood, to get pills that were the real deal. There were a lot of inconsiderate people taking pills just to get high and making it hard for a guy like Wendell to get the drugs he needed to do himself in.

Wendell thought of seeking out a drug dealer. He imagined himself walking down a dark alley and meeting his "connection," but he knew he was not imagining Big Pine. He was imagining some gritty city in a movie. The drug dealers in Big Pine would be twenty years old with huge piercings in their ears—"flesh tunnels," he'd heard them called. The name alone gave him the heebie-jeebies. Wendell tried to imagine what the fellow with the flesh tunnels would think of a seventy-two-year-old man purchasing enough of whatever the fellow was selling to do himself in. The whole project sounded overwhelming.

And, before he did any of that, he'd have to get out of bed. There was no practical way to do himself in while lying under a patchwork quilt covered in chickadees. He'd have to get out of bed and put on shoes before he could hunt down a gun or drugs, and walking around as little as he did these days, it was getting increasingly difficult to move at all. The idea of purchasing contraband sounded exhausting.

Wendell lay in his bed under the log ceiling and wondered what was going on in the real world. The Chickadee Cabin wasn't the real world, that was for sure. Neither was Loon Point. Neither was Big Pine, for that matter. Wendell lay under a patchwork quilt covered with stupid little birds and realized he'd never been in the real world. Not for a single day.

~

Mom must have gone to the potato plant after all, Lizzie figured, because she wasn't there when Lizzie got home from school.

It was getting dark, although the days were longer now. It was almost May, and the summer solstice was in June. Mr. Benson (the teacher, not her dog) had told her about how the earth went around the sun and how the tilt of the earth affected how long anyone could see the sun. That's why the days in the summer were longer. On the other end of the planet, it was just the opposite, which was wild to think about, because it meant it was super hot at Christmas. Lizzie couldn't imagine that.

But now it was getting dark, which meant Mom was late getting home, and although Lizzie had almost stopped worrying about Mom, she was now worried again. Mom was late. It was not good.

Lizzie fed Mr. Benson dinner. She wondered if she should get herself some dinner too. She wondered if Mom would be mad if Lizzie made herself some dinner before she got home—if it would look like Lizzie wasn't expecting her to come home. Lizzie didn't want her to think that.

"Mom will be home soon," she told Mr. Benson. "But you can eat now, before we do."

Mr. Benson appreciated getting dinner. Lizzie sat back down on the couch that was also her bed. She was having a hard time concentrating on her book.

Maybe Mom had gotten that new job at the bar she was talking about. Maybe they asked her to start right away. That would make sense. And if she had a job at a bar, would they give her dinner? They might. Probably a hamburger. Maybe Mom would have a hamburger and then come home.

Mom would say "Did you make dinner for yourself? That's great, Lizzie! I didn't know I'd be so late." And she'd give Lizzie a big hug, and she'd tell Lizzie she'd brought home a piece of strawberry cheesecake from the bar, and they'd sit and eat strawberry cheesecake, and Mom would tell her all about her new job and ask how Lizzie's day at school had been. Lizzie loved cheesecake, especially with strawberries.

Mom isn't coming home with cheesecake.

Lizzie knew that. She didn't know where her mom was, but she didn't think she'd gone to the potato plant today, and she didn't think Mom had started a new job without telling her. Mom was just gone—the way she was sometimes, the way she hadn't been for a while, the way she used to be before things got better.

Lizzie went to the cupboard. There were crackers, and there was cheese. There was one apple left. She cut the cheese into slices and the apple too. She put the cheese and crackers and apple on a plate, and she took it over to her bed that was also a couch. Mr. Benson jumped up and lay beside her. She heard a loon calling overhead. Tonight the loon sounded sad. Tonight there was no funny joke at the end of the song.

Lizzie fell asleep listening to the loons. She didn't wake up until she heard Mr. Benson barking and saw the red and blue lights flashing outside her window.

Chapter Ten

The concert was wonderful. Norry was pleasantly surprised.

Bud had picked her up, looking a lot tidier than usual. She did a double take when he arrived because he was not wearing a hat of any kind.

"You've got hair," she said.

"So?"

"I haven't seen the top of your head since high school. I assumed you had no hair left."

"What do you mean? I've got plenty of hair!" Bud ran his hands through his hair, making it stand on end.

And it was true. Except for a small spot thinning in the back, Bud had a full head of reddish-blond hair with curls and a noticeable tan line running across his forehead.

When they entered the armory and Norry saw the single piano on stage, she was briefly disappointed, thinking it would be a full orchestra. But then she saw the stage floor had been covered with hundreds of tiny votive lights surrounding the glossy black grand piano. The house lights dimmed, and once the first notes were struck, she did not feel she was in the pokey Big Pine Armory with the banners of civic organizations hanging on the walls, but was suddenly transported somewhere else, a place where one would routinely wear a blouse that felt like silk and listen to Chopin's nocturnes played in dim light surrounded by flickering candle flames.

"Are those real?" Bud wanted to know as soon as he saw the votive candles. Norry figured a member of the Big Pine Volunteer Fire Department was never really off duty.

"They're battery, I think," Norry said. And they were.

But Norry was going to pretend they were real. Tonight, she was going to pretend this was her real life, surrounded by candlelight and listening to Chopin.

As the first nocturne played, Bud reached for her hand and held it. He did it in such a natural way that Norry hardly noticed until her hand was within his. His hand was calloused, as it would be, and it was gentle, as it would be, belonging to the man it did, and Norry had a sudden unbidden thought.

Norry wondered if making love to Bud Gustafson would be as natural and as gentle as this. She imagined him reaching for her, and she imagined herself responding as quickly and with as little hesitation as she had when he'd taken her hand. Then she felt her insides stir with a moment of powerful desire, and she felt her hand grow damp, and she looked over at Bud—good old Bud.

She had never spent much time thinking about Bud Gustafson in all the years she'd lived in Loon Point, which had been most of her life. He'd been there when she needed help. He'd appreciated the little things she'd done for him. He made jokes about her name.

She'd judged him for the loud country music blaring from his truck, and she'd judged him because, as far as she knew, he'd never left Big Pine but lived all his life along one lake or another in the area. She thought of herself as more worldly and more knowledgeable and a bit more discerning.

But Bud could tell you what the weather was going to do, and no matter what Minnesota Public Radio predicted, her money would always be on Bud. He knew when the fish would be biting, and he sensed the presence of bear in the woods when Norry heard nothing. He would go hunting in the fall, and while Norry was not overly fond of hunting, Bud would cuss about the hunters who injured animals without finishing the job or hunted for pleasure with no intention of eating what they killed. He was a moral man, Norry thought. He was a smart guy.

And as Norry looked at his profile in the dim armory, she realized he was also nice to look at. She got wondering what the redheaded Bud would look like in the buff and felt her hand grow a little more damp. She was thinking she would never hear Chopin's Nocturne in E-flat Major in the same way again. And she decided—right then and there—she was going to invite Bud into her bed that night.

It had been a long time since Norry had contemplated any such thing. Her marriage to Alex had wounded her deeply, and it had shaken her belief in herself. She'd tried so hard to save the marriage that she'd changed as a person—and she didn't like the person she'd become. She didn't want to be that sad and hurt woman, and she'd decided, in order to avoid it, she'd stay out of romantic relationships entirely.

Coming back to the Last Resort and slowly taking the business over from her dad had provided exactly the distraction she had needed to transition from the person she didn't want to be into the person she now was—and that person was single and did not rely on anyone to meet her needs. And now this.

But Norry didn't care. The music played, and Norry felt reckless. She tilted her head back in the seat and let that music wash over her. The rules she had placed on herself had been good rules at the time. They had made her a better person. But she didn't have to live by the same rules for the rest of her life. And she didn't have to remain the same. She was a good person. She could afford to be a little kinder to herself without worrying she would no longer be independent. And inviting Bud Gustafson into her bed was an exciting thing to do for this new person she was going to let herself be.

Norry looked over at Bud. His head was also tipped back on the seat because he had fallen fast asleep. She smiled. She kept her hand right where it was and didn't take it back until intermission.

~

Lizzie woke when she heard Mr. Benson barking.

She was sure it was Mom and wondered if she was coming home with dinner—or cheesecake. But then she saw the blue and red lights reflecting on the ceiling and she knew it wasn't Mom.

Lizzie looked out the window. There was a police car stopped right outside the trailer where Mom usually parked, and Lizzie heard the sound of people talking on a radio. Then the car door slammed, and a man in a uniform came to the trailer door. Mr. Benson barked louder. Lizzie got out of bed and opened the door.

"Sorry to wake you, young lady. I'm Deputy Sheriff Calvin Webb. Are you Elizabeth Lundin?"

Nobody called Lizzie "Elizabeth," not even her mom when Lizzie was in trouble. Lizzie felt her stomach tighten.

"Uh-huh."

"Well, I'm afraid your mother is in the hospital. She's going to be okay, but she won't make it home tonight."

Lizzie stared at Sheriff Calvin. "Where's Mom?"

Sheriff Calvin took off his hat. "She's in the hospital in Big Pine, sweetie. They're taking good care of her. Do you have any family nearby where you could spend the night?"

Lizzie didn't have any family in the area, unless the area included North Dakota, and she didn't think it did. Sheriff Calvin seemed very serious. Lizzie felt the walls of the trailer start to spin as she stood perfectly still in the doorway. She wondered if her mom was going to die. This was the thing she had always feared, although she'd never said it aloud or thought about it quite so clearly.

Lizzie began to pray. *Please, God, please don't let Mom die. Please, God, please. Amen.*

~

At intermission, Norry checked her phone out of habit. She didn't expect any messages as there were no guests at the resort except for that peculiar fellow, Wendell, who had hardly spoken ten words since he'd checked in. He seemed to be happy enough, however, spending his days in the little Chickadee Cabin and recovering, Norry supposed, from the shock of losing his house.

But there was a message on her phone.

"Norry, this is Deputy Calvin Webb at the sheriff's department in Big Pine. Sorry to bother you, but I've got a young girl here, an Elizabeth Lundin, who says she knows you, and I'm wondering if you'd mind stopping by the sheriff's office when you get this message. Her mom's been hospitalized, and I'm hoping she might be able to stay with you tonight. Thanks."

Norry played the message to Bud. He was already headed to the truck before it finished. They drove to the sheriff's office, which was only two blocks from the armory.

"What's up, Cal?" Bud had worked with Calvin when he'd been a deputy sheriff and saw him regularly in his work with the volunteer fire department.

"What happened?" Norry's eyes scanned the sheriff's office for Lizzie.

"Little girl's mom was taken to the hospital. Overdose. She pulled through, but she's going to spend at least a few more hours under observation. There's no immediate family in the area, and Lizzie asked if she could stay at the Last Resort with you. She said she'd done that before, so I thought I'd give you a call. Are you friends with the mother?"

Norry had to think for a moment. "I know her," she answered. "And, yes, Lizzie has stayed with me and is more than welcome to again. Where's her dog?"

"I've got them both in back."

As they walked to the office down the hall, Calvin noticed Bud's spruced-up appearance. "Hey, I'm sorry if I interrupted your evening."

"No problem, Cal."

Norry shot a look at Calvin, saw the half smile on his face, and knew that news of her date with Bud would be all over town before the first doughnut was eaten in the morning.

Calvin opened the office door at the end of the short hallway. Sitting in an oversize chair under an enormous fluorescent light was a small girl with a dog at her feet.

"Norry!" Lizzie ran over to Norry and hugged her. "Mom's in the hospital and I didn't know who else they should call. I hope it's okay."

"Of course it's okay. It's more than okay. It was exactly the right thing to do. Have you had anything to eat?"

"I had crackers at home. And Sheriff Calvin got me a Pearson's Salted Nut Roll."

"Deputy Sheriff," Calvin corrected, not looking as if he minded the promotion.

"Well, that doesn't sound like much of a dinner. How about if we get you home—to the resort—and find you something to eat?"

Norry realized she'd said *home* as if it was Lizzie's home, and when she saw the look on Lizzie's face, her heart hurt. This kid had no home. At that moment, Norry didn't care if Cat was in intensive care. She was furious with her all ovcr again.

Bud drove Lizzie and Norry back to the Last Resort. The resort was dark except for a porch light Norry had left on and one small light burning in the Chickadee Cabin. It was nice having Wendell there, Norry thought with surprise. Having a guest made the place feel more welcoming on this dark night.

Bud parked his big red truck in front of Norry's cabin.

"Well, I'll see you soon then, I guess," Bud said, as Norry and Lizzie and Benson got out.

Norry suddenly remembered her plans for Bud and his gentle hands, and she wished she'd been given a chance to let him know.

"Yeah, I'll let you know what happens," Norry said. "Thanks for the ticket. I loved the music. Thanks for inviting me."

"Hey, I liked what I heard. I might have to play that every night when I'm having trouble getting to sleep. I think it worked better than any sleeping pill!" Bud laughed and looked into her eyes. Norry put her hand on his arm and wanted to say more.

But Mr. Benson had already run up the porch steps and was waiting expectantly for Lizzie, who was trudging behind.

"Bye, Lizzie! See ya, Mr. Benson!" Bud called to the tired girl and excited dog waiting on the stoop.

Norry watched Bud drive off in his big Ford pickup and then turned to Lizzie. That poor girl. She looked exhausted and thin and much more worried than any eight-year-old ever should.

~

Lizzie noticed Norry wasn't wearing her usual Last Resort T-shirt. She was wearing a fancy white shirt and had on a necklace made of colored beads.

"You look pretty."

"Oh! Thanks. Let's get you some dinner."

It was late for dinner, but Lizzie was hungry. Then Norry's phone rang. Lizzie's stomach tightened again. *Please, God, please don't let Mom die. Please, God, please. Amen.*

"Hi, Cat," Norry said, and Lizzie let out a breath she didn't know she'd been holding.

Norry talked to Mom for a couple of minutes and then gave the phone to Lizzie. Mom sounded really tired, but not like she was dying.

"Hey, babe. Norry said you could spend the night if you wanted to."

"I have school tomorrow."

"Can you get to the bus stop from the Last Resort?"

"Yeah, I can get there."

"Okay. I'm gonna rest now. I'll be home tomorrow."

"Love you, Mom."

"Love you. See you tomorrow."

The line went dead.

Lizzie saw Norry was watching her. "Mom said it was okay if I stayed tonight."

"I think that's a good plan."

"I have to go to school tomorrow." Lizzie felt this might need a little more explanation. "I have perfect attendance."

"Really? That's terrific. I wouldn't want you missing school. Do you take the bus?"

"It picks me up at the end of the road. By your sign."

"Oh! Right there on County Road 6. That's good. I can drive you that far. Or I can just take you to school if you like."

"No, no, it's okay. I can take the bus."

"You'll need some clothes."

Lizzie looked down at her clothes. They were cleaner than usual.

"I'm okay."

"How about a Last Resort T-shirt? Then you'll have a full set!"

Lizzie wasn't sure what that meant. All she had was a sweatshirt. But she liked the T-shirts. Norry always wore one. They had a loon on the front too.

"Okay."

Now that Lizzie knew Mom wasn't dead, she felt very tired. She finished the soup Norry had given her. It was good and had wild rice in it. She emptied her glass of milk. She slipped a piece of toast to Mr. Benson under the table.

Then Norry gave her a new Last Resort sweatshirt to sleep in. This one was blue (the other one was red) and Lizzie used another brand-new toothbrush in Norry's bathroom and went to bed in the little bedroom with the log walls. *Mom's not dead. Thank you, thank you, thank you. Amen.*

The sheets smelled like the outdoors, just like last time. *Little House in the Big Woods* was on the shelf next to all the books that came after it. Mr. Benson jumped up on the bed and made himself comfortable. He seemed to like the bed at Norry's. It was bigger than the couch that was also their bed in the trailer.

Lizzie heard Norry talking outside her bedroom door. She heard her say, "She's okay. She's going to be released tomorrow," and Lizzie felt her chest loosen. Mr. Benson sighed. *Thank you, thank you, thank you. Amen.*

The next morning, Lizzie woke to the smell of bacon.

Norry was at the stove, making pancakes again, and this time there was bacon too.

"I figured you should have something decent before going off to school," Norry said as she put a pile of pancakes on the table. Lizzie was wearing her new Last Resort T-shirt, and she saw Mr. Benson was eating pancakes from a dish on the floor.

After Lizzie finished her pancakes, the three of them piled into the Last Resort Jeep.

"I'll drop Mr. Benson off at the trailer in the afternoon," Norry said. "He can spend the day by the lake."

They stopped by the trailer while Lizzie ran in to get her backpack.

"I can walk from here," Lizzie said when she came out of the trailer.

"I can take you to the end. It's no problem."

So Norry drove Lizzie to the end of the road, and they sat in the Jeep until the bus came. When Lizzie saw the bus rounding the corner, she jumped out.

"Goodbye, Norry!"

"Goodbye!"

Lizzie hopped on the bus in her new T-shirt.

"Who was that?" Jodie wanted to know.

"That's Norry from the Last Resort. I stay there sometimes." Lizzie felt Jodie's eyes on the back of her head. *Let her stew on that for a while!*

Everything was good at school. Lizzie got 100 percent on her social studies quiz, and she aced her spelling test. But then the principal buzzed her teacher and said she had a call. Lizzie's heart sank. *Please, God, oh please let Mom be okay. Please, God, please. Amen.*

The school secretary handed Lizzie the phone. "It's your mom." She looked like she wanted to listen in. Lizzie gave her the hairy eyeball, and the secretary went back into the office.

"Mom?" Mom had never called the school before.

"Lizzie, I know I said I'd be coming home today, but I'm gonna go stay someplace for a while to get better first. I'm going to a rehab thing."

"Rehab?"

"It's for the fentanyl—it's for the drugs I've been taking. I've never been able to really get off them since I had that back injury at the grocery store and . . . oh, kiddo, I'm so sorry."

It sounded like maybe her mom was crying, and that was scary. Mom never cried.

"I gotta do this, baby. There wasn't supposed to be any space in the county facility, and they told me I was going home. Then I got another call, and I guess somebody pulled some strings. Some guy named Bud Gustafson knew somebody and put in a word for me. I don't know anyone named Bud Gustafson. That's the funny thing."

"Sure you do, Mom. He was the guy in the hat eating pancakes at Norry's."

"I met him at Norry's?"

"Yeah, when you came and said I could spend the night."

"Oh. Oh, then. Yeah. I guess I didn't remember that. Anyway, this Bud must know people at this place, because they said he made some calls and they found a spot and I can go in right away."

"Today?"

"Yeah. I guess they want to take me right from the hospital."

"Oh. But . . . where will I go?"

"Well, that's the good news. I called Norry, and she said you could stay there if you want to. If you don't, I can call your great-aunt in North Dakota. I'm sure she'd come out . . ."

"No, I wanna stay at Norry's."

"I thought you would. You like it there, right?" Mom sounded kind of sad and scared.

"Yeah. I like Norry."

"Okay. Okay, that's good."

There was silence at the end of the line. Lizzie wondered if her mom had hung up or fallen asleep.

"Lizzie, I know I screwed up. I keep screwing up. I want you to know I'm gonna do better. I just need a little time to . . . I just have to get myself sorted out . . ."

"It's okay, Mom. It's okay. I'll be okay."

"Great. Great. Norry is going to pick you up from school. You can get whatever you need from the trailer, you know, your clothes and food for Benson and . . . whatever."

"Okay. I love you, Mom."

"Oh, Lizzie. I love you to the moon and back." This time, there was no mistaking it. Her mom was crying.

Lizzie hung up the phone and headed back to class.

After school, the Last Resort Jeep was waiting for her at the curb with Norry and Mr. Benson inside. Lizzie shot a glance toward the school bus just as Jodie and her friends were getting in. Lizzie waved and hopped into the Jeep.

"Is that a friend of yours?" Norry asked.

"Nope."

"Okay then."

They drove to the trailer and parked. Lizzie and Norry went inside, and Lizzie picked up some of her clothes and all her library books.

"Is there anything in the fridge we should take?" Norry asked.

Lizzie was confused.

"Your mom will be gone for a month."

Lizzie didn't know it would be that long. She felt dizzy.

"I'm sorry. She must not have told you that. Yes, the program she's in will be for a full month. It's supposed to be a good place. They'll take good care of your mom there. But she can't leave until it's over."

Lizzie was trying to imagine not seeing her mom for a whole month.

"So, we might want to take anything in the fridge that will go bad."

There wasn't much in the fridge. Norry grabbed the last of the cheese and poured what was left of the milk down the drain. They drove to the Last Resort in silence.

Norry parked the Jeep, and Mr. Benson jumped out. He ran immediately to the shore of the lake and sniffed the water's edge, to see what he had missed, before running into the house. Lizzie brought her books in and stacked them on the shelf above *Little House in the Big Woods*. She watched as Norry put all her clothes from the trailer into the washing machine.

The washing machine started going *chug, chug, chug*, and Lizzie looked out the cabin window at the afternoon sun shining on the lake. She wondered what her mom was doing now. She saw Norry putting some oatmeal cookies on a plate.

"Thanks, Norry."

Chapter Eleven

Norry had never seen anything as bad as that trailer, at least not in person. She didn't think it was fit to live in.

The trailer itself was falling apart. She had seen that from the outside, but that was just the beginning. It smelled bad, and it was filthy. Norry saw no vacuum or broom or cleaning products anywhere in sight. The floor was covered with leaves and pine needles. The fridge had actual mold growing on the shelves. The blankets on the couch (which Lizzie called her bed) were filthy. The clothes she'd gathered, which Lizzie insisted were her "good clothes," were also filthy. Norry took one quick look into the mother's bedroom and closed the door. She didn't want to know.

She got Lizzie out of there as quickly as she could. She decided she'd buy Benson a better brand of dog food and left what was there behind. She helped collect Lizzie's library books (such big books for such a little girl!) and her schoolbooks, and Norry told her they could order whatever else she needed online.

Norry saw how lost Lizzie looked when she told her that her mother would be gone for a full month, and her heart hurt again. She was glad Cat was getting treatment (and frankly surprised she'd gotten in so quickly), but she was not feeling sympathetic toward Lizzie's mother. She was looking at this pigsty of a home with rage.

She didn't even want those clothes of Lizzie's in the house. Norry threw them all in the washing machine as soon as they got home. Then she washed her hands with disinfectant. It was awful. And try as she might (and Norry would be the first to admit she wasn't trying very hard), she could not understand how things could get so bad. What must life be like to end up living that way? It was beyond her. Drugs, she supposed. But what came before the drugs? What would make life so bad that drugs seemed better? Norry couldn't understand. She didn't want to. She put cookies on the table, and she watched Lizzie come out of the bedroom in her new Last Resort T-shirt and her filthy jeans, and she wanted to hit somebody.

"Thanks, Norry," Lizzie said.

Norry watched Lizzie eating cookies and slowly felt herself calming down. Lizzie would be here for a month. She would see that people don't sleep curled up in a pile of dirty blankets. She'd have regular meals and wear clothes that didn't smell. She'd have a room of her own, and Benson was going to the vet. Had he ever been to the vet? Probably not.

"What would you like for dinner?" Norry asked.

Lizzie looked up, surprised. "I don't care."

"I was thinking we should make a fire on the beach. I haven't made one yet this year. We could roast some hot dogs and have potato salad. How does that sound?"

"That sounds amazing."

Norry wasn't sure if Lizzie was really amazed, or if that was just something kids said. But it sounded like she approved.

"Okay, then. That's what we'll do."

Norry reached into the bottom bin of the fridge and got some potatoes out to boil. She thought it was too early for her chives to be up, but she'd check just in case. It was good to be busy.

"I'm going to go look at the lake, okay, Norry?"

"That's just fine."

"Come on, Mr. Benson, let's go."

Norry watched as the dog and the very thin girl went outside, and she saw their silhouettes against the water, now shining in the afternoon sun.

What have I gotten myself into?

It was honestly the first time she'd stopped to think. A whole month was a hell of a commitment. Calvin from the sheriff's office said child protective services would come around to check her out in the next couple of days. Unless they found some reason why Lizzie shouldn't stay (which didn't seem likely), Lizzie was here for a month.

Norry had gotten the call from the drugged-out, loopy Cat, still in the hospital, who'd asked if Norry would take Lizzie if she got into this one-month rehab program, and Norry had simply said, "Yes." That was it. They'd made no further plans.

Cat had said, "Great." Norry didn't remember her even saying "Thank you."

Norry had operated on blind instinct, and now she had an eight-year-old living with her for a month. It was one of the craziest things Norry had ever done. It was not practical at all. It was going to be hard to get all her preparations done for the season with a child underfoot, and Norry had much less experience with children than most women she knew. Honestly, now that she gave it one moment's thought, she realized what a stupid idea it had been to agree. Certainly, Cat could have found someone with a little more experience and some closer ties to Lizzie than Norry. Maybe those relatives in North Dakota could take her.

But as soon as she thought this, Norry felt her insides harden up.

No. No, she was the right person—even if she didn't look like the sensible choice. Lizzie had found her, after all. Lizzie had found her way here all on her own—with the help of Benson—and they had asked to stay. Now she needed a place to stay for a little longer, and rather than feeling put out by the inconvenience, Norry felt as if some kind of honor had been bestowed upon her. Lizzie had chosen her. This was Lizzie's new temporary home.

She wondered if Lizzie liked French's fried onions. Norry grabbed a can from the top shelf. They were always good on hot dogs. She pulled the package of good hot dogs she'd bought at the meat counter out of the freezer along with the buns and started peeling potatoes.

No, Lizzie had chosen her. Norry smiled at the thought. It was going to be a month like no other.

~

Wendell was still in bed.

He had gotten up to use the bathroom and made himself a baloney sandwich, which he then took back to bed. What he really wanted was french fries, but that was impossible, of course, as he was living in the Chickadee Cabin and might as well be living at the North Pole.

Wendell was still trying to figure out how to kill himself. He had ruled out both guns and drugs because, unless something lucky occurred (and when had anything lucky ever happened to him?), they would both require too much effort to be practical.

He could see the lake right outside his window, and he knew that lots of people drowned every year. Wendell could not swim, so it should be easy enough to drown. But the problem with drowning in northern Minnesota was the water was too damned cold, certainly in April. Even in May. Perhaps by August a person could reasonably be expected to get in the water and never get out again, but in the spring, that was pure masochism.

No, Wendell needed something considerably more convenient and less uncomfortable, and he was coming up blank. He was thinking about asphyxiation—and the inherent uncertainty involved with either a lack of oxygen or a surplus of carbon dioxide—when he was startled by the appearance of a small face in the lakeside window.

Then it disappeared.

Wendell squinted. He had his glasses on, but he'd noticed his vision had been getting worse lately. He figured he was probably going blind on top of everything else. He watched the window intently, the rest of his baloney sandwich forgotten, and just when he was about to dismiss it as a hallucination, he saw the face again.

Then he heard barking—right outside his door.

"Quiet, Mr. Benson! I think he's sleeping," the voice at the window said.

It sounded like a very young voice, and that name—Mr. Benson—rang a bell. It was that strange little girl again, the one who had been here when he'd arrived. Since she apparently thought he was asleep, Wendell figured that was the best tack to take. Let her think he was snoozing away the afternoon, which, as it happened, was not far from the truth.

He kept squinting through his almost-closed eyes at the little shape in his window. Her curly black hair was in disarray. He heard the dog make another noise. Was it scratching at the door? This was inexcusable. Wendell suddenly felt vulnerable and even a little foolish, lying under the quilt covered with chickadees in the middle of the afternoon.

He sat up. The head disappeared from the window.

"Shhh!" the voice outside said. "I think you woke him up!"

Intolerable. Wendell was going to let Norry know how he felt about this. A man could not even lie down to die without being pestered.

He swung his feet around to the floor and contemplated standing—nothing good would come from it, but he felt his hand was forced. He had so little choice about anything these days. He stood and walked to the window. There was no face in the glass, but he heard whispering. Wendell threw the door open.

"Oh!"

The small girl was sitting on the stoop with that curly dog of hers, the one with the surname.

"Hello!" she said.

"Hello." Wendell was surprised to hear his voice. It sounded a little rough. He had not spoken aloud for days. The seemingly constant chatter in his head had not made an actual sound.

"I'm Lizzie," the little girl said. "We met eating pancakes."

Wendell vaguely remembered the pancakes on the morning after the night that had ruined his life. They had been blueberry.

"And this is my dog, Mr. Benson."

That was it. Mr. Benson. Now he remembered. Mr. Benson had been eating the same pancakes that Wendell had been served. Mr. Benson, as he recalled, had been served first. And he had a last name.

"I'm Wendell."

Damn! Why hadn't he said, "I'm Mr. Eklund"? Why couldn't he at least command as much respect as this dog with the muddy paws?

"Nice to meet you again, Wendell."

Wendell figured he was supposed to say something now, and he didn't know what that would be. But, like most people, the little girl required little prompting to talk.

"I'm staying here for a month because my mom's on drugs, so now she's in rehab."

"What kind of drugs?"

"Fentanyl."

"Where did she get them?"

"I don't know. Maybe from the potato plant?"

"From a potato plant?"

"Maybe."

"No. You're thinking of vodka."

This girl was obviously not going to be helpful, Wendell realized. That would have been too much to expect.

"Me and Norry are going to roast hot dogs tonight—on a real fire. Do you want to come?"

"To dinner?"

"To the fire. Maybe Norry will have marshmallows. I think you should come."

And with that, the little girl trotted off. Wendell stood on his stoop and considered things. This was a development. Now he would not be the only guest until Memorial Day, as Norry had pretty much guaranteed. There would be another guest—two if you counted the formal little dog. Wendell was not at all sure he wanted to have a noisy little girl lurking around his cabin. But what could he do? He could draw the chickadee-bedizened curtains closed and try to shut her out, but she would still be skulking around just outside. It was unnerving. It was infuriating. It was one more nail in the coffin of his tranquility to have this little interloper literally on his doorstep, no doubt expecting attention from Wendell at every opportunity.

Wendell sucked on his teeth. *Well.*

He decided he would get dressed. Or rather, he'd change the clothes he'd been wearing for the last two days (three days?), and he'd take a shower. Maybe he'd shave. He'd picked up some razors when he'd last gone to town. He didn't know why he'd bothered. No plans to go to the opera anytime soon. Still, he had them, so he might as well use them. It would be cold, even with a fire. He'd put on that flashy sweater of Earl Söderberg's with the Last Resort sweatshirt Norry had given him. Why not? Nothing to lose. It was just a bonfire. No big deal.

And, with that, Wendell went back into the Chickadee Cabin with plans for the evening. They were the first plans he'd made since his house had collapsed, other than his plan to kill himself.

~

"So she's in rehab for a whole month?"

Norry was running cold water over the boiled potatoes. She was amazed she'd found a few chives poking up through the dried leaves and was making potato salad when Virgie called.

"Yup. I don't know how they found her a spot at the rehab center that fast, but somehow they did, and they took her straight from the hospital before she had a chance to reconsider. She asked if I could take Lizzie and the dog, and I said yes before I had any idea what I was doing. The sheriff's office let child protective services know what was going on, and now Lizzie and Benson will be staying here for a whole month."

"That's nuts, Norry! You don't know anything about kids."

Norry bristled. Maybe she didn't, but Lizzie wasn't just any kid. She was Lizzie. "Well, I guess I'm going to learn."

"You have had your share of excitement, I'd say. First Wendell and now this. I thought you'd just be moping around, painting trim on the cabins."

Norry pursed her lips. Virgie obviously didn't take her spring preparations seriously.

"I still have to do that. No, it's going to be okay. Lizzie is easy to be around. She's not a fussy eater, and everything is a first for her. I whipped some cream for the cobbler the other night, and she never knew whipped cream didn't just come out of a can. She's got all these questions about the loons and their nests, and it's fun to explain things to her. She's so smart for her age."

"Norry, you are smitten."

"Maybe. A little."

Norry looked down at thc potato salad she was making. She decided to add some hard-boiled egg. Lizzie could use the protein.

"Well, hold down the fort! I'll be back in June and want to meet everyone."

Norry had no sooner hung up when the phone rang again.

"Hey, Norry, whatcha up to?" It was Bud. Norry discovered she was more pleased to hear from him than usual. Had he always had such a nice baritone voice?

"We're having a fire on the beach and roasting hot dogs," she answered. "Wanna come?"

"That sounds great. I'll bring marshmallows."

"Excellent!"

"How's Lizzie settling in?"

"I would say she's doing well. There's been no news from the rehab place, but I guess that's normal. Right now she and Benson seem like they're having a good time outside. So far, so good."

"Well, I'll see you soon, then. I love Last-minute plans!"

Norry shook her head and headed outside to the lake. She piled up some driftwood in the firepit, along with some birch logs that had been curing behind the cabin. Lizzie and Benson appeared from out of the woods.

"Norry! I told Wendell he could come to the bonfire. Is that okay?"

Norry did a calculation and was glad she had a large pack of hot dogs.

"That's just fine. Bud is coming, too, and he's bringing marshmallows."

"Marshmallows!" Lizzie jumped up and spun around in the sand and looked for a moment like the eight-year-old she was yet so rarely resembled.

This is how things should be when you are still eight years old, Norry thought. *There should be bonfires and marshmallows and days by the lake. There should be pancakes in the morning and a shelf full of books to read. You shouldn't have to be worried about whether your mother will make it home at night or whether you have heat or whether there's anything to eat in the kitchen. It shouldn't have to be that hard.*

The paper birch caught fire in an instant, and the driftwood started up right afterward.

Norry heard Bud's truck pulling in and felt an unfamiliar stirring in her stomach. Then she saw Wendell loping his way over. He was wearing the same loud argyle cardigan he'd been wearing when she met him, this time paired with a Last Resort sweatshirt and her father's shoes. She realized she had hardly seen Wendell outside his cabin and hadn't spoken a word to him. It was good Lizzie had thought to invite him.

"Hey, Wendell!" Bud hollered. "How's it hanging?" Bud was carrying a bag of marshmallows and a case of root beer.

Wendell looked up, startled.

"Have a seat, Wendell," Norry urged as she set some chairs up around the fire.

Lizzie went to work immediately, roasting her hot dog, which looked as if it would be completely black by the time she was done.

Norry brought out the potato salad and paper plates. Bud passed around the root beer. Wendell settled himself heavily into a chair with his back to the lake.

The sun was setting, and it was one of those gorgeous slow-motion sunsets that you only see in extreme latitudes. The smell of wood smoke was wafting into the air, and at that moment, a loon called from one end of the lake and was answered by another on the other side. Benson was settled into a spot under Norry's chair and had already scored half a hot dog that had fallen on the sand.

"This is the life, isn't it?" Bud said, finishing up his potato salad and throwing the paper plate into the fire, where it burst into flame for a moment and then crumbled.

This is the life.

It truly was. It was the same life Norry had always had, and yet it was somehow different. It was the same Bud Gustafson, and yet he didn't look like the same old Bud. He looked like a handsome stranger, sitting there with a can of root beer in his hand and a seed cap on his head. He looked exactly the same and completely different.

Wendell looked like many of the campers she'd had over the years, dressed in the fancy sweater and Last Resort sweatshirt, and yet Norry sensed there was something different about him as well. She had thought he was just kind of an introverted guy, in shock over losing his home. Maybe there was more going on beneath the surface. Maybe he was lonelier than she had realized. She saw in his face a kind of sadness that she hadn't picked up on when she'd first met him. She suspected it had always been there. She just hadn't noticed.

And sitting across the fire from her was Lizzie, intent on roasting two marshmallows at once, both of which were on fire. Her hair was messy, and she had bits of burned marshmallow on her face, and she was watching those marshmallows like they were the most interesting things in the world.

It was true, what she'd said to Virgie. Showing Lizzie things she had taken for granted had forced Norry to see them in a new way. When she saw the first marsh marigolds blooming along the shore, she found herself thinking she'd have to show the bright-yellow flowers to Lizzie. She thought she should get the pontoon out earlier than usual and take a spin around the lake with Lizzie. She wondered if Lizzie would like to go fishing with Bud—once the northern season started. She imagined taking Lizzie to pick raspberries—until she remembered that no, Lizzie would be gone by then.

Long before the first raspberries were ripe, and with any luck at all, Lizzie would be living in a decent house with her mom, probably in Big Pine, maybe farther away. Cat would be working a better job, and she'd hopefully have a cleaner place to live. This month together would be almost forgotten by the time the raspberries were ripe.

Kids don't remember things, Norry reminded herself. *Kids live in the moment.*

It had seemed as if the Last Resort never changed and Norry didn't change either. But she no longer thought this was true. At that moment, she was thinking that things changed almost too much, almost too quickly.

Norry got up and put another log on the fire. Wendell was roasting a marshmallow, and it had just caught fire. He didn't seem too happy about it. Bud finished his root beer, crushed the can, and pushed a log closer to the center of the fire with his foot. Benson let out an enormous sigh.

Right now, Norry. That's what you have. You have this moment right now.

A loon called again, closer this time. The sun finished its long trip and disappeared below the surface of the lake. Norry smelled the wood smoke and promised herself she would remember everything.

Chapter Twelve

Things were pretty good for Lizzie after that.

For the first couple of days, Norry drove her down to the bus stop with Mr. Benson in the cab, and then she walked home from the corner in the afternoon.

On the second afternoon, Lizzie said, "I can walk both ways."

So, on the third day, she started a little earlier and walked all the way to the corner on her own with Mr. Benson. She walked by her old trailer about halfway to the bus stop, and she thought it looked worse than she remembered. The sides were all rust stained, and parts of the roof gutters were falling off. The windows were covered with a film of dust. It didn't look like anybody was living there—because no one was. But it also didn't look like a place anyone had lived in for a long time.

Mr. Benson followed Lizzie to the bus stop and waited with her for the bus.

"Goodbye, Mr. Benson!" she said when she got on. "Go on home!" Mr. Benson waited for the school bus doors to close; then he turned around and headed back the way they came.

That afternoon, when Lizzie got off the bus, Mr. Benson was there on the corner, waiting for her.

"Did you send Mr. Benson to meet me?" Lizzie asked Norry as she entered the house.

"No! Twenty minutes before your bus was due, he just headed off in a hurry, like he had an appointment. I had no idea where he went."

Mr. Benson looked up at Lizzie, his mouth a little open, a smile on his face.

"He's a smart dog," Lizzie said.

"He is," Norry agreed.

The days went on like this for a couple of weeks. Sometimes Bud came to dinner, and sometimes Wendell joined them outside when the sun went down. Lizzie got some new clothes, and Jodie got less annoying. There was a new girl named Bri in the fifth grade, who had just transferred into their school, and Jodie and her friends got to tease her all day long. Bri sat at the front of the bus with Lizzie in a miserable little heap.

But school was going good, and Lizzie still had a perfect attendance record. She'd talked to her mom a couple of times. Mom sounded a little tired and maybe a little sad, but she said she was "learning new skills," and Lizzie thought that sounded good. Lizzie liked learning new skills.

It was now the middle of May, and the days were getting longer and longer. Lizzie had to go to bed before it was even dark. Norry would pull the curtains closed, and Lizzie would ask if she could read one more chapter, and Norry would always say, "Just one more. That's all."

One night, Lizzie finally finished *Little House in the Big Woods*. She'd been saving it, only reading a little at a time and reading other books in between. But finally, she read the very last story about how Pa didn't shoot the deer with the big antlers, and then he didn't shoot the bear, and then he didn't shoot the mother deer with the fawn.

And Pa apologized because he said they wouldn't have any fresh meat and Laura whispered that she was glad he didn't shoot them, and Mary said they could eat bread and butter for dinner and Pa hugged them both and they went to bed.

Then Laura lay in bed and thought that this—Pa playing his fiddle and the wind in the big trees and the cozy little house with the firelight on the walls—all of this was now.

When Lizzie read that, she started to cry, and she didn't know why, because it wasn't a sad ending at all. It was happy.

"This is now," Lizzie said, as she closed the book with the picture on the cover of the happy family inside the home with walls made of logs. Lizzie looked around at the log walls around her, and she listened for loons. But tonight it was quiet.

"This is now."

She put the book back on the shelf with the rest of them. She would start the next one tomorrow—or maybe just take a look at it tonight.

That's when she heard a noise outside.

She pulled open the curtains that faced the lake, and she saw Wendell was still outside, but he was no longer sitting in his lawn chair. He had fallen down—chair and all—and he was lying in the sand, making a bad noise.

Lizzie dashed outside. She had real pajamas on—a nightgown that Norry had ordered online—and she looked exactly like Laura in *Little House in the Big Woods*.

"Wendell! Are you okay?"

Wendell did not look okay. His face was red, and he was gasping for breath and lying in a funny position in the sand. Lizzie ran back to the cabin.

"Norry! I think Wendell is in trouble!"

Norry and Lizzie came running back out of the cabin together. Norry took one look at Wendell and grabbed the phone out of her pocket.

"Hang on there, Wendell," she said as she called 911. Then she called Bud, just to make sure.

Norry knelt beside Wendell. She had lifted his head up, and he seemed like he could breathe a little better.

"Is he going to be okay, Norry? Are you okay, Wendell?"

Wendell didn't say anything, and Lizzie didn't know what to do.

"I'll tell the ambulance where he is when they get here!" she told Norry, and she dashed off to where the driveway entered the resort.

She stood there at the edge of the wood in her long white nightgown until she heard a siren and saw the red and blue lights. She remembered how the sheriff had come to tell her when Mom had been in the hospital with an overdose. But this time, it was Bud in an ambulance with another man and Sheriff Calvin in a squad car.

"They're on the beach!" Lizzie yelled, feeling important.

The men ran straight there. They put Wendell up on a stretcher and hauled him back to the ambulance. Lizzie thought they must be strong, because Wendell was a pretty big guy.

Lizzie watched as the younger man started asking Wendell questions and Bud came around and closed the back of the ambulance, and Sheriff Calvin started his siren and headed down the driveway first.

"Goodbye, Wendell! Get better soon!" Lizzie yelled as they pulled out of the driveway. She watched the red and blue lights disappear and listened until she couldn't hear the siren anymore. And then it was very quiet.

"I think he had a heart attack," Norry said. "It was so good you found him when you did."

She put an arm around Lizzie, and Lizzie hugged her back. Norry was shaking—and so Lizzie hugged her for a long time.

It was still light over the lake, although the sun was down, and Lizzie finally heard a loon call, and it was one of the slow, sad calls.

"I hope Wendell is okay," Lizzie said.

"They'll take good care of him," Norry said.

"Wake me up if the hospital calls, please?"

"I will. I'll do that."

Then they went back inside, and Lizzie went back to bed, even though she was much too worried to sleep. *Please, God, please don't let Wendell die. Please, God, please. Amen.*

Then she fell asleep.

~

Wendell felt himself going down.

First came the terrible pain and the shortness of breath, and then he felt himself sinking, sinking into the ground, and he realized that it was not his imagination but that the back legs of the plastic lawn chair were, in fact, sinking into the sand and taking Wendell with them. Then he was on the ground and in terrible pain, all alone on the beach.

After that, he didn't remember any more.

Wendell had heard of a phenomenon where people who come to the brink of death had a sudden realization of how dear life was. They may have been feeling depressed or even suicidal, but coming to the threshold of death's door created a new appreciation for the preciousness of life.

Wendell did not have that experience. Wendell woke in the hospital and discovered—to his great disappointment—that he was still very much alive.

Well, this is just great, he thought.

Wendell had wanted nothing but a quiet death since the night his house collapsed. He'd been thinking about it more or less nonstop. Oh, things had gotten marginally better, if he had to be completely honest. The nightly sunset viewings were better than nothing, he supposed. Anything was better than sitting inside the cramped Chickadee Cabin twenty-four hours a day.

He'd gotten in the habit of sitting on the beach until the sun was all the way down and then going straight to bed. He hadn't figured out how to kill himself yet, but he figured something would turn up. Even a guy with the worst luck in the world was bound to catch a break, eventually. And then, miraculously, he had.

He hadn't known what was happening at first, but he'd suddenly felt he could not breathe at all. He reached for his inhaler, but then he felt his chest growing tighter and tighter, and his vision—never the best—blurred over completely. Then there was a sudden very sharp pain in his chest, and he was thrown back and started to fall. That must have been when he let out a gasp, or a yell, or some unfortunate noise, because it attracted the attention of the nosy little girl in the white nightdress. The miniature Florence Nightingale had come running out of the cabin and alerted the authorities, and the next thing he knew, Wendell was in Big Pine Hospital, attached to all sorts of monitors and gizmos, and some doctor, who appeared to be about eighteen years old, was telling him he was "a very lucky man."

"You are a very lucky man, Mr. Eklund," the juvenile doctor said. And the only thing that Wendell didn't hate about the pronouncement was that, for once, someone had referred to him by his proper name. "You got here in the nick of time. A few minutes longer and I'm afraid things would not have turned out as well for you."

Wendell eyed the doctor, or what he could see of him. He was a fresh-faced youth in a white jacket with a bobbing Adam's apple. That was about all he could make out.

The doctor now seemed to be waving his arms from side to side.

"Wendell, can you see me?"

This seemed like a foolish question to Wendell, and he wasn't sure he had to answer. Especially now that the teenage doctor was referring to him by his first name.

"Wendell, when was the last time you saw an eye doctor?"

Wendell thought about this. When did he get his last pair of glasses? He remembered that Medicare wouldn't pay for them, and that had really pissed him off because they were crazy expensive and he'd thought they would pay after he turned sixty-two—so he'd been sixty-two. He was seventy-two now. So. That was simple.

"Ten years."

The juvenile doctor didn't say anything, and Wendell couldn't make out his face clearly, but he could sense disapproval. Doctors always thought you should see other doctors. They probably gave each other kickbacks.

"Are you still driving?"

This did not seem to have anything to do with the heart attack. This seemed like meddling to Wendell. Still driving. What an insane question. Of course he was still driving. He was currently being warehoused in a cabin at the far end of the back of nowhere. Without a car, he'd starve to death.

"Yeah."

"There is an eye clinic downstairs. I'm sending you down as soon as you've stabilized."

This was preposterous. Wendell didn't think this doctor even had the right to do this. He had a good mind to get up as soon as this doctor left, yank all these gizmos off, and . . .

Then Wendell realized he had come by ambulance. His car was still at the Last Resort, and he had no way of getting back to the Chickadee Cabin. Not that he really wanted to go there. He had nowhere he wanted to go. Wendell wondered if it was too late to die. The hospital seemed like it would be a handy place to do it.

Wendell was going to tell this doctor that his eyes were fine and he didn't want any further treatment and that they needed to arrange for transportation for him to get home because he was here against his will and he had a right to do with his life what he wanted and . . . Wendell realized the doctor had left.

Damn. Damn, damn, damn.

Wendell had come so close to meeting his goal. If he hadn't unexpectedly let out a groan when the chair tipped over, that meddling little girl would never have heard, and he could have quietly died on the beach in the setting sun. Wendell imagined it as the final scene in a movie. There he'd be—in Earl Söderberg's fancy sweater, the last of the sun shining in his face.

"Goodbye, world. You never gave me a goddamned thing and I'm glad to leave you."

The audience (who would have seen Wendell's life played out in the previous reels), would understand that this was the end of a cursed but noble man, a man who had done his best against insurmountable odds and was now left alone—as always, alone—on the beach, (which was, of course, a metaphor for life). It was the culmination of years of wretched misfortune and cruel chance. Now he was alone on the beach in the setting sun, and the music would swell. The audience would cry for this man who had been so mistreated by fate and never appreciated by his peers. They would see how fitting it was that he was alone in the end, as he had always been. There would be no pesky little girl dressed like Pollyanna, hopping over and getting emergency services involved. She had ruined it. She had ruined a perfectly good ending. Wendell squeezed his eyes tight and thought he was going to cry in frustration, but instead, he heard a squeaky sound, and he opened his eyes in surprise.

It was shoes. It was squeaky shoes worn by another figure in white. This one was shorter. It was a nurse.

"I'm supposed to take you down for an eye exam."

Wendell sighed. The indignities would never end.

A few minutes later, a new person in a white coat was asking the same inane question.

"Are you still driving?"

This time it was an optometrist, and she was informing Wendell that his vision was severely impaired by cataracts and more or less implying that Wendell was an idiot for not realizing this sooner.

"You absolutely are not fit to drive until you've had this addressed," the latest bossy figure in white told him. Wendell squinted at the optometrist with the grouchy voice. She appeared to be rather beautiful, from what he could make out.

"I'm going to try to get you in for cataract surgery as soon as you're released. In the meantime, you better find someone who can drive you."

He was then wheeled back to his room, reattached to gizmos, and given a glass of juice.

As bad as the Chickadee Cabin had been, Wendell was forced to admit this was worse. But it went downhill from there. Wendell was still working on his juice when he heard a thump-thump-thumping noise and looked up to see Bud Gustafson. At least he figured it had to be Bud. It was a little hard to make him out. Wendell figured they must keep the lights on low in the hospital to save electricity. He was having a hard time seeing anything.

"How you feeling, buddy?"

Bud was not Wendell's buddy. Bud was the guy who had twice prevented Wendell's life from ending when it should have. He would never have ended up in the Chickadee Cabin if it hadn't been for Bud, hauling him ass over teakettle through a hole in the roof. If he had just been left to die, he wouldn't have to go through any of this. Wendell looked at Bud. His nemesis had made himself comfortable in the chair by Wendell's bed and was holding his hat in his hands. If this were a movie, Bud would be played by Willem Dafoe. They did not bear a striking resemblance, but Bud had that same malevolent smile.

"I'm fine."

"Well, get some rest, will you? I understand they're working hard to get you in for cataract surgery as soon as you're well enough to be checked out. I'll keep in touch with the hospital staff and be here to pick you up, and we'll get you back to the cabin whenever they're through with you. Don't worry about a thing."

Did Wendell get any say in any of this? Was he simply a cadaver to be carted about from one procedure to the next? Was there no such thing as bodily autonomy anymore?

Bud leaned in and gave Wendell a pat on the shoulder. "Hang in there, Wendell. You'll be back to normal in no time flat."

With that, Bud put on his hat and headed out the door.

Back to normal? Wendell considered the utter absurdity of the phrase.

What on earth was normal? Had Wendell ever had a normal life? As far back as he could remember, his life had been just one crushed dream after another. Failure followed by disappointment followed by betrayal followed by disaster. The trajectory of his life had started at a low ebb and taken a sharp nosedive as soon as he'd turned eighteen.

At seventy-two, his "normal"—as Bud so blithely put it—was below water. Underground. Beneath the earth's crust. Wendell had never experienced what Bud considered "normal." Bud waltzed in here, blowing sunshine and rainbows out his ass, spouting his two-bit philosophy. He didn't have a clue. Bud was a fool. They were all fools—everyone who insisted that "things were looking up" and the "best days were yet to come" and "everything would work out in the end." How in God's name could they keep up the pretense that any of this was true? How could they pretend this bore the slightest resemblance to the real world?

This is how the majority survived, Wendell realized. This is how clueless, deluded, ignorant idealists like Bud got by day after day. They pretended life was not the shithole that it was. They saw rainbows when the sky was black. They went looking for a pony in the pile of horse poop. There was no rainbow. There was no pony.

It was only a handful—people brave enough to tell the truth—who would admit that life sucked. It was short and painful and lonely. Hope was a delusion. Love was a hoax. Happiness was a lie. People said they were happy so that gullible people would believe that life could be something other than what it was. Wendell was part of the tiny minority who knew the truth.

For a moment, Wendell's whirling thoughts stood still.

Maybe—knowing what he knew, seeing what he saw—maybe he could blow the lid off the whole stinking shebang and tell the world what he understood so clearly, what so few seemed willing to believe. The idea gave Wendell a shiver.

He could always kill himself later. In the meantime, Wendell decided he was going to get busy setting the world straight.

~

"Yes! He had a heart attack right on the beach," Norry told Virgie.

Bud had called her from the hospital in the morning, and Norry had woken Lizzie with the good news that Wendell had pulled through. They weren't saying much about his condition yet, but he was still alive and apparently able to speak—although Norry wasn't sure how they would know since he never seemed to have a thing to say.

Norry had made pancakes to celebrate, and as soon as Lizzie and Benson headed off to the bus, she called Virgie to tell her the latest.

"No one would have known a thing until morning if Lizzie hadn't heard a noise and gone out—in her nightgown!—to investigate. Bud said we got him in the nick of time, and while Wendell was in there, they discovered he has terrible cataracts. So he's getting that done before he comes back."

"Wow," Virgie said.

"I know!"

"And I thought this was your slow season."

"I just feel so bad. He must have had some symptoms, but, you know, he's so quiet. I don't think he'd complain about anything, no matter how bad things got. I never even noticed he had cataracts behind those thick glasses. I've hardly spent a moment alone with him. He's just this mild-mannered guy, and the idea that he could have ended up dead on the beach last night just destroys me. I'm going to make a point to keep a closer eye on him from now on."

"It sounds like you have plenty to keep an eye on already."

"You know, I thought it was kind of a nuisance when he moved in. But by now, I've gotten so used to having him here, I can't imagine it any other way."

Norry realized, as she said this, it was true.

She would go to the hospital this afternoon and see what Wendell might need when he got home. When she imagined him sitting alone in the Chickadee Cabin, it made her heart hurt.

"He obviously likes it here, Virgie. I think he should just stay in the Chickadee Cabin forever."

"Forever doesn't last."

"Well, for now. For as long as now lasts."

Chapter Thirteen

Lizzie heard Norry calling her from the house.

"Lizzie! Would you like to visit Wendell in the hospital?"

"Can we?"

"Yes, they say he can have visitors. We probably shouldn't stay too long, but he's supposed to be doing better and could be released the day after tomorrow. But then he's going to have his cataract surgery."

"Surgery?"

"Yes, he has cataracts in his eyes, and they have to be removed so he can see better."

Lizzie didn't know what Cadillac surgery was, but Norry didn't sound too worried.

"Do you want to visit him?" Norry asked again.

"Yes!"

Lizzie and Norry piled into the Last Resort Jeep and drove into Big Pine. They found Wendell in bed wearing a pale-blue hospital gown that matched his eyes exactly. He looked lonely, and Lizzie sat on the edge of his bed to talk to him.

"How're you doing?" Norry asked.

"We miss you!" Lizzie added, before he had time to answer.

"I understand you're going to get cataract surgery in a couple of days," Norry said.

Wendell opened his mouth, as if he might say something.

“I wanted to find out what we could get for you,” Norry continued. “I’m headed to the grocery store.” Wendell looked at the piece of paper Norry was waving in his direction, and Norry laughed. “I’m sure the last thing on your mind is food. Tell you what—I’ve got some basic things on my list, and if anything else comes to mind, you let Bud know when he stops by, and we’ll make sure you are all provisioned.”

Wendell opened his mouth again. There was a pause.

“A notebook,” Wendell said softly.

“Wendell said something,” Lizzie told Norry.

“What was that, Wendell?” Norry leaned in along with Lizzie.

He cleared his throat.

“A notebook. I’d like a notebook. And a pen.”

His voice sounded raspy.

“Oh! Wendell, what a great idea,” Norry said. “I’ll bet it’s hard to talk right now, and that would come in handy. We’ll pick up a notebook at the grocery store and drop it off before we go home.”

“I’ll pick it out!” Lizzie said. She looked at Wendell’s watery-blue eyes. They had a film of white over the top of them. Those must be the Cadillacs, Lizzie figured. They were white Cadillacs.

“Okay, Wendell!” Norry squeezed Wendell’s arm, and Wendell jumped. “I think you’re looking fine today. It seems like you’re getting great treatment. Wasn’t it lucky the doctor noticed you needed your cataracts treated? One-stop shopping! You’re going to be a new man by the time you get home.”

Wendell’s mouth opened again, but this time, he didn’t say anything.

“Okay, Lizzie, let’s go shopping. Don’t worry about a thing, Wendell. We’ll see you in a little while and bring a notebook. We’ll have everything ready for you when you get back home.”

Lizzie was watching Wendell closely. She’d never really looked at him up close before. “I’m just so glad Lizzie found you when she did,” Norry said softly. “And I want you to know how much you mean to all of us.”

Then Norry took Lizzie by the hand, and they headed out the door.

"Goodbye, Wendell!" Lizzie called as they left. She thought Wendell looked sad.

~

The choice presented to Wendell was not good—but when was it ever?

The little girl, Lizzie, who had no compunctions about sitting right on his hospital bed, and the bossy Norry, who appeared to take his misfortune as license to be bossier than ever, returned within the hour. Lizzie spread the offerings on Wendell's bed.

"What do you think?"

Well, he couldn't see much. That was the truth. What the beautiful doctor had said about his eyes might have a grain of truth in it, because he'd noticed it was getting a lot harder to make out details and colors. But it appeared he was being asked to choose between three notebooks.

One had a cartoon puppy on the cover and said *Be Silly. Be Honest. Be Kind. ~Ralph Waldo Emerson.* Wendell had a vague notion who Ralph Waldo Emerson was, and he sincerely doubted he would ever have said anything so foolish.

The second notebook said *It is never too late to be what you might have been. ~George Eliot.* Wendell had no idea who this George Eliot person was, but he was obviously an idiot.

The final one had no text on it, which was a relief, but it did have a cartoon unicorn. Wendell had in mind a simple black spiral notebook with no distracting nonsense on the cover at all, but that was too much to ask in his compromised position.

He took a closer look at the unicorn and ran his hand over it. The surface was scratchy. The unicorn was standing in a field of various shades of gray and looked rather forlorn. Wendell decided that was the best representation he was going to find for the thoughts he intended to write and chose the unicorn.

"Oh, good!" Lizzie said. "I was hoping to keep the puppy one. Doesn't he look like Mr. Benson?" The dog did look a bit like Mr. Benson. At least, it looked as stupid.

"Now you get to pick a pen!" Lizzie had several pens of various styles in her hand and gave them to Wendell. There were a couple of click pens and a couple with caps and one uniball pen. That was the best. He uncapped it and tested it. It wrote effortlessly. Good.

"Okay," Norry said. "We better get back to the Chickadee Cabin and put your dairy stuff in the fridge before it gets warm. If there's anything else you need, just give me or Bud a call."

Wendell wondered what would happen if he requested a loaded handgun but suspected a unicorn notebook was as good as it was going to get.

"See you soon, Wendell!" Lizzie hollered on her way out.

Much too soon, was his guess. And much too often.

The noisy pair headed out the door, and Wendell uncapped his new pen and hesitated.

Wendell's life was one long hesitation. He had hit the pause button at around eighteen years of age and never really started it up again.

He didn't know where to start, so he started at the beginning—or the beginning, as he perceived it: his adolescent memories of never measuring up to what his father wanted. Wendell's father had died right after Wendell graduated from high school. But Wendell remembered how little his father had encouraged his idea of writing movie scripts and novels.

"How you gonna make a living doing that?" his father had asked.

Wendell had no answer, as he recalled. What else had his father said? He must have said something awful to set Wendell on his downward trajectory. He must have mocked him for his aspirations. He was sure his father was largely responsible for his failure to succeed. If you start out with a supportive parent, you have it easy. What might Wendell have accomplished if he'd had a parent who believed in him?

But instead of remembering the harsh words his father had used to crush his dreams, Wendell remembered something quite different. He remembered another notebook. This one, happily, had no unicorns on it. This one had been leather and worthy of his ideas. It was a grown-up, serious writer's notebook, and his mother had given it to him as a graduation present.

Why had he forgotten that? What had he written in that notebook?

Wendell chewed on the end of the pen, trying to remember the long-lost notebook. He wondered if it had still been in the house when it was crushed, and then hauled off to the landfill. Somehow, that seemed fitting—to have all record of his dreams carted off to decompose with dirty diapers and lawn clippings and rotting mattresses.

But his mother had given him that. He remembered that now. She'd said something about him needing a place to put his thoughts, and she'd bought it at a fancy stationery store in the Twin Cities and given it to him as a graduation present.

He noticed his eyesight must be getting worse as he tried to see the lines in the notebook. Then he realized he was crying.

He was thinking of his mother, whom he'd lived with until her death, and honestly, he couldn't come up with anything she'd ever said to discourage him. She'd always at least pretended to be delighted when he had one of his petty successes, some short-lived respite from the endless string of disappointments that dogged his life. When he sent in the manuscript to the contest. When he joined that writers' group. He'd lost the contest. The group had disbanded. Nothing ever worked out, of course. But he remembered—before he knew how hopeless it all was—how excited his mother had been.

"Good luck, Wendell!" she'd call out the door. Amazing. She'd actually said that, he remembered. She had wished him good luck—the man with the worst luck in the world. She must not have known. She must not have suspected what a complete and total failure he was.

Wendell put the cap on the pen. Then he took it off again.

I received a leather-bound notebook from my mother, Wendell wrote. The pen was nice. It flowed across the page. *I didn't know what to do with it at the time and I still don't.*

This was not what Wendell had intended to write, but now that he had started, he might as well continue. After all, he had nothing else to do.

~

Norry was cleaning the Chickadee Cabin and preparing for Wendell's return. She was surprised how few personal possessions he had. Bud had mentioned his place had been kind of cluttered when the roof fell in. Wendell had even said something about going to retrieve "his stuff." But Bud said Wendell had ended up deciding there was nothing worth saving. There was no indication that the Chickadee Cabin had an occupant other than a handful of food items in the fridge and a few of Earl Söderberg's clothes hanging in the closet. Kind of sad, not to have a single memento of your past life, Norry thought, as she put the milk and bread and cheese and some lunch meat into the fridge.

She changed the towels and the sheets and swept the floor and cleaned the kitchen. She'd been doing this for so long that she sometimes finished before she realized what she was doing. It was a kind of meditation, cabin cleaning. She didn't need her mind to engage—unless it was simply filthy, or something had been broken. But there was nothing like that in the Chickadee Cabin. Wendell had left almost no sign he was living here.

As she mopped the floor, she was thinking about Bud and what she should do about him. Of course, she didn't need to do a thing. They'd gone to a concert. She'd had a few titillating thoughts. Things might have ended differently if they hadn't gotten the call about Lizzie that night, but since then she'd been busy caring for an eight-year-old, and now this excitement with Wendell, and it was already the middle of May, and soon the first guests would be coming, and . . .

Norry knew she was putting Bud off. She wasn't quite sure why.

Bud was a good guy, and she liked him a lot. Maybe too much. Maybe that was the problem. Caring too much for people was not necessarily a good strategy. Right now, after just over two weeks, she was already dreading Lizzie's departure. Cat had called one night after Lizzie had gone to bed and said she was doing well in the program. Norry never got calls at night and almost didn't answer it. Cat said she needed to apologize for her behavior. Norry figured this was some kind of twelve-step thing she was required to do.

"I really screwed up," Cat explained. Norry did not contradict her. "I've just had a lot of problems lately, first with the injury and then just feeling like I'm in the wrong place or time . . . I'm sorry. I know that doesn't make a lot of sense. But I'm sorry I never thanked you for everything you've done. I know Lizzie loves staying with you, and I just wanted you to know how much I appreciate you."

Norry listened. She did not feel like telling Cat she understood, because she did not. She didn't feel like telling her it was nothing, because it was not nothing. Taking care of Lizzie was a big deal—but something she was happy to do—not for Cat's sake, but for Lizzie's. Norry didn't know what to say, so she listened, thanked Cat for calling, and hung up.

She probably thinks I'm a bitch, Norry thought. And Norry was a little crabby. That was the truth. For ten years, since she'd returned to Loon Point, she'd been content on her own. She interacted with the guests, but there was a clear boundary between their lives and hers. No one was on the inside but Norry. And now Lizzie had broken in, and Bud was threatening to do the same, and even Wendell—poor Wendell—was almost breaking Norry's heart, and she didn't know what on earth was happening to her.

Maybe she needed to have a talk with Bud—tell him he was a nice guy but she couldn't see herself getting into anything like a relationship now, tell him how much she appreciated him as a friend. But when Norry imagined this conversation, she felt an odd stirring of defiance.

She didn't want Bud as a friend. She wanted more. Norry had gone for a long time not wanting anything other than what she had, and now to her surprise—and consternation—she wanted more.

The cabin smelled of lavender and disinfectant. It was ready for Wendell's return. Lizzie's bus was due any minute now. Bud said he might come by this weekend with dinner. The walleye and northern opener was Saturday, and he would almost certainly have some luck. Fresh walleye sounded wonderful.

Norry stood on the stoop of the Chickadee Cabin. Soon, the lake would be filled with boats, and there would be kids playing on the beach and people grilling on the barbecues outside their cabins. There would be noise and guests asking for more towels and dogs running around. But for another week, it would be quiet.

And then Lizzie would leave.

Norry realized she felt much sadder about this than she had any reason to feel. Just then, she saw Benson jump up from the deck of her cabin, where he had been sleeping, and trot down the road to meet the bus.

"Forever doesn't last," Virgie had said. And it was true. But Norry wanted right now to last forever.

~

"You will need to make some lifestyle changes," the teenage doctor was telling Wendell.

Wendell was not listening. They wanted him to start taking some medications, and he was supposed to exercise and lose some weight. Wendell was annoyed because he'd just started to write in his new journal when the doctor came in with a stern expression and lots of unwanted advice about what Wendell should do in order to live longer. Wendell had no desire to live longer. He wondered what would happen if he took all his new medications at once. Probably nothing. Not with his luck.

"Start slowly, a little walk every day. See if you can go a bit further each day."

So tedious. These doctors were so tedious. Did they not understand that life was not this precious thing to be hoarded and preserved and extended at all costs? If Wendell had wanted to live any longer, wouldn't he have given some indication by now? No. The assumption of all these medical types was that life was the one thing no one could get enough of. It was the ultimate gift, and they were in the business of prolonging it, so of course they had a high opinion of themselves.

"Your prescriptions are ready for pickup now, and I understand you can get in this afternoon for the first of your cataract surgeries. Take it slow. You've had a major cardiac event. It will take some time to get back to normal."

That phrase again. *Back to normal.* Wendell involuntarily shook his head.

"I understand," the doctor said, understanding nothing. "It's difficult when we are faced with an event of this kind. It is not unusual to experience some depression and emotional fatigue. Just let us know if you need any assistance. We're here to help you on your healing journey."

Healing journey? What kind of doctor says *healing journey*? Had he entered an ashram? Wendell felt the quality of medical care at Big Pine Hospital had taken a sharp downward dip since the days he used to take his mother here for her appointments.

The doctor left, and Wendell remembered taking his mom to this hospital, near the end, how she always thanked everyone just for doing their job. How she never seemed to mind all the intrusive procedures and impertinent questions they asked. She would smile and comply, and then they'd go out for lunch at the diner, and she'd have a tuna fish sandwich and say how lucky she was to have such good care. Wendell had never paid much attention to what she was saying. She was an old woman without much to be happy about. That was his feeling at the time.

He was almost as old as she had been then, he realized. Had his mother really been happy?

He didn't see how she could have been, widowed so young and, at the end, living with a grown son who had never amounted to anything. She never did anything important or went anywhere interesting. She'd had her church groups and her charities and a handful of friends she'd known since she was young. It wasn't much of a life, as far as he could see.

Wendell got out his notebook again. The unicorn was bothering him less. He thought there might be something fated about it, this unicorn, because it was how Wendell saw himself. He was an oddball, a freak of nature, the one who never fit in. He had struggled with feelings of being alone and outside the herd for as long as he could remember, and things had only gotten worse with time. This unicorn standing alone in the gray mist was a fitting symbol.

He tried to pick up where he'd left off with his musings. He had planned to write his treatise in this book. He wanted to explain to the ignorant idealists of the world—the fools who went around all day with their heads in the clouds while they were stepping in shit. He wanted a record of both his suffering and his insights.

But when he opened the book, he again remembered his mother. He remembered her last years, when she had been so frail. He'd been impatient, he recalled. He'd felt as if she took up a lot of his time—although he couldn't remember what he had been doing that would have kept him so busy.

He recalled one night after he'd come back to live with her, when she was near the end. She'd had a bad night and had somehow fallen on the way back from the bathroom. He'd picked her up (when he could still do that), and he'd carried her back to her bed. He'd been worried. He remembered that now. He'd been worried he was going to lose her, which, of course, he did shortly thereafter.

"You're a good son," she'd said.

"No, not really."

"You are a good son and a fine man, Wendell," she told him.

But it was much too late for that, as Wendell recalled. He knew he was not a fine man, and he never would be, and this was just the sort of thing a mother would say, especially as she lay dying.

"I want you to be happy," she said.

And Wendell remembered that at the time, he'd had no idea what she meant. He had no idea how he was supposed to do this thing his mother wanted. He had never known how to be happy.

Chapter Fourteen

The surgery went well. At least, that's what they told Wendell. He still had an eye patch on and was not supposed to take it off for a while, so he looked like a pirate when Bud came in that oversize red truck of his to take him back to the Chickadee Cabin.

"All set, Wendell?" Bud asked. Bud had a gift for asking stupid questions.

Wendell had his new notebook and pen and the bottles of pills he was supposed to take. He'd be returning in two weeks' time to get the second eye done.

"Why don't you do both eyes at once?" he'd asked a nurse.

"It's better this way in case something goes wrong."

This did not fill Wendell with confidence, but he didn't see he had much choice, and he figured he'd still have one good eye if they messed up. He looked briefly out of the "new eye" when they checked it, but everything was blurry. The doctor seemed pleased. As if doctors knew anything.

It wasn't until the next morning, in the Chickadee Cabin, that Wendell got up the nerve to remove the eye patch to see how bad his vision was in the new eye. If he hadn't already been in bed, he'd have fallen over.

Everything was different.

They told him he might not need glasses after the surgery, except maybe for reading, but Wendell hadn't believed that for an instant.

Doctors loved to overpromise. He remembered how his mother had been given "up to a couple of years" to live and had been dead by Christmas. Doctors thought they were gods and never wanted to deliver bad news. But whatever he'd been expecting, Wendell was not prepared for this.

He could see.

Not only could he see, but everything was a different color. More precisely, everything was suddenly in bright colors. When he closed the eye that had just had surgery and looked through what he thought of as the old eye, all the color was sapped from the room, and it became an indistinct fog—what he was used to. Then he closed the old eye and looked through the new eye. Everything was crisp and ridiculously colorful—absurdly, unnecessarily colorful. He'd had no idea those chickadees on the curtains were red. He'd assumed the logs of the cabin walls had grayed with age. He hadn't known his quilt was made of calico in sixteen different shades. The whole place was crazy with color.

Wendell had to close his new eye. It was too much.

He waited a few minutes. He tried again. He closed his new eye again. Crazy. That's what it was. Wendell's view of the world had gone crazy.

He struggled out of bed. He was tired. He was more tired than he remembered being. That's when the bossy Norry came by and told him he should get outside more and that she'd put a table and chair right outside his cabin, in the shade of a big Norway pine. Wendell looked out the window and saw a rustic wooden table and a chair with a brilliant-red cushion.

He looked with his old eye. Then he looked with his new one. Too much.

But later that day, he made his way outside. He hadn't gotten far with his writing project since he left the hospital, so he brought his notebook. But that was different too. Wendell looked at his lonely unicorn in disbelief.

It was pink.

The unicorn was pink, and it had sparkles on it. Wendell had felt something rough, but he'd had no idea it was glitter. It was pink glitter. The unicorn was standing in a field that was also pink, and there were rolling hills in the background of varying shades of pink and violet. It was the most embarrassing notebook Wendell could imagine, and it was made worse by the fact that he had selected it himself.

He opened the cover and saw the few words he had written. He couldn't believe it could be worse, and yet it was.

He'd been writing in purple ink.

~

For the next two weeks, Lizzie was busy. The first guests would be coming to stay in the cabins for the fishing opener, and Norry had said she wanted to "do everything" with Lizzie before they came, while there was still time. So that's what they'd been doing.

Norry had the pontoon boat delivered early. It was in storage in Big Pine over the winter. It was an old-fashioned pontoon boat, with a canvas roof over the top and upholstered seats and a shiny wooden steering wheel. Two guys from Big Pine delivered it right to the sandy beach in front of the resort, and Norry took Lizzie for a ride right away.

"Let's go look for loon nests," Norry said as they toured slowly around the lake. The sun was warm, but the water was still very cold. Lizzie had walked in it before she got into the pontoon, and her feet had turned white.

"When will the loon chicks hatch?" Lizzie asked.

"Oh, not until the end of June, usually."

Norry told her how the male loons came back first and looked for a place for the nest. Norry said loons lived up to thirty years, and they often stayed with the same partner for most of their life—although there were loon divorces.

Mr. Benson (her teacher, not her dog) had told Lizzie's class that loons were more closely related to penguins than ducks. Their feet were way at the end of their body, which was why it was hard for them to walk on land. But they were excellent swimmers, and they flew more than a thousand miles when they migrated.

Lizzie watched the loons in the distance, ducking beneath the water, then popping up in a different place, sometimes very far away. She wondered what it would feel like to be at home deep below the surface of the water or high above land in the air.

They'd been all around the lake and were almost back to the point where the resort sat. Lizzie could see it in the distance and thought how funny it was to see the eight cabins lined up, all surrounded by giant pine trees that towered over them. The cabins looked tiny on the sandy beach.

Norry was scanning the shore. "There. Look."

Lizzie picked up the binoculars and saw activity on the shore. She couldn't make out what it was, but she saw two loons in the water. They let the pontoon float silently closer. Lizzie looked out over the water at the loons, busy doing something in the reeds at the lake's edge.

"They had a nest there last year," Norry whispered.

Soon there would be baby loons riding around on their parents' backs, and later, the loon parents would fly off by themselves and the baby loons wouldn't follow until they were old enough.

But Lizzie wasn't going to see any of this.

Mom was getting out. She would still be going in for counseling, but things were going to be better, she promised Lizzie. "I've learned a lot, kiddo," Mom said on the phone. She didn't want to stay in Big Pine. "Too many bad memories," she'd said.

She told Lizzie they were going to move to the Twin Cities, and she was going to get a better job. "I've lived in the sticks too long," Mom said.

Lizzie wasn't sure what the sticks were, but she guessed Mom meant the woods. Wherever they were going, it wasn't going to be in the woods. Lizzie liked where she was. She didn't like the trailer much, but she was learning about the birds and the berries and the trees. She liked being on the lake. But she knew Mom needed a job, and she hadn't been happy working at the grocery store, where she hurt her back, or the potato plant, where she got back on drugs. She wasn't sure what Mom was going to do, but whatever it was, it was going to be somewhere else.

Lizzie looked up at Norry and couldn't imagine not seeing her again.

Norry always looked serious, but Lizzie knew she had a great big heart. Norry loved the Last Resort, and she loved the forest, and Lizzie thought she even loved Wendell—she was always so worried about him.

Wendell had made it home from the hospital, but he wasn't walking around very well. He was weak and he got tired, and Norry said he should try to get more exercise, to walk a little every day. Wendell had said he was too tired for that, but Lizzie knew Norry was not going to give up. Norry never gave up on anything, as far as Lizzie could tell.

Norry had set up a table and chair in front of Wendell's cabin. "Now you don't have to sit inside," she'd explained.

Wendell had started sitting at the little table outside his cabin for much of the day. He was there when Lizzie got home from school, and she was happy to see he was writing in the notebook she'd gotten for him.

"Whatcha doing?" Lizzie asked him.

"I'm writing the story of my life and death."

"Is it a good story?"

Wendell looked down at the page of purple writing. His handwriting was loopy and curvy, and Lizzie couldn't read it, but it looked like he had a lot to say. Wendell had his mouth puckered, as if he was thinking seriously about Lizzie's question.

"I don't know yet."

The next weekend was the big walleye and northern fishing opener, and Norry had her first guests. Two guys from the Twin Cities came, and they knew Norry. They said they used to come up when her dad was still alive. They had their own boat, and they were on the water as soon as it was legal to start fishing.

A little later that Saturday morning, Lizzie heard someone calling from the lake.

"Hey, Lizzie! Are you gonna come and help me catch dinner, or what?"

It was Bud, and he was in a boat. Lizzie went out to the end of the dock, and Bud pulled the boat in. He told her they were going fishing, and he helped her into a life jacket and even let her hold his pole. She reeled it in, and he helped her cast it out again. It was the most exciting thing ever.

"Maybe I can get my own fishing pole next year!" Lizzie said. And then she remembered.

But just then, she felt a tug at the line, and Bud helped her pull in a big fish. It wasn't a walleye, Bud said, sounding a little disappointed, but it was a big northern. When they returned to shore, Bud showed her how to fillet the fish, and Lizzie thought she could probably do it herself and wished she could get a chance to try. Bud cooked the northern, and Norry made a big salad and a blueberry crisp. They ate outside and welcomed the two fishermen back at the end of the day. They hadn't caught anything, but it seemed like they'd had a good time.

Then Norry made another bonfire and Wendell came over from his cabin. He'd still had only one eye operation, so he kept opening one eye and closing it and then looking through the other eye.

"Why are you doing that?" Lizzie asked.

"Doing what?"

"Blinking like that."

"I'm just seeing things a little different, that's all."

"Do you like it?"

"I'm not sure."

The next week went really fast, and pretty soon Lizzie only had one more week of school left. Jodie Johansson had started hassling Bri again.

"Hey, Bri! Is that what they're wearing in the hood these days?" Jodie called out when Bri got on the bus.

"Oh, shut up!" Lizzie hollered back. "Like, Big Pine is the fashion capital of the world?"

Jodie was so surprised she just made a face and whispered something to one of her friends. But she left Bri alone for the rest of the ride home. Lizzie knew it wouldn't last, but school would be over next week.

Wendell had his second Cadillac removed and seemed like he was spending more time sitting outside, writing in his unicorn notebook.

"How's the story coming?" Lizzie asked.

"The story?"

"About your life and death."

Wendell looked down at his notebook for a long time.

"I think I might have some writing left to do," he finally said.

And at the end of her last week with Norry, Lizzie started packing.

She hadn't come with a suitcase, and now she had a lot of stuff she hadn't owned when she got there—new jeans and tennis shoes and underwear, her *Little House in the Big Woods* nightgown, her new notebooks and pens, and some books. Norry gave her a brand-new duffel bag to put it all in.

Lizzie made her bed the way Norry had taught her to, and put the duffel bag by the door. Then, all of a sudden, it seemed real. The stuff in the duffel bag was her real life. Everything that came before the duffel bag didn't seem real anymore, and Lizzie wasn't sure she wanted any of it. "I'm going to come to stay again sometime, aren't I?" she asked.

"I hope so. You and your mom can come and stay anytime you like. Maybe you can come up during the summer and we'll make blueberry jam."

Blueberry jam sounded wonderful, and Lizzie was about to ask where the blueberry bushes were when she heard Mom's old car pulling up at the Last Resort. Mom got out, dressed in jeans and a sweatshirt that was too big. Lizzie had forgotten how small she was. She looked kind of frail and a little tired, but not loopy.

"Mom!" Lizzie ran to her and gave her a huge hug. Mr. Benson danced around them. Mom just stood there, and Lizzie realized Mom had started to cry.

"Oh, kiddo, it's so good to see you!"

Mom came into the cabin, and Norry told her what they'd done while Lizzie was there. Norry was talking a lot, Lizzie noticed. She told her mom how they'd gone out on the pontoon boat and seen where the loons were nesting and how Lizzie had helped Bud catch a big northern. Mom just nodded, and she didn't seem like she was understanding everything. She was looking around Norry's house and saying "Uh-huh," and if Norry stopped talking, there was silence.

Then Norry gave Lizzie a big hug, and when she was through, Lizzie didn't let her go and she hugged her a little longer.

"I'm going to miss you so much," she whispered into Norry's ear, because she didn't want to hurt her mom's feelings. And Norry gave her one last squeeze.

"Thanks for everything," Mom said, and she walked out of Norry's house and put Lizzie's duffel in the back seat. Lizzie climbed in the passenger seat, and they were headed down the driveway when she realized she had not said goodbye to Wendell.

"Wait, Mom, wait!"

Lizzie jumped out of the car and ran over to the Chickadee Cabin, where Wendell was still working on his unicorn notebook, and she gave him a big hug. Wendell seemed surprised.

"I'm going to miss you, Wendell!" Lizzie said. And Wendell opened his mouth like he was going to say something, but Mom tapped on the horn and Lizzie had to leave.

They drove out of the Last Resort, and the last thing Lizzie saw was Wendell, sitting at his little table with his mouth still open.

~

Norry didn't leave the house to watch the car pull away.

She'd imagined she would, but at the last moment, she found her feet rooted to the cabin floor. She heard the sound of the car start and then stop a few feet down the driveway, and she had this ridiculous idea that Cat had thought better of the whole thing. Maybe she needed a little more time. Maybe they were going to look for a house in Loon Point. Maybe she just wanted Lizzie to finish her final four days of school living at the resort. Four days! It wasn't much.

But none of that happened. The car stopped, and Norry stood in the cabin, listening intently. After it had stopped just long enough for her to become convinced they were—improbably—coming back, she heard a car door slam and the engine start up, and the car drove away.

And Norry was alone.

She'd talked to Cat briefly on the phone the day before. Cat told her she'd been applying for jobs in the Twin Cities. Summer vacation started on Friday, and Cat had expressed the opinion that the last four days of school were not particularly important. Norry had told her that perfect attendance mattered a lot to Lizzie and surely four more days wouldn't matter. Cat had sighed and said she supposed this was true, but she was not going back to that trailer—which Norry thought was a good idea. Cat had a friend from the potato processing plant who'd let them stay for the last week of school. And that was all.

Norry sat down. She was aiming for a chair but instead found herself sinking down to the kitchen floor, and she was sadder than she could remember being in a very long time.

She tried to sort out her feelings. The end of May was always going to come. Cat's treatment was always going to end. Cat was so fortunate to have gotten into that center. The wait to get in was usually months, from what Norry understood, and who knows what life would have been like in the meantime. No. Everything had worked out exactly as it was supposed to. Better than could be expected. Norry had done a good thing and helped a little girl when she needed it. There was no reason whatsoever to be sitting on the kitchen floor. And crying. Now she was crying. So dumb.

While sitting on the floor, Norry used her vantage point to examine the kitchen. It could use a better cleaning than she'd given it in a few months. It was amazing how much grime you could see on the cabinet fronts when you observed them from a new angle. And the baseboards all around could use a scrub. Norry got up from the floor and headed over to the sink. She filled a bucket full of hot water and soap and started scrubbing. Cleaning was what she did when she needed time to think.

She saw the coffee drips on the cabinet fronts and remembered that first morning after the spring blizzard when she'd served Wendell and Bud coffee and made pancakes for everyone—even Benson. And she remembered how Wendell had poured half a pitcher of cream into his coffee and she'd had to refill it. She remembered Lizzie hadn't even known that a person picked blueberries. Norry had never gotten a chance to pick blueberries with Lizzie. The thought made Norry absurdly sad.

Lizzie was going to live in the Twin Cities. She didn't need to know how blueberries were picked. She would soon know all sorts of things Norry had never known as a child. Maybe she'd get to go to concerts and plays. Probably she would. Norry scrubbed harder, thinking of all the things Lizzie might do in Minneapolis or St. Paul. She'd go to the Children's Theatre, and she'd visit the Minneapolis Institute of Art, and she'd get to hear the Minnesota Orchestra. Norry was picturing a full life for Lizzie in the Twin Cities, a life far away from Loon Point, filled with wonderful things. A bigger school. More opportunities. Lizzie would thrive. She was such a good reader, she'd be able to get into advanced classes that would challenge her more than they could at Big Pine Elementary. They'd have special programs for kids like Lizzie.

But in her heart, Norry didn't believe this.

Because she honestly didn't think there were other kids like Lizzie. There was only Lizzie. There was Lizzie, and then there was nobody else. Norry's baseboards were spotless. Her cabinets were pristine. But she still felt she had a lot to do. She had a lot of feelings and nowhere to put them.

Oh, Lizzie. Why did you have to come here at all?

Just then, Norry heard another vehicle driving in. Not more guests. They weren't due till later in the week. Not Cat's car. (Of course it wasn't Cat's car. Why would it be Cat's car?) This one sounded bigger, anyway.

Norry dumped the dirty water down the drain. Those baseboards had really needed it. Maybe she should do the baseboards in the bedrooms next. Norry saw the red truck outside her window. Bud. She wiped her face. She realized she probably looked as if she'd been crying.

"Hey! Anyone here?" Bud called.

"I'm here. Just me."

Bud walked in the door, and Norry's efforts to stay calm and nonchalant evaporated.

"She just left."

"Oh. Oh, Norry. I'm so sorry."

And she went over to Bud, and he hugged her, and he hugged her hard. And Norry wondered why on earth she had never been hugged by Bud Gustafson before, because it was the biggest and surest hug she'd ever had in all her life.

Chapter Fifteen

They decided to eat indoors.

Even though the night was beautiful and Norry generally opted to eat outside whenever it was possible, she wasn't in the mood to make conversation with the two guest fishermen, and she didn't want a bonfire without Lizzie. So she and Bud had walleye and asparagus and wild rice, as if they were in a fancy restaurant in Bemidji. Except they were just sitting at Norry's kitchen table, enjoying the view of her spotless kitchen cabinets.

She didn't have a lot to say.

Her reaction to Lizzie's leaving was unreasonable. She knew this. Norry was not generally an unreasonable person. She prided herself on being able to look at most things in a rational way—possibly too rationally. But it had gotten her through her difficult divorce and the loss of her dad and her new life here. She had enjoyed what there was to enjoy while she could, and she'd always been aware, from the time her mother died, that life was short, and happiness of every kind would eventually come to an end. And so she had steeled herself for loss, and she'd been able to handle it when it came.

And now she wasn't doing well at all.

The walleye was delicious. She'd let Bud cook, and he had some combination of seasoning she'd never tried. It certainly couldn't be any fresher, since he'd caught it that day. Asparagus was in season, but that didn't mean much as far north as Big Pine. It was still ridiculously expensive, she was sure. But Bud had shown up with a pound of it, and they were having it with wild rice, and Norry had to admit it was a terrific dinner.

Bud kept quiet. Norry was so far into her thoughts that when he asked if she wanted another piece of toasted bread, she jumped. Then she realized she was not being very good company. Then she realized how glad she was that she was not alone.

"Thank you," she said.

"Thank you," he said.

"For what?"

"For being who you are and doing what you do." He handed her the bread.

"I'm not sure I do much."

"You made a big difference to Lizzie."

Norry looked down at the table. She noticed that as good as the meal was, she hadn't eaten much.

"And you make a big difference to me," Bud added.

Norry looked up at Bud and noticed he'd taken his hat off. She smiled. This was only the second time she'd seen him without a hat. He looked almost naked. Norry found the idea of a naked Bud very nice.

It took a long time to finish dinner. After dinner, they had some coffee and Norry got out some leftover blueberry cobbler, and they took their cups and bowls out to the deck. The fishermen had gotten in long ago. They'd built a small fire in front of their cabin, and she could hear them laughing and see them drinking beer in the firelight a few yards off.

"Can I get you more cobbler?" Norry asked as she took Bud's bowl.

"No, but I'd like something else."

"What's that?"

And Bud stood up and pulled her toward him and he kissed her—before she could say a thing about it, with a coffee cup in one hand and two cobbler bowls in the other. He kissed her very gently, and then he held her shoulders and he looked right into her eyes.

Norry looked deep into Bud's. She saw the fine lines around them and the way the sun had left lines upon his face. She saw the way he looked into her eyes as if he could see everything she might be thinking and didn't want to change a thing. She saw he wanted her, and she realized she had not wanted anyone like this in a very long time—if ever. She heard the cobbler bowls rattling together and was rather surprised she had managed to hang on to them at all.

"Norry Last. At last."

And Norry knew she was smiling, and she knew he was following her as she went into the cabin, carrying the dirty dishes, and she felt his hands around her waist as she rinsed the bowls in the sink, and she felt him pull close behind her as she put down the sponge, and she felt his size and his warmth and his breath on her neck. And she reached for his hand and took him straight into her bedroom.

~

Lizzie and her mom were going to stay at Bonnie's house for a week, while Lizzie finished school. The guest room only had one bed, so they were going to share it.

"Should I hang up my clothes?" Lizzie asked.

"I wouldn't bother," Mom said. So Lizzie left all her clothes in the duffel Norry had given her.

The next morning, Lizzie walked to school. It was only four blocks from Bonnie's house. Bonnie had a yard that was fenced in, and Mr. Benson had to stay in the yard.

"I'll be back in the afternoon, Mr. Benson," Lizzie promised. Mr. Benson didn't look happy.

Nothing much was happening in school. Friday would be the first day of summer vacation. They spent a lot of time on art projects and were allowed to read in class if they wanted to, but they had to return all their library books. Everyone was talking about what they were going to do this summer. Some of the kids were going to summer camp. Most of them were spending time on the lake. Lizzie wondered what she was going to do all summer.

When she got home, Mr. Benson was very happy to see her, but Mom was on her way out the door. "I'm going to meet with a counselor at the center," she said.

Bonnie was home from work and had a puzzle set up on the kitchen table. Lizzie helped her put the pieces together since she didn't have any homework or library books. Mr. Benson stayed under Lizzie's chair, and when she left the room, Mr. Benson followed.

"You must be excited," Bonnie said as she filled in the edge of the puzzle, "moving to the Twin Cities. I've never lived in the Cities before. I've got a sister who lives in Bloomington, though, so I've been there plenty."

Lizzie wasn't sure where Bloomington was, but it seemed like there were a lot of cities in the Twin Cities, not just two.

Mom got home an hour later, and she looked more tired than she had been before. "I'm going to bed," she told Lizzie and Bonnie.

"Don't you want any dinner?" Bonnie asked, but Mom said no, so Bonnie and Lizzie had a frozen pizza.

It was the first week in June now, and that meant the sun was up until late. Lizzie dug a book out of the duffel Norry had given her. She had wanted to save the book to read once summer vacation began, but she didn't have any library books and Bonnie only had magazines. The book was all about the animals in northern Minnesota. It wasn't a kids' book. That was because Norry thought Lizzie was smart and could read books for adults.

Lizzie started reading, but the book made her sad. She knew she wasn't going to be seeing many animals in the Twin Cities. There weren't going to be any loons, and if they saw a bear in the city, they'd probably shoot it. Lizzie wondered if there were deer or squirrels. Probably there would be rabbits and field mice, anyway. There were rabbits and mice everywhere, as far as Lizzie knew.

The sun was low in the sky, but still not all the way down when Lizzie went to bed.

"It will get dark a little earlier in the Twin Cities," Bonnie told her. And Lizzie wondered how far away the Twin Cities were. It sounded like another country. It sounded too far away.

Lizzie and Mr. Benson both climbed into bed next to Mom, who was snoring a little. She saw Mom was in her clothes, and Lizzie remembered she'd always slept in her clothes until Norry got her the *Little House in the Big Woods* nightgown. She wondered if she should put it on. She realized she'd forgotten her toothbrush.

She wanted to pull the curtains closed, but there weren't any curtains, just a window shade, and it was up too high for Lizzie to reach. The sheets weren't crisp, like Norry's. They were slippery. Lizzie tried to remember this wasn't her home, but she didn't know what kind of home they'd be going to. When Lizzie tried to imagine it, there was nothing.

So, instead, she imagined the cabin at the Last Resort and the walls that were the color of maple syrup (the real kind that comes from trees) and the sound of the loons flying overhead and the whistling sound the Norway pine needles made when the wind blew through them. She wondered how the loons' nest was doing, and if they'd laid eggs yet. She wondered how Wendell was doing and if he'd finished his story in the unicorn book. She wondered about Norry and Bud.

"Everything's going to be okay, Mr. Benson," Lizzie whispered. That's what her mom had told her.

"Everything's gonna be okay, kiddo," Mom had said as they drove into Big Pine. Mom had seen Lizzie was sad to leave the Last Resort. "We're going to have a brand-new life. It's going to be great."

But when Lizzie asked what the brand-new life looked like, Mom didn't have any answers. "I guess we'll just have to find out!" she'd said. And Lizzie didn't think Mom looked as sure as she sounded.

If Lizzie didn't know better, she'd say Mom looked a little afraid.

~

It was midmorning, and so far, Norry had not made it out of bed.

"Well. That was worth waiting thirty years for," Bud announced.

"You were not interested in me thirty years ago!" Norry protested.

"Of course I was. You were just too smart and in too big a hurry."

"I couldn't have been too smart if I didn't know you were interested in me."

Norry wasn't sure how there was room for both of them in her small bed, as Bud seemed to take up most of it, but she found the remaining space was enough. More than enough, actually. And curling up to this big man was something she'd wanted to do for most of her life and had just never realized it. Until now.

"You know, Virgie is due back tomorrow," Norry said. "No, wait. Today! Virgie is due back today."

"So?"

"So? What am I going to say?"

"Why do you need to say anything?"

"She's my best friend. And you dated her!" Norry pulled the sheet over her face. She felt as if she were sixteen years old—and not in a good way.

Bud pried the sheet loose from her fingers. Sunlight was shining on him. They had not pulled the curtains shut last night. He was a furry man, Norry had discovered. He was a reddish-blond man from the top of his head to the tops of his furry toes. And in the dappled sunlight coming through the window, Bud seemed to glow. He was a big, furry, glowing naked man, and Norry was delighted he was in her bed, kissing her again.

"To hell with Virgie," Bud said under his breath.

"To hell with Virgie," Norry agreed.

Quite a bit later, Norry was up making pancakes. Bud had fallen asleep again, and it was almost ten o'clock. Ten o'clock! This was a guy who got up before dawn to go fishing every other day. She was making pancakes and frying bacon, and she figured the smell would eventually wake Bud up. And she was right.

"Well! Top of the morning to you," he said.

He'd put on his jeans and nothing else. Norry decided that serving pancakes to a topless man was perfectly fine in her book. In fact, she might need to make a habit of it.

"You're such a liar. You never noticed me in high school," she scolded.

"You're such a smarty-pants. Of course I did. But I didn't spend a whole lot of time getting my hopes up. You couldn't wait to get out of here."

"You're right. I was in a hurry."

"And now? Are you happy here now?"

Norry didn't know the question was an earnest one until she looked at Bud's face and saw he was genuinely worried. She sat down at the table across from him.

"I am. I love my life here. But I have been lonely. Having Lizzie live here was . . ."

What was it? She tried to put her finger on it.

"I never felt as if I was really needed before. My dad didn't need me until the end, and he expected me to sell the place after he was gone. My marriage was . . . my marriage was with someone who needed something, but it wasn't me. Having Lizzie here was different. I didn't feel I was alone until she came here. Then I realized how lonely it had been."

Bud stopped eating blueberry pancakes long enough to take her hands in his.

"You've been alone too long, Norry."

She felt herself blushing, and she felt things were moving too quickly, but she didn't want to chase him away—not now. Maybe not ever. So she kept her mouth closed, and she looked down at the maple table and squeezed his hands. It was enough. It was enough for now.

Bud finished his breakfast and stood up to stretch. Norry wondered again how she'd had such a gorgeous man in her sights all these years and never noticed. Of course, she'd never seen him without a shirt. Hell, she'd never seen him without a hat.

"And what are you up to on this fine day, Mr. Gustafson?"

"Oh, I suppose, after I kiss a lovely lady a couple more times, I better head off to look at an Evinrude I promised to fix sometime today."

"I think I'm going to give Cat a call and see how they're doing. Maybe invite them by at the end of the week before they leave for the Cities."

"You're hurting."

"I am a little. Isn't that silly?"

"It is not silly. You have a big heart."

Bud gathered his clothes up from various parts of the bedroom—finally locating a sock beneath the bed—and headed for the door.

"One more Last kiss."

"So I should make this kiss last?"

"Oh, I don't think you'll be able to do that. I'm pretty sure I'll be back for another before you know it."

Norry stood in her kitchen and heard Bud's truck start up. She never imagined the sound of a Ford F-250 could make her heart constrict. She smiled. Then she frowned. She figured she was going to have to face Virgie.

~

Things were changing. That was Wendell's impression. Wendell was trying not to get involved, but it was hard not to notice some changes going on.

First, that old car had pulled up, and Wendell had assumed it was just more cabin guests. He already had to put up with the two drunken fishermen just two cabins down. It was not a cabin guest, but a young woman who must have been Lizzie's mother. He vaguely remembered her from the morning he'd first come. She was kind of scruffy, from what he remembered.

She looked a little more cleaned up this time around, and she was driving off with Lizzie, but not before the child jumped out of the car and hugged him. It had all been a little too emotional. And unnecessary. But it was kind of sweet, he had to admit. The woman had not come back, and so Wendell had to assume Lizzie was gone for good. He was sad about that, for some reason. She had been a pest, but he'd gotten used to her and her dog and her silly questions. Now it was just the fishermen and Norry. But then it wasn't.

That Bud Gustafson was always hovering somewhere around, and last night, he'd parked his pickup right in front of Norry's cabin and had never left. Wendell knew because he watched. The big red truck stayed right where it was all night long. Well. That had never happened before. That was a development for sure.

Now Bud had driven off in his truck. The two fishermen were back on the lake. And little Lizzie had not returned. She must have gone for good. Yup. Things were changing. That much was obvious.

Wendell was back out at his table under the big Norway pine. He had been working on his unicorn notebook, but it was not going the way he wanted it to. He was not sending the message he intended. It was frustrating because he knew he had a lot to say, but every time he tried to make the argument—to explain the things he needed to explain—his mind drifted off and he ended up looking at the lake or listening to the loons.

Norry said they had a nest just around the corner. She said she'd take him to see it in the pontoon. Wendell wouldn't normally have gone in for a thing like that—getting in a boat and tooling around. He wasn't that kind of guy. But it was different, with the new eyes. Wendell figured he would be able to see the nest, and the eggs inside it, and probably the baby loons inside the eggs. Wendell had something like x-ray vision now, as near as he could tell, and this was causing him to notice all sorts of things he hadn't noticed before.

Today he hadn't written a word. The notebook was lying on the table, and the glitter on the unicorn was sparkling in the sun. And Wendell knew it was stupid, but he was thinking that unicorn looked good, all glittery like that. He didn't know why he had thought it was such a sad beast. It was a happy unicorn—how could it not be? All pink and shiny, surrounded by pink and purple hills.

Wendell figured he must be losing his mind.

Dementia didn't run in his family, but there was always a first. That teenage doctor might be good at picking up problems with vision, but Wendell doubted he'd have a clue if his patient was a few shingles short of a roof.

But then Wendell wondered if it really mattered. They treated him as if he were half demented as it was. Even with his vision back, Norry would stop by and see what he needed when she drove into Big Pine for groceries. He'd made sure he paid for everything. He made her keep the change, and he tried to give her something for gas. He wasn't a total charity case, after all.

But she'd said she didn't mind, and she brought Wendell his groceries, and since Norry was picking them up for him, he got kind of embarrassed living on chips and frozen dinners, so he had her pick up some things he didn't usually eat. Potatoes instead of potato chips. Cheese instead of Cheez-Its. Some chicken. Some fruit. Wendell even used the grill outside and cooked up a chicken breast. He got one of those salads in a bag. It wasn't that hard. It reminded him of something his mother would have made. He thought of all her recipe books lying at the bottom of the county landfill. It was sad, but honestly, Wendell probably wasn't going to use his mom's recipes. He'd discovered they had recipes on the internet. Wendell could just look on the fancy new smartphone he got last week and find out exactly how long it took to cook a chicken breast on the grill. He could find recipes for the soups he remembered eating back when his mom made soup. It was all there on the internet. Pretty amazing.

Wendell realized, while he had been planning the soup he was going to make tonight, he'd forgotten all about his writing project. This was no good. This was not how things got done. He needed to get to it. Even if no one ever read it (and he doubted anyone would), he wanted to get it all down—all the frustration and humiliation of being in a tiny minority who understood the unfairness of life.

But as he mulled it over, he wondered if Norry might not understand some of this. Her mom had died when she was young, and her dad died a few years back. If he was to believe the gossip in Loon Point, she'd come back to the Last Resort after her husband left her. For almost ten years, she'd been running this place all on her own, and now that he'd had a chance to inspect the operations, he realized a lot went into keeping a resort like this going. It was a hell of a lot of work for a single gal. It was kind of amazing she'd made a go of it. Maybe it was okay if a guy like Bud showed up now and then. Bud was a pain in the ass and a doofus, but he probably could help her out.

Then Wendell had a thought. He realized he had been helped quite a bit himself over the last month or so. Take the whole house thing—that was a disaster, of course. But Norry (and even Bud, he had to admit) had been helpful. They had done a lot of things for him they hadn't needed to do. And maybe he hadn't been quite as aware of it as he should have been. It kind of ruined his mood for writing about all his bad luck.

Instead, he thought about that little Lizzie and Norry—and even Bud—and he picked up his (purple!) pen and let it write whatever it wanted to write. And the purple pen wrote *I have had the good fortune to meet some kind people.*

Chapter Sixteen

"So, what is it that you and Bud are doing?" Virgie asked.

Virgie was clueless. Or she was pretending to be clueless. Or Norry was just really bad at explaining this.

"We're . . . well, we've started . . . we're kind of . . ."

"Are you sleeping together?"

"Well, yes, but that isn't the point. The point is . . ."

"Of course it's the point. Congratulations! It's about time."

Norry sighed. She knew Virgie was going to think whatever she wanted. And she would have liked to have had a little more time to figure out what, exactly, she and Bud Gustafson *were* doing. But Virgie was back today, opening up her shop, and there was no point in delaying the inevitable.

"Seriously, I think this is long overdue," Virgie said. She had just finished cleaning the windows of the shop, which hadn't been washed since she closed up in the fall. The inside was remarkably clean, as Virgie covered everything up in bed sheets, making the place look like a little haunted house until she removed them in the spring.

Virgie was filling her shop with new inventory. In addition to her handmade jewelry, she also had an impressive collection of used books, a few new books recommended for summer reading, and assorted bric-a-brac that Norry couldn't imagine anyone needing or wanting, but every summer they did. By the end of the season, Virgie would have sold off all her inventory—except for the used books. Then she went back to Mexico and got more supplies.

"I mean, it's not as if there is a huge selection of men up here in the winter," Virgie continued. She was setting up a display of bangles and bracelets and necklaces. They all seemed a little flashy to Norry, but Virgie knew what tourists liked. "And you know what they say about men in the Northwoods," she added. "The odds are good—but the goods are odd!" Her friend laughed heartily.

Norry didn't think Bud Gustafson was odd in the least, but she wasn't in the mood to debate the matter with Virgie.

"So, the little girl, Lizzie, she's gone now?"

"As far as I know. They were supposed to leave for the Twin Cities this morning. I invited them to come by for a farewell picnic, but Cat—that's her mom—never replied."

"She sounds like a flake."

"She might be. But she got through the rehab program, and she says she wants to get into a new environment and get a better job. I mean, she's saying all the right things."

"But?"

"But . . . I think Lizzie deserves better. That's all. I know it's not a nice thing to think, and I suppose I have no business saying it, but I don't think that girl has gotten a fair shake."

"This girl has really gotten under your skin."

"She has. I felt as if I had been treading water for a long time. I let Lizzie into my house and things changed. I could see my life looking different. I started to feel I had a lot more choices."

"And sleeping with Bud was one of them!"

"Okay, yes. Possibly yes." Norry was pretty sure she was blushing, and she hated that.

Virgie was now pulling out a selection of bright Mexican tablecloths and placemats. Even Norry could tell those would sell like hotcakes.

"I've had several distinct pivots in my life," Virgie said, "and at each of them, I've become somebody I didn't expect to be. If you'd known me fifteen years ago and saw me working corporate, in my black suits with my black briefcase and all my frequent-flier miles, you would never recognize me."

"I don't think I've ever seen you in black," Norry agreed. Virgie was wearing a bright-yellow skirt, a red tank top, and sandals with blue stones on them. Norry always felt a little underdressed around her.

"No, I got rid of all my black clothes when I transformed myself from a high-flying international businesswoman to an itinerant Mexican jewelry maker. No looking back!" Virgie was smiling. "And you've had your major pivot, too—leaving your marriage, moving back up here, taking over the business."

"Alex left me, not the other way around. I'm not sure it counts as a 'pivot' if you come home to find your husband has packed up and moved out."

"Sure it does. Some of us just need a nudge from the universe. I actually think we're changing all the time. We're changing and evolving, and the big changes—the changes that people notice—are just the outward signs of things that have been brewing on the inside for a long time. It seems sudden, but I don't think it usually is. I think we're always changing and then suddenly realize—for whatever reason—that life has done us a favor, because the life we were in doesn't fit us anymore." Virgie stood back and surveyed her shop. "Done."

Norry had to admit the overall effect Virgie had created was nice. A few minutes earlier, the shop had looked abandoned. Now it was filled with color and life. It looked as if she was ready for business.

And, on cue, the bells hanging on the door jingled, and a woman stuck her head in. "Are you finally open?" she asked. She gravitated directly to the Mexican tablecloths, unfolding several, and throwing Virgie's careful display into disorder. "Ooh! These are nice."

"Okay, I've got campers getting settled into the Black Bear Cabin now and more checking in to the Moose and Raccoon Cabins tonight," Norry said. "I better scoot."

"See you soon. And give Bud a squeeze for me, will you?"

Norry was about to protest but stopped herself. "I will do that. I'll do that the first chance I get!" Then she smiled and waved as she headed out the door. She could hear Virgie laughing.

Let her laugh. Squeezing Bud sounded like a fine idea.

~

It was Friday, and Lizzie was supposed to be moving to the Twin Cities.

Yesterday, Lizzie had gotten her award for perfect attendance, but Mom didn't seem as excited as Lizzie was hoping she would be. She said she was anxious to leave Big Pine. This morning, she'd gone out to get a few things before they left. While she was gone, Lizzie packed up the duffel Norry had given her, made the bed in Bonnie's guest room, fed Mr. Benson, and took him for a walk.

Mr. Benson hadn't been on a leash much at the Last Resort, but he liked it. He liked to show off, trotting next to Lizzie. He walked by her side and looked straight ahead, only glancing up when he saw squirrels unacceptably close. Then he had to tug at the leash a little and let out a bark, to let the squirrels know that under ordinary circumstances, they would be dead meat. But he had more important things to do at the moment than chase their hairy behinds because he was walking with a Very Important Person. At least that's what Lizzie thought he was saying.

Lizzie took an extra-long walk because she did not want to go back to Bonnie's. Bonnie smoked, and her house smelled like smoke, and she was listening to a radio station where everyone was yelling at each other. Plus, Lizzie didn't want to leave. She wanted to leave Bonnie's, but she didn't want to leave Big Pine or go to a different school than Big Pine Elementary. She'd finally gotten Jodie to shut up, and she had a perfect attendance record for two years straight. They wouldn't know that in the Twin Cities. And, next year, she'd be in fourth grade, and she already knew the teacher, Ms. Hart (which sounded like *heart* but wasn't spelled that way), and she was super nice—as you would expect, with a name like that. Lizzie wanted to be in Ms. Hart's classroom, and she wanted to stay in Loon Point—or at least Big Pine—so she could visit Loon Point and Norry and Bud and Wendell and be close to the lakes and the forest and the loons.

Lizzie was getting kind of worked up about this, wondering why they had to go at all, and she knew she was walking Mr. Benson too long, and Mom would be back from her errands and she would be mad because Lizzie had made them late. But when she got back to Bonnie's, Mom wasn't back yet.

"She must have decided to get some stuff at Walmart," Bonnie said.

Lizzie was glad she wasn't in trouble, but now she was worried about what was taking Mom so long.

She read for a half hour and then went back into the kitchen.

"Maybe your mom went to counseling at the rehab center," Bonnie said.

"Maybe."

Lizzie knew Mom hadn't said anything about going to counseling, and she knew Bonnie knew this too. They were both wondering where Mom had been for the last three hours, when they were supposed to have left for the Twin Cities first thing in the morning.

Lizzie went back into the guest room and started reading her book from Norry again. She was reading about bats and how a single brown bat can eat one thousand mosquitos in less than an hour. She wondered who got to count all the mosquitos the bats ate and what kind of job that would be, watching bats eat mosquitos. She was about to start the chapter on gray wolves when Bonnie knocked on the door.

"You want some lunch?"

"Is it lunchtime?"

"It's after lunchtime." Bonnie didn't sound happy.

"Sure. Thank you."

Lizzie came out into the kitchen. The kitchen was smoky, and Bonnie was still listening to the loud radio program, but she had made a baloney sandwich with a lot of mustard and sweet pickles. Lizzie loved sweet pickles.

Lizzie finished lunch and went back to her room to read. Mr. Benson climbed up on the bed with her and put his head in her lap.

By midafternoon, Lizzie was worried. Bonnie knocked on the door again.

"So"—Bonnie stuck her hands in her pockets—"I'm going out tonight. I'm meeting some friends at the Legion."

Lizzie wondered why she was telling her this.

"So, if your mom isn't back by then, we're gonna have to figure something out."

"But it's only . . ."

What time was it? Lizzie looked at the digital clock by the bed. It was after three o'clock. When had Mom left? It'd been early. The sun had been up, but the sun came up early now. It was almost the solstice.

"Don't you think she'll be back by nighttime?" Lizzie asked, and then she was sorry she did. Now Bonnie was going to tell her what she thought, and Lizzie had a feeling she already knew what Bonnie thought.

Bonnie made a face and looked down at her feet. "Let me make a phone call."

She left, and Lizzie tiptoed to the door to eavesdrop.

"You haven't seen her? Well, she said she was leaving for the Cities today, and her kid, Lizzie, is still here. Uh-huh. Yeah, that's what I was afraid of too. Uh-huh."

Lizzie leaned in closer.

"Okay, yeah, if you hear anything, let me know. Yeah. Thanks."

Bonnie hung up, and Lizzie dashed back to the bed.

"I don't know where your mom is," Bonnie said. She looked like she was going to say something more, but then she didn't. She was making that face again, the one that made Lizzie wish she was someplace else.

"If you have to go, I could wait for Mom at the Last Resort," Lizzie offered.

"The resort?"

"Yeah. The Last Resort. With Norry?"

"Yeah, I know who Norry is. Why would you stay there?"

"That's where I stayed when Mom was in rehab. If she's . . . I mean, if you have to go, I could go there."

Bonnie looked a little relieved.

"Okay, let's give her a couple more hours. Then, if we don't hear from her, you'll either have to go to the Last Resort or come with me to the Legion."

"The Legion?"

"The American Legion."

Lizzie wasn't sure what the Legion was, but she knew she'd rather see Norry than go with Bonnie. She had a feeling Bonnie was tired of having her around.

Lizzie went back to reading, but this time she wasn't really reading. She was reading the same two paragraphs about gray wolves over and over and looking at the little clock by the bedside. It had red, square numbers, and they clicked when they changed. *Click!* Another minute had passed. *Click!* This went on for a very long time until the clock said *4:55*. Then Bonnie knocked on the door again.

"Okay, Lizzie. I gave Norry a call, and she's gonna come by and scoop you up in a few minutes. My girlfriend is here to pick me up, so maybe you could wait on the stoop."

Lizzie knew she had suggested calling Norry, but she had somehow been sure Mom would come back—late and out of breath, with news that the car had needed a repair or that she had gone to see a counselor at the rehab center or . . . Lizzie knew none of these things made sense. Mom would have called. The only time she didn't call was when she was doing drugs.

Lizzie put on her shoes and made sure she had everything from Bonnie's room. She put Mr. Benson back on his leash, and he looked all excited, ready to take another walk and see more squirrels. She hefted her duffel bag over her shoulder and made sure the guest room looked tidy.

Then she went out into the kitchen, where Bonnie was waiting. Bonnie had on a black T-shirt that said *Bitch* in sequins on the front and had her keys in her hand.

Lizzie and Mr. Benson went outside. The sun was still high in the sky. There was a car outside, waiting for Bonnie. She locked the front door behind her.

"Norry said she'd be by in no time," Bonnie said as she got in the car.

The car drove off. Lizzie sat down on the concrete stoop. It was hot in the sun. Mr. Benson sat beside her. The street was quiet. Maybe Mom would come before Norry got here. They could pretend she hadn't really gone missing. Mom could call Norry and tell her they just got a late start and now they were on their way to the Cities. Norry would say it was no problem and they should come and visit sometime this summer before school started. Lizzie and Mom would drive up in July and visit Norry and Bud and Wendell, and they would stay in a cabin like regular guests, except they would be special because Lizzie would know the owner and so would Mr. Benson. Lizzie tried to imagine Mom sitting at the campfire, maybe having a marshmallow. It was hard to imagine. Mom didn't do things like that.

Then Lizzie heard a car.

Turning onto the street was a familiar big, dark-green Jeep. It said **The Last Resort** on the side. Mr. Benson stood up. The Jeep stopped. The window was open.

"Oh, my gosh, Lizzie," Norry said. "Get on in."

Lizzie threw her duffel into the back seat, and she got into the passenger seat and Mr. Benson jumped onto her lap. Norry reached over and squeezed her hand, and they drove off with the windows wide open and the wind blowing in Lizzie's face.

When they pulled off County Road 6, Lizzie saw the trailer she used to live in, and then, just a little farther, they pulled into the Last Resort. Mr. Benson jumped out without even waiting for Lizzie. The afternoon sun was making diamonds on the water, and the pontoon boat was tied up at the dock. It felt like Lizzie had been away forever and it had only been a week.

"Make yourself at home," Norry said.

Lizzie carried her duffel into the cabin and back to her old room and she saw the bed with the red blanket on it and the books all lined up on the shelf, and she sat down at the end of the bed and breathed. She felt like she'd been holding her breath all day.

Norry had taken her phone onto the front deck, and Lizzie could hear her leaving a message for Mom. Lizzie didn't think it sounded like a friendly message, and suddenly Lizzie became worried that maybe Norry hadn't wanted her to come back. But after Norry hung up, she came back into Lizzie's room (or what Lizzie thought of as her room), and she sat on the bed next to her.

"How are you?" she asked, and she took Lizzie's hand.

Lizzie was happy to be back. She was glad to be out of Bonnie's house, although Bonnie hadn't been mean to her. She was worried about Mom, and she was a little mad at her, too, because she'd said she was just going out for a minute, and she had lied. Lizzie didn't know what to say.

"My clothes smell like smoke" is what she finally said.

"Let's get them washed. I think you're due for another Last Resort T-shirt, anyway. I just got the new ones in. I don't think you have a yellow one yet."

Norry gave Lizzie a brand-new yellow T-shirt, and Lizzie put on her shorts and gave Norry all her dirty clothes, and she went outside to look for Mr. Benson, who was checking to see what he had missed while they'd been away.

A couple of hours later, everyone was there. Everyone except Mom.

Norry and Bud and Wendell and two fishermen were there—they were different fishermen, but they were nice. And Norry's friend Virgie, who Lizzie had never met, arrived. Virgie was dressed in seven different colors (that Lizzie counted) and had on at least a dozen bracelets that jangled together. She had a loud laugh. "I'm glad you could join us!"

Virgie told Lizzie, and she sounded like she meant it. But Mom still hadn't gotten there.

They had a big fire on the beach, and Norry said they were going to make their own dessert.

"What are we having?" Lizzie asked.

"We are having moose pies!"

"No!"

"Yes."

Norry brought out some heavy iron things, like little cast-iron pans on the end of sticks, and she showed Lizzie how to butter both sides of a piece of bread and put it in the pans, with raspberries on the inside, then clamp the pans shut.

"Then what?" Lizzie asked.

"Then you put them in the fire."

"No way!"

"Yes."

And Lizzie made her first moose pie—and did not burn it like she usually did with the marshmallows. It popped right out of the cast-iron mold, a perfect little browned pie with raspberries inside. Norry put a scoop of ice cream on top, and it was the best thing Lizzie had ever eaten in her entire life.

Then Bud made one, and when Norry put ice cream on his moose pie, he gave Norry a kiss—right in front of the bonfire—and Virgie let out a whoop and applauded, and Lizzie applauded (because Virgie did), and Mr. Benson started barking, and Norry looked embarrassed. But she looked happy. Then Norry made a moose pie for Wendell.

"Aren't they good?" Lizzie asked.

"They are very fine," Wendell agreed.

"Have you written more in your unicorn notebook?"

"I have."

"Are you still writing your story?"

"I am."

"What kind of story is it?"

"It's got a lot more surprises than I expected."

"I love stories with surprises, don't you?"

Wendell looked down at the paper plate where his moose pie had been a moment earlier. "I think I do. I'm not sure I used to, but now I think maybe I do."

And all the while, Norry had her phone resting on the arm of her lawn chair, and Lizzie felt like it was a little bomb waiting to go off. Mom was going to call. Or someone was going to call about Mom. No matter what happened, Lizzie didn't think it was going to be good. But she wanted to know that Mom was okay.

The phone didn't ring, and the sun went down, and just as it did, Lizzie heard a loon call—very loud and very close. It made the hair on her neck prickle.

Bud kicked a log over in the fire but didn't add any more wood.

"Probably time for bed," Norry told Lizzie. "We don't know what tomorrow will bring."

Lizzie felt like she would never know what tomorrow would bring, ever again. She went into the cabin and saw her *Little House in the Big Woods* nightgown had been washed and all her other clothes were folded up on the dresser. Mr. Benson's food and water bowls were back on the kitchen floor. But still, there was no Mom.

Lizzie brushed her teeth and got into bed. Norry said she could leave the curtains open to watch the last of the sun go down.

"Good night, Norry," Lizzie said.

"Good night, Lizzie. I'll let you know if there's news."

"Thank you."

But Norry didn't need to do that, because later that night, Lizzie heard the sound of a car driving in and then she heard a loud crash. Mr. Benson jumped off the bed and started barking. Lizzie heard a car radio playing, and then she heard swearing. Lizzie ran out onto the deck.

It was Mom.

She had driven into a cluster of birch trees at the end of the driveway. The car lights were still on, and the car radio was playing loudly.

Mom got out of the car, and Lizzie worried she might be hurt. She wasn't walking right.

"Where is she?" Mom yelled. "What the hell have you done with my daughter?"

Chapter Seventeen

It's not as if Wendell could sleep with all that commotion.

First, he heard the crash. Then he heard the screaming. Lots of profanities. It sounded like a woman. Wendell got out of bed and peeked out the window, but it was dark, and all he saw were some headlights illuminating the beach. Wendell had recently become the owner of a pair of slippers—more castoffs, these also from Norry's father, apparently—so he slipped them on and headed outside to see what was causing all the ruckus.

As soon as he got outside, he saw the lights from the car were off kilter, and as soon as he got close to the car, he saw why. The car was wrapped around the clump of birch trees that grew next to the sign that said **The Last Resort**, right at the entrance. A couple of feet farther to the right and the sign would have been taken out as well. But as it was, the birch looked as if they'd taken the full velocity of the car. The car must have been moving at a pretty good clip because the front fender and hood were crumpled around those defenseless trees, which were now standing at a significant angle.

Well, that's no good.

Wendell padded over in his new slippers to see who had perpetrated all this mayhem in the middle of the night. The car door was now open, and there was a woman—a rather small one—staggering toward Norry's cabin. She appeared to be drunk, and she was stumbling and staggering forward as she swore. As Wendell drew closer, he caught the drift of what she was saying.

"I got a message you have her!" the woman hollered. "Give me back my goddamned daughter!"

This did not seem like a good idea to Wendell. A person unable to avoid perfectly stationary birch trees probably should not be chauffeuring around an eight-year-old. Or be behind the wheel of a car at all, for that matter. That was Wendell's opinion.

Now she was making her way to Norry's cabin, and Wendell wondered if he was expected to do something. Should he try to subdue her? Wendell had very little experience subduing anyone, and although this person was quite small, she was also inebriated and belligerent and looked as if she might put up quite a fight.

But a moment later, Wendell was relieved to see this would not be necessary. Bud Gustafson appeared from out of Norry's cabin, and now Wendell saw Lizzie was there too. Bud was approaching the woman across the lawn. Things were getting interesting now. Wendell was glad he wasn't going to be called upon to do any heroics. He wasn't feeling particularly heroic. He'd just woken up, after all.

Bud was speaking quietly to the woman, who was not lowering her voice.

"You've stolen my daughter! I'm gone for a couple of hours, and you think you can fucking come and take her? I'm gonna call the sheriff's office and tell them you kidnapped my daughter!"

At this point, Wendell saw the lights of the Raccoon Cabin pop on, and the curtains pulled open. Then he saw Norry on her front deck with Lizzie. Everyone wanted to see the show.

"Where is she, asshole?" the woman demanded. "You bring my goddamned daughter out here or I'm gonna call 911 right now and tell them you kidnapped my kid!"

Wendell saw Norry was gripping Lizzie's shoulders, and Lizzie's eyes were wide.

"You're bleeding," Bud said. "I think you should get checked out at the hospital."

"Fuck you!"

Bud was standing very close to the woman, and she was looking up at him, swaying in place. But it seemed the effort to remain upright was too great, and she plopped down on the grass and started to cry.

"Come on, come on. Let's get you to the hospital," Bud said.

He scooped the woman up off the ground as if she were a doll. Wendell remembered Bud was strong. He had hoisted Wendell through the hole in his roof. Wendell had not appreciated it at the time, he now recalled. The woman sagged in Bud's arms, her head hanging loose. She appeared to have passed out. Wendell saw the car was still running. He crept a few feet closer.

"Kill the engine, would you, Wendell?" Bud said.

Wendell reached into the crashed car. He turned off the ignition and switched off the headlights. The car lights went out, the music stopped, and it was suddenly much darker and quieter. Bud nodded at him, and Wendell felt a flush of pride. He was helpful. He was assisting in an emergency.

"I'm gonna take her into Big Pine," Bud said to Norry and Lizzie.

"Do you need help?" Norry asked.

"No, you stay here with Lizzie. I'll give you a call when I get there and let you know what's happening."

Norry nodded, and Wendell could see that Lizzie's eyes were wide. Poor kid. This was no way to see your mother. Wendell wondered what else this little girl had to put up with.

Bud carried the unconscious woman to his big red truck and put her in the passenger side, fastening a seat belt around her. By this time, the two fishermen had come out of the Raccoon Cabin and were standing on the lawn in their boxer shorts, watching the action.

Lizzie was standing in front of Norry, and Norry had her arms wrapped around her. The truck started up and Bud took off with the woman. It was a narrow squeeze to get out of the driveway beside the crashed car, and Bud had to drive into the ditch to make it, narrowly scraping by a Norway pine. And then he was gone.

"Come on, Lizzie. Bud will call with news as soon as he gets to town," Norry said.

The fishermen went back into their cabin, and Norry and Lizzie went back into theirs. Wendell stood outside in the dark by himself.

There was a whole world of things that people didn't know about. That was what Wendell was thinking. There was every kind of trouble happening at any given time, and there were folks stepping up and helping people when you'd never suspect they were doing it. Wendell realized that he might have gotten some help along the way that he had not fully appreciated at the time. It was something to think about, that was for sure. Wendell stood outside long enough for the lights in the fishermen's cabin to go out. Then he saw the light at the far end of Norry's cabin go out. He figured that must be Lizzie's room. Then there was just the one light on, in Norry's kitchen. That light stayed on.

Wendell looked out over the lake. The moon was almost full, and it was reflecting on the water. A cool breeze picked up, and Wendell could smell the lake and the sap in the trees, and the last of the smoke leftover from the bonfire that night. As he thought over the day, he had to admit it had been a pretty good one. He had written in his unicorn book, but it had ended up being mostly memories of his mother. She had been a fine woman, no doubt about it. He thought about this woman trying to take Lizzie tonight, and he remembered his own mother, Eunice Eklund, and what a good person she had been. He'd been lucky to have a mother like her.

Then he'd been invited to the bonfire, and he'd been afraid it would be a big crowd, with two new fishermen he didn't know and this Virgie woman, who seemed a little loud. But they had all been nice to him, and he felt like he fit right in, which was unusual for Wendell. And then Wendell had eaten a moose pie. He'd never heard of such a thing. It was delicious. Wendell figured he could eat a moose pie every day of his life. It had been a great night, really.

And now this. That little girl Lizzie didn't deserve to have a mother who smashed into birch trees at two o'clock in the morning, and Bud shouldn't have to drive her to the hospital in his truck.

Wendell looked down at his feet and remembered he was wearing new slippers. They were fine slippers, they really were. They had hardly been worn. Wendell realized he'd never thanked Norry for the slippers. Then he realized, with an uncomfortable feeling, that he'd never really thanked her for any of it—not for the Chickadee Cabin or the moose pie or the slippers or . . . well, any of it.

Wendell felt something shift. He was unlucky, no doubt about that. No lucky person has their house fall on their head and loses all their earthly possessions. But he had some things in his life that weren't all bad. He had to admit it. There were a few things that were not terrible.

He looked out over the lake again. He had new glasses, but he didn't need them anymore except to read. He'd forgotten to even put them on when he came outside, and with his new eyes, he could see far out onto the lake. He could see the moon and the clouds reflecting its light. He could see the pine branches waving in the moonlight. He could see in the window of the Chickadee Cabin and the bright cabinets inside and the log walls.

His old house had been kind of dark, as he remembered. Not when his mother was living there, but later on. It had been a little dingy. Maybe a little crowded. Of course, he no longer had any possessions, so there was nothing to fill his home now except Earl Söderberg's old clothes, and his unicorn notebook, and an assortment of pills he was supposed to be taking. But still. The Chickadee Cabin was adequate. It met his needs. Wendell was not, after all, a complicated man.

Maybe that was the trick. Maybe that's how people always managed to stay so much happier than Wendell had. They didn't complicate things—the happy ones didn't, anyway. They knew what they needed, and they decided to be grateful for what they had. It was a new idea. It was kind of a simpleminded idea. Wendell wasn't quite ready to drink the Kool-Aid. Not yet. But as he thought of that poor Lizzie with her drunken mother, he realized that a couple of things had gone his way, after all. He just hadn't had time to think about them until now.

Wendell went back to bed. He turned the light off on the bedside table. He was sure he would be asleep in a moment. Instead, he lay awake for a long time. He heard a loon call from far away. He heard the tree branches overhead. And he wondered what would happen to Lizzie's mother. It was too bad, Wendell thought. It really was.

~

Norry waited in the kitchen. There was no chance she was going back to sleep, and so she waited at the table with her phone for Bud to call. Lizzie went back to bed.

"They'll take care of her at the hospital," Norry said. Lizzie nodded. She looked sad. And scared. And maybe a little embarrassed. It was a lot for an eight-year-old. Norry thought Lizzie would be awake for the rest of the night, but when she checked a few minutes later, she was sound asleep, her arms around Benson. Norry closed the door.

A few minutes later, Bud called. Cat was in the hospital and would be there at least for the night. She was still out cold when he'd brought her in. The doctors said she had a concussion, a fractured arm, a few cuts, and some bad bruises. They'd done a blood test, and she had a number of things in her system, including opioids. They were going to do another assessment in the morning, but for now, she was sleeping.

"When will she be released?"

"I'm guessing tomorrow."

"Then what happens?"

"I don't know."

After she hung up, Norry went back to bed and tried to sleep. She knew Bud would go back to his place, but she wished he was with her. It would be good to hold him right now. After a long time, Norry finally fell asleep, thinking about Bud and wondering how many times he'd done this—stepped in to help without ever being asked.

In the morning, Norry heard Lizzie's door squeak open and the sound of Benson's toenails on the kitchen floor. "Good morning!"

Lizzie looked like she hadn't slept well. Her face was pale and her dark eyes were serious.

"How's Mom?"

"Your mom is still in the hospital, but she's going to be okay. She got a pretty good knock on the head. Bud will be checking in on her again this morning."

Lizzie nodded. She looked much too serious for an eight-year-old.

"How about if I make us some toast and eggs while we wait for the tow truck?"

"Tow truck?"

"Your mom's car is blocking the driveway right now, and I think the Eliots in the Black Bear Cabin will want to get out this morning. Plus, we've got new folks coming in to stay in the Beaver and Deer Cabins later today and a big family is coming to stay in the Bald Eagle Cabin tomorrow."

"That's a lot of people."

"That's summer in Minnesota." Norry looked closely at Lizzie. She looked as if she had aged two years overnight.

"Are you okay?"

Lizzie shook her head and looked at the floor. "I didn't want to go. I didn't want to go to the Twin Cities, and I was wishing we wouldn't go, and now Mom is in the hospital and the car is smashed."

"None of that is your fault."

"No. But I got what I wished for, and I feel bad."

Norry looked at the small girl with the wild black hair wearing a long white nightgown. She got down on her knees and realized Lizzie was crying.

"Oh, Lizzie. None of this is your fault. You hear me, honey? None of this. Your mom is sick. She has an addiction, and that is not your fault. She's gonna have to fight really hard to get well, but hopefully, she can get some more help."

Now Lizzie was crying a little harder, but she was hanging on to Norry.

"You did exactly what you should have done. It was a responsible thing for you to do—letting Bonnie know you could come here yesterday. I'm very proud of you."

Slowly, Lizzie stopped crying.

"Better?"

"Uh-huh."

"Want an egg?"

"Uh-huh."

"Sunny-side up, scrambled, or shipwrecked?"

"What's a shipwrecked egg?"

"It's a cross between sunny-side up and scrambled. It's the best. I'll make you one."

The tow truck arrived a half hour later, just about the time Bud called from Big Pine Hospital.

"I can't get her back into the rehab center for at least a week," Bud reported.

"You called the rehab center? That was nice of you."

"I'm a nice guy."

"I know that."

"No, I used to work with the manager there, back when I was a deputy, and he was able to squeeze her in last time, but this fentanyl thing is raging—it's hit them hard. I think they'll get her in as soon as they can, but they don't have a single free bed right now."

"So, what happens?"

"Well, I don't think they're going to release her today, after all. She wasn't wearing her seat belt, and she got a good knock on the head when she hit the birch trees. They want to observe her for a day, at least, to see if there's any serious injury."

"And then?"

"No idea. I haven't talked to her. I don't think that car of hers is going anywhere."

"No, I don't think so either. I'm having it towed to Mick's Garage."

"I could have pulled it out."

"And put it where? This way, she can have them sell it or scrap it. Either way, it won't be sitting around here."

"Good plan."

"Bud, thank you."

"For what?"

"For being a nice guy."

"Oh, that. It's just a bad habit I picked up."

There was a pause.

Norry felt she should say something. She knew what she wanted to say. She wanted to tell him she loved him, because she thought maybe she did. But she didn't think she should tell him this over the telephone.

"Well . . . thank you."

"You bet. See you soon."

~

Lizzie and Mr. Benson watched as the tow truck arrived. The car made a bad crunching noise when they pulled it loose from the birch trees.

It had beer cans in it that hadn't been there before. The whole front of it was smashed in, the windshield was cracked, and the hood was crumpled up. The car already had been rear-ended last winter, so the bumper in the back was missing. Now the car was pretty much wrecked. So were the trees it ran into.

Last night was bad.

Lizzie had heard what her mom was saying. She'd heard all the bad swear words, and she heard Mom say that Norry was wrong to have taken Lizzie to the Last Resort. Mom said Norry was a kidnapper. Mom said she was going to have her arrested. It made no sense. If Norry hadn't come, Lizzie would have had to go to the American Legion, and she knew Bonnie didn't want her there.

Now the tow truck was pulling Mom's car up onto a trailer. It looked even worse up there. Lizzie wondered if the car would ever drive again. Probably not. She wondered if Mom was going to be okay.

But Mom was wrong.

Lizzie had done the right thing, calling Norry. She knew it. Norry was Lizzie's friend, and Mom should not have been driving if she was high on drugs. Lizzie thought Mom would probably be sorry for the things she said last night. Lizzie loved her mom, but Mom was wrong about this. Mom had a problem. But it still hurt, thinking of those things she said.

Mr. Benson cocked his head as Mom's car was locked in place on the trailer. The birch trees were still bent over with big gashes in the trunks. Lizzie felt bad for the birch trees. And she felt lonely.

"It's just us, Mr. Benson," Lizzie said.

She wondered if she would still be going to the Twin Cities. She wondered where she would live when Mom got out of the hospital. The resort was almost full. Norry was going to be busy. She probably didn't want an extra guest in her house when she had all these other guests. Lizzie wondered what was going to happen next. Just then, Lizzie saw Wendell coming out of the Chickadee Cabin. He had slippers on, and his bright plaid sweater.

"Hi, Wendell," Lizzie said. Wendell looked over at her. "You don't have your glasses on."

"I don't need them."

"You don't?"

"No. I have new eyes."

"Really?"

"Yup. I can see everything and it's all different. Everything is in bright colors."

"Wow. That must be fun."

Wendell raised his eyebrows and seemed to be thinking this over. "It is."

He came over, and they watched together as the tow truck pulled away and Mom's car disappeared down the drive.

"That was a bad accident," he said.

"My mom was high."

"I'm sorry to hear that."

"She went to rehab, but then she got high again."

"That can happen, from what I understand."

"I think she was doing drugs and drinking beer."

"That is very dangerous."

"Yeah. I know. She's in the hospital."

Lizzie could see the two fishermen from the bonfire last night getting into their boat. They were joking and laughing. It was going to be a nice summer day—even though it was not officially summer until the solstice.

"I'm sorry you have to go through all this," Wendell said. "It's . . . I'm sure it's . . . I mean, it has to be hard for you."

Lizzie looked up at him.

"I think . . . I think Norry will take care of you. I mean, for now. I mean, until things get better. She's a very considerate person. She's helped me. And I think . . . I think you're a good kid and you will be okay."

This was the most words Lizzie had ever heard Wendell say at one time.

"Thank you."

Lizzie liked Wendell. She'd liked him from the first moment she met him wearing his big red shoes. If Wendell thought things were going to be okay, Lizzie figured that maybe, somehow, they would be.

Chapter Eighteen

Cat did not look great.

Norry looked at this woman who was, objectively, an attractive person, and thought she looked bad in about every way there was to look bad.

She had a fractured left arm in a sling. She had a nasty cut on her forehead under a bandage. She had stitches above her right eye, which was swollen shut and purple colored. Her lips were puffy, and there were still traces of blood in her blond hair. When Norry and Lizzie walked into the hospital room, Cat's gaze darted off in the other direction. She only had one working eye at the moment, and that one was not making eye contact.

When Lizzie saw her mom, she hung back behind Norry.

"How're you doing?" Norry asked. She felt foolish as soon as she said it. It was pretty obvious how Cat was doing.

Cat cleared her throat. Her voice came out not much above a whisper. "I've been better."

"Yeah. I can see that."

"Hi, kiddo."

Lizzie went over to her mother. She seemed afraid to touch her, which, given her injuries and her recent behavior, did not seem like an unreasonable reaction to Norry.

"Hi," Lizzie said. "The car is wrecked. They towed it away."

Cat looked up questioningly.

"It's at Mick's," Norry said. "You can talk to them if you want to see if it can be repaired."

She felt a flicker of guilt, knowing Cat could almost certainly not afford a car repair bill right now. She also could not afford to be without a car. Norry reminded herself that none of this was her problem.

"Okay," Cat said.

"It smashed the birch trees," Lizzie said.

"Yeah. Sorry about that."

Cat leaned her head back and stared at the ceiling with her one good eye. Norry noticed how slim her neck was. It looked like Lizzie's neck, like the neck of a girl, not a woman. She wondered how old Cat was. Not old. Much too young to have seen so much trouble.

She decided she was going to have to address the elephant in the room.

"I'm fine having Lizzie stay at the Last Resort until you are released and get back on your feet again. Lizzie is a wonderful guest, and she's no trouble. But I don't want any issues with you about it, Cat."

"No. I got no issues."

Norry thought this was a patently ridiculous statement. Cat obviously had a lot of issues. Cat was nothing more than one giant ball of issues as far as Norry could tell. But seeing her in the hospital bed forced her to feel something—not precisely sympathy, but sadness. Norry felt a terrific sadness for this young woman with this wonderful daughter who seemed to think she had nothing in the world to live for. She wanted to shake her—broken arm and all—and say "Can't you see what you have here? Can't you see you are young and smart and have this amazing daughter and all these years ahead of you to do whatever you want? Don't you know that life is full of love and beauty and astonishing surprises?"

And at that moment, Norry was sorry she had not told Bud she loved him because she realized she *did* love him, and here she was, wasting a day without telling him. Then she remembered Bud was trying to help Cat—and had helped her before without Norry even knowing about it.

"I guess Bud is trying to see if there's an opening for you at the rehab center. It sounds as if they're pretty full now, but he's going to try."

Cat didn't say anything. She was still looking at the ceiling. The hand that was not in a sling started tapping on the rail of the bed. Lizzie was looking at her mom. There was a long silence, with only the tap-tap-tapping of Cat's fingers on the metal rail.

"But I guess they want you here for some more tests today anyway," Norry added.

Cat sighed. "Yeah. They said I have a concussion."

"Well, call if you need anything. We'll come by tomorrow to visit."

"Okay."

Lizzie was still standing by her mom's bedside, looking at her. Cat was still staring at the ceiling. Norry felt the time ticking by and wondered if Cat was sedated or brain damaged or just trying to process everything that had happened in the last twenty-four hours. Maybe all of the above.

Finally, Norry said to Lizzie, "I think maybe we should let your mom rest."

Lizzie nodded. "I love you, Mom."

Cat's good eye flickered and looked down at Lizzie.

"I love you, kiddo. I love you to the moon and back."

And in that moment, Norry saw the mother that Cat could have been and must have been at some earlier time. Lizzie laid her head on her mom's stomach and wrapped her arms around her slim hips. Cat stroked her daughter's hair with the hand that wasn't in a sling.

Norry stepped back and looked at the mother and daughter. She felt her heart hurt with a cocktail of emotions that were hard to identify. *It shouldn't have to be this hard* was all she could come up with. It shouldn't have to be so hard to be a mother—or a person. And Norry wondered what Cat had been through in her short life that had caused her so much pain. And she knew she had not been fair to her. She'd been angry, and she'd blamed her. Norry still felt there was good reason for both anger and blame. But she hadn't stopped to think of what Cat's life must have been like to make these drugs a better alternative than living without them—better than living alone inside herself.

The door opened, and a doctor entered. Lizzie got up from the bed and Norry took a last look back at Cat. She was watching Lizzie with her one good eye. She looked impossibly sad.

"See you tomorrow," Norry said.

Cat didn't respond. She just watched as Lizzie left the room and headed down the hall.

~

It looked to Wendell as if that little girl, Lizzie, was back.

He saw her go off with Norry, after her mother's car was towed, and Wendell thought maybe that was the last he'd see of her. But now she was back, playing on the beach with her dog, Mr. Benson. Life goes on. That was Wendell's observation.

He sat down at the kitchen table where he had made himself a tuna fish sandwich for lunch. Bud had called him, while Norry and Lizzie were away, to tell him that an apartment was available at Sleepy Pines, in the senior housing facility in Big Pine. There was always a waiting list, but Bud had been keeping in touch with the manager, apparently, and there was a ground-level unit that faced the park open right now if Wendell wanted it.

Wendell wasn't sure what he wanted.

He was so accustomed to not getting what he wanted that suddenly having to choose anything seemed like a terrible burden. He had been so angry when he moved in to the Chickadee Cabin—it was so small and secluded. He couldn't get chicken wings or Cheez-Its or french fries. He was always being bothered by Norry or Bud or Lizzie or all three. Even the fishermen who came and went felt like they needed to shoot the breeze with Wendell and tell him what the fishing was like that day or what the weather was supposed to be like tomorrow. It was all very annoying. He had no privacy at all.

But now that he had the opportunity to move, Wendell felt a curious reluctance to leave the Chickadee Cabin. It most likely was just inertia. As he looked back on his life, he realized he had seldom moved toward anything he wanted. He'd always said he had big dreams and goals, but when he looked at it honestly, he knew he had refused to engage. He had dug in his heels, and whenever life threatened to take him with it, he had steadfastly refused to take part. Wendell was a nonparticipant in his own life.

By now, he figured the habit was pretty well set. But here was Bud, telling him he had a choice. He could ask Norry about staying longer at the Chickadee Cabin. Or he could move in to Sleepy Pines—open spots were hard to get, to hear Bud tell it—and in one of the better units at that. Wendell knew where it was and could just about picture it. The park was by a lake, and that first-floor corner unit would look out on that park. It would be handy to the grocery store and the Dairy Queen that Wendell used to frequent. It was a good deal, Wendell had to admit. For a guy who had lost his house through no fault of his own, it was about the only option available, and Wendell knew he had to move on it right now if he was going to.

He took a bite of his tuna fish sandwich. It wasn't bad. He'd made it with sweet relish. Wendell liked sweet pickles.

The thing was, he didn't want to leave.

Oh, sure, Norry was bossy, and Bud—well, Bud was a pain in the ass, and the way things were looking with him and Norry, he was likely to be around a lot more. Lizzie was always coming by and pestering him, and now that summer was in full swing, there would be a nonstop parade of nosy parker guests asking about the weather and the fishing and all kinds of nonsense. But by now, Wendell was sort of used to it. And he liked his view out the window of the Chickadee Cabin, and even though it was a single room with a bathroom (which was small),

Wendell didn't have a lot of possessions anymore and—if he was going to be totally honest with himself—he was beginning to like it that way.

The apartment at Sleepy Pines would be a lot bigger. He'd have a separate bedroom and a dining area and a larger kitchen. There was a "rec room," where people played Ping-Pong and built puzzles and played cards. There would be a lot of people his age. Wendell didn't like the sound of any of it.

But life was nudging him on, and Wendell did not know how to resist the current. He'd been floating too long.

"Sure thing," he said to Bud. "I'll take it."

~

"Your mom is getting out today," Norry told Lizzie the next morning over breakfast. "She'll be by to pick you up around noon."

Lizzie looked surprised. Norry didn't blame her.

Cat had made faster progress than expected. She was getting released today, she told Norry, early this morning. She said she had a car she could use, and they were going ahead with plans to move to the Twin Cities.

"Did you want Bud to check and see if the rehab center had a spot for you?" Norry had asked her.

"No. I know what they have to say. This was my screwup, and I'm going to fix it."

She sounded determined, and it didn't sound like Norry was going to change her mind. Cat had been released from the hospital. There were no charges filed. She'd told child protective services that she had a job to get to in the Twin Cities and she wanted to get there as soon as possible. They would be following up with her, once she was settled, but in the meantime, there was little anyone could do to stop her. The near-comatose woman from yesterday was gone, and this was a new Cat sounding like she was ready to fight. Norry wasn't sure exactly what she was going to fight, but it was clear she was not going to let Norry stand in her way.

"But there's an issue," Cat went on. "I've got a place lined up to stay, but they don't take dogs."

Norry felt her heart sink.

"I'm going to have to bring Lizzie's dog to the shelter unless you want to keep him."

Norry listened carefully to the tone of Cat's voice. She had to know this was going to destroy her daughter, but she gave no sign. Norry thought of the curly-haired dog currently curled up beside Lizzie and wanted to scream.

"You're sure you can't take Benson?" she asked quietly.

"No. No dogs. I was lucky to find a place to stay, and they have a bullshit no pets policy."

"Okay."

"Okay?"

"Okay, I'll keep Benson. Maybe Lizzie can come and visit him later in the summer."

"Yeah. Maybe. I'll be by around noon."

There was a longish silence. Norry wondered what she was supposed to say.

Cat continued in a slightly lower voice. "And thanks. Thanks again for what you've done. I'm sorry I screwed up, but I'm making it right. I promise."

"We'll see you around noon," Norry said. And the line went dead. Now Norry had to tell Lizzie.

"So, there's a problem," Norry began as she gave Lizzie another pancake. "Your mom called, and I guess they don't take dogs where you're going in the Twin Cities. She asked if Benson could stay here."

Lizzie said nothing.

"I'm happy to keep him for you. He's your dog. Maybe you and your mom can come and visit him in a couple of weeks after you're all settled."

Lizzie had stopped eating her pancakes. Benson had heard his name. He was looking from Norry to Lizzie as if maybe he was going to get a treat.

"I'm sorry, honey. I know your mom is doing her best. It's hard to find a place that takes pets."

Lizzie's eyes were now large, as if she was just taking in what was being said.

"No." Lizzie put her fork down. "No. I'm not going without Mr. Benson."

"I'm sorry. I'm just so sorry. But I promise I'll take good care of him. He'll be here to visit whenever you come back."

Norry knew she should shut up. There was an excellent chance Cat would not want to come back, and some very good reasons why she shouldn't. If she wasn't going back into rehab, getting out of town and away from her triggers was probably the smartest thing to do. But making that child leave behind her dog, after what she'd been through, was just not right. It wasn't fair. Norry knew this and bit her tongue.

"No!" Lizzie threw herself on the floor and wrapped her arms around Benson. Norry joined them on the floor and wrapped her arms around both girl and dog.

"I'm so sorry," she whispered in her ear. "I'm so, so sorry." Benson licked her face.

"I don't want to leave," Lizzie said, and now she was crying. "I don't want to leave you. I don't want to leave the Last Resort. I don't want to leave Mr. Benson. I don't want to go."

"I know, honey. I know." Norry had a lot of things she wanted to say, but none of them were useful. None of them would help.

"Hey, how would you like to take a pontoon ride?" she asked.

Lizzie looked up, confused. "Do we have time?"

"We do. We do if we leave right this minute."

Lizzie and Norry and Benson went straight out to the pontoon boat. They left their dirty dishes on the table, and Norry didn't care. The guests in the Bear Cabin were planning to use the boat this morning. She didn't care. She had three cabins that were supposed to be cleaned before noon, and she didn't care about that either. She didn't care if she pissed off every camper at the resort. Right now, she and Lizzie were going on a boat ride.

As soon as they left the shore, everything seemed calmer. As soon as the resort faded from view, Norry had the sense that she and Lizzie and Benson were in a world separate from everything else. The weather was perfect. Norry took the pontoon out to nearly the center of the lake so that the shore on all sides was a distant tree line, the cabins invisible in the distance.

Norry was thinking of all the things she wanted to say, and she couldn't think of anything that wouldn't either put Lizzie's mom in a bad light or make Lizzie cry again. So she steered the boat around the lake. They didn't go fast. They just watched the water and the shore. Benson was sitting in the front of the pontoon, his curly hair blowing in the breeze, and Lizzie was sitting with her arm around him, her own curls catching the wind.

Finally, they made it almost all the way around the lake. Norry had resisted looking at her watch, but she knew they didn't have a lot of time left. She killed the engine in front of the loon's nest.

"They haven't hatched yet," Lizzie said.

"Not yet. They will soon."

"I was hoping to see a baby loon."

"I know."

"Mr. Benson—my teacher—he told us how they ride on their parents' backs and the loon parents can't dive under the water until the babies are big enough to dive on their own."

"I think you're going to be okay, Lizzie." Lizzie looked down at the floor of the boat. "I know this is hard. But you're a smart girl, and you're tough. You have good sense. No matter what happens, don't forget that."

Lizzie said something that Norry didn't hear. So she left the steering wheel and joined Lizzie in the front of the pontoon. She put her arm around her, and the three of them sat, looking at the brushy area on shore where the loons were nesting.

"Thank you, Norry."

"Oh, honey. It was such a pleasure. You have no idea."

Norry slowly brought the pontoon back to the resort and pulled it up to the dock. As expected, the family from the Bear Cabin was gathered on the beach, waiting for the boat. Norry gave them the keys and took Lizzie by the hand. They packed up Lizzie's few belongings in the duffel once again. Norry gave her a bottle of maple syrup and a jar of raspberry jam she'd made last fall. Then she grabbed *Little House on the Prairie*, the second book in the series, and gave it to Lizzie.

"Here. So you have something to read until you get a library card."

"But . . . it goes with the other books."

"No. It goes with you."

Lizzie tucked the book into the duffel. She was packed and waiting. Norry made her a baloney sandwich. She put in extra sweet pickles because she knew Lizzie liked them, but Lizzie didn't finish it.

It got to be a quarter after twelve, and Norry started to wonder if Lizzie was going to go through a repeat of two days ago. But this time, she would not be alone. The idea that Cat might not show up filled Norry with a combination of feelings, none of which made her particularly proud.

Just then, she heard a car coming down the driveway. Norry looked out the window. It was about the same vintage as the car that had recently smashed into her birch trees, but this one did not seem to have a muffler. Cat parked and hopped out. Her arm was still in a sling, but the bandage was off her head, and it looked as if her hair had been washed. The swelling was down and both eyes were open. She had a couple of small stitches that ran through her eyebrow and still a lot of bruising. But her eyes were focused, and she was very much awake. Norry had never seen her quite this alert.

"Hey, kiddo," Cat said.

"We gotta take Mr. Benson," Lizzie said.

Cat took a deep breath and looked at the ground for a moment. Then she looked up at Lizzie.

"We can't. We can't take the dog. I'm sorry. But I never actually said you could have a dog now. It's not a good time. We'll get a dog later on when we're settled."

"I want Mr. Benson!"

"Maybe Benson can come down and live with us once we get a different place. But I gotta get down there and start work. We're lucky to find a place to stay at all."

Nothing about this sounded lucky to Norry, but she bit her tongue.

Lizzie was crying as Norry took Lizzie's duffel out to the car, which was in worse shape inside than out. She put the duffel in the back seat, and Benson tried to jump in with it, but Norry held him by the collar as Lizzie knelt to hug him. Then she hugged Norry. Then she hugged Benson again.

"Come on, we got a long way to go," Cat said.

Norry looked at her and tried to sympathize. She was terribly pale and thin. She was injured, and she didn't look as if she should be driving.

"Cat, if you'd like to spend a few nights here, just to heal a little more . . ."

Norry couldn't believe she was saying this. She had no empty cabins, only the room that Lizzie was in. But she could stay in the spare room and give Cat and Lizzie her double bed. They could make that work for a few days at least.

"No. No, thanks. I gotta go. I've got a job lined up and a place to stay. I gotta get away from this . . ." Her voice trailed off. "I'll be in touch," she finally said.

Then she got into the driver's seat and threw the car into reverse. The car made a noise that didn't sound good to Norry. Lizzie had both arms hanging out the passenger side window, and she was crying. Benson was pulling on his collar, trying to follow her.

"It's okay, Benson. It's okay," Norry said.

But as the car made its way down the driveway, Norry didn't think it was okay at all. It was the furthest thing from okay.

Chapter Nineteen

"Bud told me about an opening at Sleepy Pines," Wendell told Norry.

"Oh, my gosh, Wendell. You know you can stay here as long as you like. You can stay here forever, as far as I'm concerned!"

Wendell was surprised how sad Norry seemed to be. He wasn't paying her much. He didn't figure she would miss the cabin rent. She looked like she was going to cry. Wendell wasn't sure what to do, but then she brought him a couple of cardboard boxes, and in no time at all, he had his possessions loaded up and in Bud's truck. And, although Wendell was sorry to leave, the realization that he had made a decision was heady.

Then Bud drove him to Sleepy Pines, and he met with the manager, who seemed like a friendly enough person. The apartment was furnished—right down to the dishes—so Wendell didn't need to buy much. The next thing he knew, Wendell was sitting in a recliner in his new living room, looking out his sliding door on to the park. Life goes on. That was Wendell's observation.

Wendell walked down the hall to check out the rec room. There were half a dozen geezers in there, complaining about their aches and pains and talking politics. Wendell stood near the door for a while, then headed back to his apartment.

He noticed it was quiet. No one was starting up any boat motors or throwing sand on the beach. Wendell remembered his unicorn notebook. Maybe this would be the time to get started writing in earnest. He went to fetch it, then sat back down in the recliner, pen in hand, ready for inspiration to strike.

Instead, he just looked at the notebook. The sun was coming in through the glass door and it hit the notebook's cover. The notebook sparkled in the sunshine. A unicorn. It was funny. It was the dumbest thing ever. He'd thought this was some kind of symbol of lonely isolation instead of what it was—a bubble gum–pink little girl's notebook with a large-eyed unicorn covered in glitter, standing in front of hills in various shades of pink and purple. It had to be the most cheerful little notebook on the market, and Wendell had deliberately selected it to hold his musings on the dismal nature of life and the essential unfairness of existence. It was a hoot. No wonder he wasn't getting far.

Wendell found himself chuckling. He couldn't remember when he'd last found anything funny, but this was really funny, now that he thought about it. He thought that unicorn looked so sad. He thought it was a dreary gray. Then he'd gotten his eyes fixed. But maybe there was a little more to it than that.

He had seen that unicorn as a sad and lonely beast because he was looking for a sad and lonely beast. That's what he was. He was an expert at seeing sadness and loneliness. He had honed his skills. Just like that buttinsky Bud Gustafson had honed the skill of helpfulness. Bud was always getting himself involved in other people's problems and helping them out, whether they wanted help or not. By now, Wendell figured Bud couldn't stop himself if he wanted to.

Meanwhile, Wendell had been working just as hard on a different project. He'd been working on the making-himself-miserable project, and it had been an unqualified success. He had become far more miserable than he'd ever imagined possible.

Wendell had gotten his new eyes at just about the time he started reconsidering a few things. Taking a fresh look, so to speak. He was never going to believe his life was a bowl of cherries. He was never going to be one of those folks who assumed the glass was always half full. If the glass was half full, it would be empty soon enough. Glasses emptied. That was the nature of glasses, in Wendell's experience.

But still, getting out of his house—even losing his stuff—hadn't been as terrible as he'd believed it would be. When Wendell tried to remember the valuables he had lost, he couldn't come up with enough to fill the two boxes that Norry had given him this morning. He had to assume most of the stuff he'd lost was not stuff he needed. This was a new thought for Wendell.

And there was a lot of other stuff—not the stuff he kept in boxes, but the stuff he kept in his head—a lot of that got hauled off to the county landfill at about the same time. Wendell used to be sure about a lot of things, and now he wasn't sure he knew much at all. It had made him comfortable, thinking he was a little smarter than most folks, knowing he had the inside scoop—even if the scoop was that life started out as a pile of shit and got worse with time. It wasn't great news, but Wendell got a sense of satisfaction from knowing the truth. He was willing to accept things other people were just too timid to admit. He was part of a small minority who knew more than most people. He was special.

And now he wasn't sure he knew a damned thing.

All his stuff—the stuff he'd stored in his head and the stuff he'd stored in boxes—all of it was gone, and he was left with nothing but Earl Söderberg's snazzy clothes and a pink unicorn notebook. Wendell had no idea who he was anymore. But somehow, this was not a tragedy. It didn't feel like one today, anyway.

Wendell had not been looking for a new life. His life had been terrible, but he'd been completely satisfied with terrible. His days had been gray, and he'd been alone, and he'd had no expectations of anything good ever happening. But now Wendell was looking at things with new eyes. He had fewer expectations than ever before. He wasn't expecting rainbows and unicorns, but he wasn't expecting constant disappointment and betrayal either. He wasn't expecting anything at all. He was living in a state of near-constant surprise.

Wendell looked down again at the unicorn and smiled. He had grown very fond of this little notebook. This little notebook was worth more than the dozens of boxes rotting in the county dump.

There was a little blank spot in the upper right corner. Wendell uncapped his purple pen—and chuckled again as he did it. Purple. It was funny. He thought he was such a serious guy, and all the while, he'd been writing in purple ink.

Wendell Eklund, he wrote.

He admired his handwriting. *That's me. The oldest living pink, sparkly unicorn.*

~

Norry suddenly found herself alone.

Of course, she wasn't alone. Every cabin but the Chickadee Cabin had guests in it now and would stay that way until the end of summer. There was a lot to do—cabins to clean, wood to stack, towels to distribute and collect. Some camper was always wanting something—a spatula or a measuring cup or a corkscrew or a knife. And even though Norry made sure there was extra of everything on hand, something always went missing or something new was needed, and there would be a knock on the door and a barefoot camper asking, "You don't have a can opener, do you?" And of course, she did.

But these were guests, who would come for the weekend or the week or possibly two weeks at the longest, and be gone. Yes, she had known some of them a long time—like the Eliots, who'd been coming before her father had passed. But they didn't live here. Wendell and Lizzie had lived here. Norry wondered how Wendell would do on his own at Sleepy Pines, but at least she could stop by and visit him. Lizzie was just gone. And Norry had to accept that she might never hear from her again.

She was behind on her cabin cleaning, and there was a line of campers with questions and requests for firewood and moose-pie makers and marshmallow sticks and more towels. Norry kept busy all day, catching up. Busy was good. Busy kept her from thinking every minute about the car without a muffler headed down to the Twin Cities.

Cat had seemed so determined. Like she was going to do this and do it on her own. Moving away from Big Pine probably was a good decision, but her borrowed car did not look like it was ready for a long trip, and neither did she. She was dragging Lizzie off without her dog, which Norry thought was just about the most heartless thing a parent could do—especially given what Lizzie had been through in the last couple of months.

But Norry knew she was being hard on Cat. Presumably, she had done just fine for the first eight years of Lizzie's life. They'd rented a nice little house in Big Pine. Lizzie had pointed it out one day when they were in town. Cat had been involved with Lizzie's schooling and worked a steady job at the grocery store. Then she'd been injured and got hooked on painkillers. She went through rehab. She had one very bad day. And now she seemed dead set on getting on with her life. Norry had to do the same.

She had finished up the cabins and was now having a late-afternoon cup of coffee. Benson had followed her from cabin to cabin, as if Lizzie might be hiding out in one of them. Now he sat alert on the deck, watching the people come and go, convinced Lizzie would be back at any moment.

"Hey, Benson, come here, sweetie."

Benson came inside and let Norry scratch him between the ears. There had never been a dog at the Last Resort, and Norry wasn't sure why. It was a good place for a dog. The campers enjoyed having him around. He barked when there were bear nearby at night and played with the kids on the beach during the day. Benson would fit right in—once he realized Lizzie was not coming back.

"Poor sweetie," Norry said. But she wasn't thinking about Benson. She was thinking about Lizzie and the way she looked, driving off in that rattletrap car. Norry had asked for this. She'd let herself get way the heck too attached to a little girl she knew would not be around for long. She had somehow imagined that Lizzie would stay in Big Pine, maybe spend the summers at the resort, visit on the weekends. She had built up a fantasy that had Lizzie being in her life much longer than this spring. She had imagined something like forever. *Forever does not last.* And, just as she thought that, she saw the familiar red truck pull up in the driveway.

You are probably going to regret this too, she admonished herself.

But at that moment, Norry did not care.

She remembered how completely alone she had been before the night Lizzie had knocked on her door. She hadn't been aware of her solitude at the time, but she had been like a mosquito caught in the varnish of one of the resort's vintage deck chairs—immobilized, stuck in time.

She maintained the cabins so they looked just as people expected cabins built in the late 1930s would look, just as her father had refurbished them to look in the 1980s, just as they had when she took over the resort ten years ago. Everything remained fresh and newly painted or varnished, and yet the same. That was how Norry thought of herself. She had not let herself fall apart after her divorce. She was healthy and active. She had a few close friends and a business she was proud of. It was a perfectly fine life. No one could say it wasn't.

But it never changed.

She never visited Virgie in Mexico. She didn't even have a valid passport. She never went to the Twin Cities for the weekend, although she loved music and theater. She never cut her hair differently or wore anything other than her Last Resort gear and jeans. She felt as if—except for the few years she had been away at college and then briefly married—she had always been here. Always Norry No Last Name. Always reliable Norry.

The red truck was now parked in front of her cabin, and Bud was sitting inside, checking his phone by the looks of things. He had a hat on, and his face was sunburned. With his reddish complexion, Bud would burn before almost anyone, and he spent a chunk of every nice day out on the water. Under the hat, his forehead would be white. He had a farmer's tan that extended from his shoulders to his toes. Bud was not a guy who wore sandals. He was not a guy who wore shorts. He wasn't someone who went to concerts or plays, and if he did, Norry was sure he'd nod off as fast as he had at the Chopin concert. That's just who Bud was.

For a brief, unbidden moment, Norry remembered her former husband, Alex. She spent as little time thinking about him as possible. He was the one who introduced her to classical music and theater and art. He had never loved her. That was her belief. But she had provided him with a kind of stability that he needed to keep his life and his emotions from flying off in all directions. The always-reliable Norry had been there to pick up the pieces and hold the center in place, to assure him—and then reassure him—at every opportunity. She would always be there. She would never leave him. She would always forgive whatever he had put her through most recently. Of course she would. And then he left.

Norry shook her head. She had not asked for this reverie. She didn't need anything from the past right now. Right now, she needed something new. And even though she'd known him for almost thirty years, the fellow in the red pickup looked like someone new to Norry. It probably wouldn't last. It might even be a bad idea. But she liked what she was seeing, and she was not letting any more of her life go by without a few changes.

"Hey, handsome. You looking for some dinner?" she called out.

Bud looked up from his phone, and his face broke into a smile. That big, childlike smile squeezed Norry's heart.

"That would be great. Can you believe I got skunked today?"

"That has to be a first."

"Not quite, but close."

"I've got a hunch your luck is about to change."

Bud scrambled out of his pickup and Norry held the door open for him.

~

Lizzie thought they were going to drive forever.

Mom was tired, she could tell, but she said they were going to make it before dark. Lizzie didn't care. She didn't care where they were going. All she could think about was Mr. Benson, straining to come with her, and Norry holding him back and looking so sad and worried.

The car made a lot of noise, and it smelled like smoke. Mom was focused on the highway and didn't say much.

"I'm sorry," she said a couple of times.

"I'm going to make it right," she said a few minutes later, but it sounded to Lizzie like she was talking to herself.

They pulled off to get gas, and Mom bought her a hot dog off the hot dog roller machine. Lizzie put a lot of pickle relish and mustard on it. She liked the relish, but the hot dog had been on the roller too long. It was chewy. She remembered the sandwich she'd left uneaten at Norry's. She was beginning to think she hated her mom.

"Why do we have to go to the Twin Cities?" Lizzie asked when they got back in the car.

"Because I can get a better job."

"You had a job in Big Pine."

"Well, I don't anymore. And I need to get away."

Mom's knuckles were white on the steering wheel. She was holding it with one hand because the other was still in a sling.

"I like it in Loon Point."

"Loon Point is for rich people. We are not rich people."

"What are we?"

"We're people who don't feel like answering a whole lot of questions right now, okay?"

Lizzie bit her lip.

"I'm sorry," Mom said. "I'm just really tired and I've got a headache and we need to get to Laura's."

"Who's Laura?"

"She's someone I knew at the grocery store. She's working at a store in the suburbs, and she got me a job. We're going to stay with her for a little while."

"Laura is the name of the girl in the *Little House in the Big Woods* book."

"Good. Then you'll probably like her."

Mom didn't sound like she wanted to talk. Lizzie didn't care. She was mad.

"Laura in *Little House in the Big Woods* had a dog," Lizzie said. "His name was Jack."

"Look, enough with the dog already! Laura is doing us a big favor taking us in, and I couldn't ask her to take a dog too."

"You didn't even ask her?"

Mom was focused on the road. Lizzie knew the answer. Now Lizzie knew she hated her mom for sure.

Mom turned on the radio. Lizzie watched the scenery go by. There were more towns now. The road was bigger. There was more traffic. Then Lizzie must have fallen asleep, because when she woke up, it was dark and the car was taking a lot of turns. They were on smaller streets now. Mom was looking at her phone and turning when it told her to turn.

Finally, they came to an apartment building, and Mom parked the car.

"This is it," she said.

Lizzie looked around. It didn't look like they were in the Twin Cities. There were no tall buildings. This looked like some kind of neighborhood. There was a gas station and a KFC. The apartment building was bigger than any apartment she'd ever seen. It took up most of the block.

Mom turned off the car and her head dropped forward. Lizzie realized she was exhausted. "Are you okay?"

Mom didn't say anything for a while. She looked up, but she didn't look at Lizzie. "I don't know. I don't know what I am."

Laura met them outside and led them into the apartment. She had twin beds in her guest room.

"There are a lot of kids here you can play with," Laura told her.

Lizzie nodded. She was still mad. On the way in, she heard a dog barking. There were definitely dogs in the apartment building. Mom had lied. Now Mom was tired and wanted to sleep. "We'll look around tomorrow," she said.

Lizzie brushed her teeth and put on her *Little House in the Big Woods* nightgown.

"Look at you!" Laura said. "You look like you're going to a costume party."

Lizzie looked down at her nightgown. She didn't think it looked like a costume. It was a nightgown. She thought it was what people who wore pajamas slept in. Now she wasn't sure. Lizzie wasn't sure of anything.

Mom was asleep by the time Lizzie climbed into bed. No Mr. Benson.

Laura was watching television in the living room. The windows were closed and Laura had air-conditioning, but Lizzie could still hear sounds from outside the window. There was a siren, and there were some traffic noises. A car went by with the radio really loud. There was some talking in another apartment on the other side of the wall, and she could hear the sound of their TV, along with Laura's.

She didn't want to be here.

She didn't want to be in Laura's spare bedroom or anyone's spare bedroom except Norry's. Mom was acting strange, and Lizzie was afraid. She wasn't sure what she was afraid of, but it had to do with the city and the strange sounds and the fact that she had no idea what was going to happen next.

She wanted to wake Mom up and ask her what their life was going to be like and if she was going to get a library card and if she would make friends and where she would go to school in the fall. She wanted to know if they were going to live in an apartment like Laura's or in a house like they used to. She wanted to know if she would ever see Norry and Mr. Benson again.

Lizzie sat up and looked at her mom. Mom had gone to bed in her clothes. She had stitches on her forehead and her lips looked dry. She was snoring a little. And even if Lizzie could wake her, she knew Mom wouldn't answer her questions. Mom wouldn't answer because Mom didn't know.

And that was the scariest thought of all.

Chapter Twenty

Wendell looked up from his notebook to see Lucille Munson, his former neighbor, knocking on his patio door.

As usual, she was wearing some brightly colored muumuu kind of thing, and she had apparently bypassed the front door and gone around the back, through the park, and she was now standing outside with a metal casserole pan balanced in one hand, knocking on his glass door with the other.

What the heck?

Wendell closed his notebook and slid the door open a crack, as if this might deter her from making a full entry into his apartment.

"Wendell! It's so good to see you. Aren't you looking fine? It looks like you've lost some weight. I heard about your heart attack and was going to visit you, but they released you so fast I never got a chance. I just heard you had moved in to Sleepy Pines, and I thought I better stop by and bring you a housewarming gift!"

Wendell could see he had no choice.

"This is a heart-healthy recipe someone brought to a church circle meeting—chicken and wild rice and low-sodium cream of mushroom soup." She pushed her way in, handing him the hotdish as she did.

"Oh! Isn't this nice?" Lucille said as soon as she had finagled herself fully into the apartment. "This is so nice! I know these units fill up so quickly. That Bud Gustafson was a saint to get you to the top of the waiting list the way he did. My goodness! What a view you have, looking out over the park. It must be so nice for you to have a place of your own again."

"Um . . . yeah."

"Oh, and you're going to love the complex. You know there are so many people our age living here. I'd be here myself if I could stand to give up my garden. But goodness! Keeping up a house is a lot of work. Well, you know that. You know all about that, with your roof troubles."

Wendell did not particularly want to be reminded about his roof troubles.

"Have you seen what they've done on your lot? I'm sure you have. It is just scraped clean. Not a sign there was ever a house there. My! I thought that was a little drastic. It seemed to me they could have saved it somehow and made a nice home for somebody. But too much water damage. That's what I heard. They just scraped it clean. Oh, it broke my heart, it really did. But you seem to be doing just fine now, Wendell."

Wendell wondered where his inhaler was and realized he had not needed it in a long time. Until now.

"Well, I shouldn't keep you. I could see you were working. Oh! Would you look at that? Isn't that just about the cutest notebook ever? Where did you get that, Wendell? I'd like to get one of those for my granddaughter. She loves everything to do with unicorns."

"I don't know. It was a gift."

"Oh, well, I'll have to keep my eyes open for one like that. That is just adorable."

Wendell could feel the hotdish was still warm. He wondered if it still would be by the time Lucille left.

"Well, I'll be seeing you around soon, Wendell. I'm here almost every day to visit someone. I think half my church circle lives here already, and we play bingo every Wednesday. Maybe you'd like to join us. It's a nice group of women and it would be fun to have a fellow join us for a change!"

Wendell tried to imagine anything worse.

"You take care of yourself, Wendell. Watch your diet! I don't want to hear you've had any more issues. I'm so glad you landed on your feet."

And with that, Lucille let herself out the sliding door and headed off across the park. He saw she didn't make it more than a few yards before she met someone else she knew.

What a bother! What a bother that woman was. She had been a bother for as long as he had known her, and he'd known her almost all his life. She had been by almost every day when his mother was ill, toward the end. She'd always been stopping by and bringing food and taking his mother's laundry over to her place. She even made his mother's bed, now that he remembered it. She and his mother would talk, with Lucille bringing her the news from town when she was too ill to go out. She was always nattering on about something or another and she . . .

She'd made his mother's life a lot better.

Wendell couldn't believe it. But it was true. He thought about the loud woman in the muumuu who had just invaded his home, and he knew, beyond a doubt, she'd made the last years of his mother's life much better while he stood by and watched. Wendell was no good with small talk. He never had been. Small talk was how feeble-minded people killed time because they had nothing better to do, nothing more important to say. Wendell was focused on more important things. Although, at the moment, he was having a hard time remembering what those things were.

What was he doing that was so important, those last few years his mother was alive? He couldn't remember. He remembered being annoyed with her constant needs and requests. He remembered Lucille had done things for him without him even realizing it. He was terrible at making the bed the way his mother wanted it. He had never really learned to cook, and after his mother became too ill to do it, it never occurred to him to try. He would have made her a grilled cheese sandwich seven days a week if he'd had his way. But Lucille never showed up empty handed—she always brought food. And he'd eaten a lot of it. Actually, Wendell had probably eaten most of it.

And he'd never thanked her.

She'd even helped with his mother's funeral. Wendell was no good at that. He didn't know about that kind of stuff. The Methodist church had put on a buffet in the basement. And a lot of people came. Wendell remembered standing in a line by the buffet table and having one person after another tell him how wonderful his mother had been, and he'd nodded and wondered how long it was going to go on. It was awkward, having to talk to all those strangers. And then Lucille had packed up the food for him to take home and she'd been by nearly every week afterward, bringing something by for him to eat or just standing on the stoop and taking up his time.

She'd been the only friend he'd had.

He looked up to see if she was still in the park. Wendell felt a crazy compulsion to do something—flag her down, thank her for the hotdish, tell her he appreciated everything she'd done all those years. But she was gone. The pink-and-green muumuu had vanished, and all that was left in the park was the sunshine filtered through the giant oak trees and a couple of red-winged blackbirds hopping around a park bench. Wendell could see the brilliant red on the tops of their wings. They were ordinary birds, blackbirds. They were nothing special, but Wendell had never noticed how beautiful they were.

Wendell looked down at his notebook. He had more things he wanted to write now, and they had nothing to do with how smart he was or how much he knew. He wanted to figure out how he'd managed to have a friend like Lucille in his life—nearly all his life—and had never once seen her as anything but a nuisance.

~

Norry woke the next morning next to Bud and Benson. She remembered inviting Bud into her bed, but Benson had somehow snuck in and found a spot as well. They both were snoring softly. It was nice, waking up with Bud lying beside her. She decided she could get used to this. He was a sound sleeper. Usually Norry woke to the calls of loons on the lake, or a car pulling in late, or a voice outside at night. Bud slept through it all.

Already this morning she could hear campers out on the beach, the hollow thumping sound of a boat hull hitting the side of the dock, the small motor of a fishing boat puttering just offshore. She stretched. She had a busy day ahead. Every day was busy this time of year. And she imagined Bud had a few errands he'd be eager to get to as well—so he'd have time for a little fishing on the lake at sunset.

She wondered where Lizzie had spent the night. She hoped it was someplace decent. She knew it was not supposed to be her worry, but it was. She wondered how Wendell had done in town in his new apartment. Bud said it was nice. He said Wendell would have company. It was going to be strange not seeing him sitting at his little table outside, writing in that glittery pink notebook of his.

Norry realized that a lot of life was letting go of things. She hated letting go. She knew she could never stand to see her father's business sold after he died. She'd had to keep it going the way it had always been. She had hung on to her marriage far longer than was sensible because the idea of giving up on it was unthinkable. Now, in such a short time, she'd become attached to this little girl who had needed help. Likely, that was all that was required of Norry—to help her through a difficult time, to see her through a rough patch. Instead, Norry had visions of Lizzie always being around, always being a part of her life.

"At least I have you, Benson," she whispered to the sleeping dog, who heard his name and nuzzled her.

She curled closer to Bud and hugged him.

"Hey, beautiful," he said, and stretched.

"Hey, yourself."

"How are you doing this morning?"

"Oh, you know, the usual. Worried about Lizzie."

Bud frowned. "Yeah, me too. I talked a little to the rehab folks. Having a relapse is the norm, unfortunately. It's not the end of the road. Most people take at least a couple of tries to get clean. But she's probably gonna need some help."

"And she was still injured."

"I know. I wish she could have given it more time."

"I thought after she totaled her car, she'd stay put for a little while, anyway."

"She was in a hurry," Bud said. "She told me she'd gotten a loaner car from a friend, and she was getting out of here. I think her intentions are good, but I don't know how much support she has down in the Cities . . ." Bud's voice trailed off.

Norry knew what he was thinking. He was wondering how much support Lizzie would have if her mother took off again.

"You did a good thing," he said, squeezing her hand.

"I did nothing. Lizzie showed up on my doorstep."

"People show up on someone's doorstep in one way or another all the time. You didn't have to do what you did."

Norry heard a knock on her door. "Oh, Lord. The day has started." She threw on a Last Resort T-shirt and jeans.

Bud shook his head. "You are amazing, you know that?"

Norry leaned over and ran a finger from his breastbone down to his furry navel. "No, you are the amazing one." She kissed him. "You know that, right?"

"Shhh. I don't want the word to get out."

There was another knock at the door. "Coming!"

Norry helped the camper from the Bald Eagle Cabin operate the pump to fill the inflatable raft. It must have a slow leak. One more thing to add to the list. By the time she was through, Bud was already in his truck.

"See you soon," he said as he pulled out.

Norry felt her heart lurch and wondered how it had come to this.

She thought she'd been content on her own. She was pleased by how well she'd done without help, without company. There was a proud history of women living on their own in the Northwoods, and Norry was happy to be one of them. But today, all she could do was wonder how the little girl with the wild black curls was doing while she counted the hours until she saw Bud again.

Was she happier like this? Attached so deeply to people, feeling a little bereft every time she was left alone for a few hours?

Then she realized she was not alone. Benson had trotted along beside her like a shadow and was now looking straight into her eyes.

"I forgot your breakfast, didn't I?"

Benson nudged her hand to let her know he could be patient, but it was certainly past breakfast time by now.

"Okay, Benson. Let's start this new life together, shall we?"

Benson and Norry had breakfast, then they headed out to Big Pine for supplies. Norry stopped at Virgie's shop on her way back.

"So, she just took off, huh?" Virgie was putting some new used books on the shelf when Norry got there. Business had been good, Virgie said. There were always regular customers eager to see what she'd brought back from Mexico. "I should have brought twice as many tablecloths!" she said as she rearranged the dwindling display.

"Yup. She took off in that beater car with her daughter crying and the dog whimpering next to me, and I'm telling you, it was not a good day." Norry didn't feel the need to mention that the day had at least ended well, with Bud in her bed.

"Well, that sucks," Virgie declared. "I don't see how moving to the Cities is going to help her keep clean."

"I don't know anything about it and—you know what? At this moment, I don't care. I know I should care about Cat, but all I can think about is that little girl having to leave her dog behind. I mean, Lizzie loved it here, and she was doing so well at Big Pine Elementary. I don't see how moving to the Cities is going to make anything better. I just don't get it."

Benson was checking out Virgie's used books. Some of them must have smelled like dogs. They were very interesting.

"At least you were able to take in Benson. You've never had a dog before, have you?"

"Nope. But Cat was ready to drop him off at the shelter. Can you believe that?"

"No, I honestly cannot. But then, I can't imagine any of what's going on in her head right now. I know I did some stupid things when I was in my twenties. She's young and she's got a drug problem, and the odds are good she's had some pretty serious problems before this. Where's Lizzie's dad? Has there ever been any mention of him?"

"Nope. I asked Lizzie once about her dad and she said she didn't have one. That was it."

"Well, lots of kids do just fine with one parent. And some kids need a little help. You were good to step in when you did, Norry."

"That's what Bud said. I didn't do anything. That little girl literally knocked on my door—with her dog! Now she's gone, and the dog is here, and I'm half out of my mind."

"And how is Bud?"

Norry smiled in spite of herself. "Bud is good. Bud is . . . great."

Virgie laughed. "'Bud is good. Bud is great.' You are hysterical. I'm glad to hear it."

The last of the books were on the shelf. Benson seemed to have satisfied himself with their provenance. He lay down in the middle of the braided rug in Virgie's shop and looked perfectly at home. Virgie bent down and stroked his head.

"I think you're going to like having a dog," Virgie said. "And a boyfriend."

"Hmm."

"You've done all you can do right now for that little girl, you know that."

"I do. But I don't feel good about it."

"No, and I don't blame you. It's not a great situation. It could get better. I hope it does. But it's not ideal, that's for sure. Come here."

Norry crossed the room into Virgie's open arms. They were not generally the hugging kind of friends, but Norry suddenly felt how badly she needed a hug. In fact, she may have stopped at Virgie's store for the sole purpose of getting one.

"You're a good friend, Virgie. Have I ever told you that?"

"You're my bestie, Norry. I only want the best for you."

Norry took a deep breath. She wasn't great with big emotional scenes. But maybe that was changing as well.

"Okay. Gotta go. I'll keep you posted on the never-ending drama of the Last Resort."

"Please do. And give Bud a squeeze for me, will you?"

"I will. I will certainly do that."

~

Mom left for her new job with Laura in the morning.

Lizzie took *Little House on the Prairie* with her as she walked out with them. There was a woman in the building named Cindy who kept an eye on the kids in the summer. Laura said she didn't charge much. She had all the moms' phone numbers.

"It's not really a day care," Laura said.

"That's fine. Lizzie is very independent."

Lizzie met Cindy before Mom left.

"Hi, Lizzie," Cindy said. She was an older woman, and she was sitting in front of her TV, watching a game show. "There're snacks on the table. Don't leave the building without telling me."

Lizzie waited for more instructions. It didn't look as if there were going to be any. Lizzie stood there for a few minutes.

"Where should I go?" she finally asked.

"You can go out in the yard if you want," Cindy said. "Just don't leave the apartment complex."

"I don't know how to get back in."

"Don't you have a key?"

Lizzie had been given two keys, but one didn't look like a key. It was round and gray.

"I don't know how it works."

Cindy rolled her eyes and said something under her breath. She got up and went with Lizzie to the front door. "Here. Just put it in front of the little light and the door will open."

Lizzie tried it. It worked. She went outside. The sun was bright. It seemed a lot hotter than in Loon Point. In back of the apartment, there was a yard and a small playground. There were two girls on the swings.

"Who are you?" the bigger one in braces asked.

"I'm Lizzie."

"That's a funny shirt."

Lizzie looked down at what she was wearing. It was one of her Last Resort T-shirts. That was about all she had now, but she had them in three different colors.

"Why funny?"

"You know, 'the last resort'? That's funny."

"It's a real place."

"No, it's not."

"Yes, it is. I used to live there."

"You're a liar. 'The Last Resort' is a joke. Don't you get it?"

"It's not a joke. It's a real place. My dog is still there."

"You left your dog at the last resort?" The girl laughed, and it wasn't a nice laugh. Lizzie decided she'd go back into the apartment. Cindy was still watching TV.

"Can I read here?"

"You can do whatever you want."

Lizzie opened *Little House on the Prairie*. It was the book that came right after *Little House in the Big Woods*. She opened it to the first chapter where Pa and Ma and Mary and Laura and baby Carrie were packing up their little house in the Big Woods of Wisconsin. She couldn't believe what she was reading. They left the little house all alone and lonely in the middle of the forest and they moved away and they never came back.

Lizzie hadn't seen that coming.

She figured Laura and Mary were going to stay in the big woods forever. Lizzie read a little farther, and Pa said he wanted to move out where there weren't any trees. Lizzie had liked Pa. Now she thought he was kind of stupid. They had a perfect little cabin in the woods surrounded by animals, and now they were going to leave it lonely and empty and never see it again.

Lizzie closed the book. This was a sad book. She didn't want to read any books about girls getting taken away from the woods. She thought about the log cabin she had left behind. She wondered what Mr. Benson was doing. She wondered if Norry had made pancakes this morning. She wondered how Wendell was doing with his unicorn notebook.

Tomorrow will be better. Lizzie was sure it would be. It had to be.

Chapter Twenty-One

Norry and Bud were having dinner. In a real restaurant.

She was having something Italian that she couldn't pronounce, and Bud was having ribs. They were both dressed up more than usual. Norry found a sleeveless blouse to pair with jeans. Bud had his hat off. Lizzie had been gone a week and Benson had settled in. He still watched the driveway every afternoon, but the rest of the day he trotted beside Norry as she did her chores, taking brief breaks to swim in the lake when it got warm.

The solstice was next week, so even though it was fairly late, the sun was still high in the sky. Norry and Bud sat out on the deck of the restaurant. Their server was trying very hard to pretend he was not in Big Pine—maybe not in Minnesota at all, possibly in New York or Paris. He called Bud "sir," which didn't happen often. Norry was amused. Bud told him he didn't need a glass for his beer. The server brought one anyway.

Norry was nervous because Bud seemed serious. He'd suggested they go out. They'd only been out once before, the night of the Chopin concert, and he said it was time. This place was new. Norry was having a hard time imagining it would make it in Big Pine, but there were a lot of folks with money who spent the summer in the area. Maybe it would. Norry always wished the best for new businesses.

Over dessert, Bud suddenly looked at her very seriously.

Uh-oh. Whatever it is, here it comes, Norry thought.

"You know I care a lot about you."

Norry took a forkful of tiramisu. It was good. They were splitting it, but now Norry was wishing she'd ordered her own. Good tiramisu was hard to find. She felt like she should say something—Bud was twisting his cloth napkin into a knot—but she channeled her inner Virgie and reminded herself she didn't have to do anything. She listened. This way, she got more tiramisu. Win-win.

Bud was definitely having trouble, she could see. The normally white part of his forehead above the hat line was now red as well. She waited. She ate more tiramisu.

"Oh, damn—Norry, I love you, is what I'm trying to say. I've known you forever and I've always carried a torch for you. Neither of us is getting any younger—although I'm getting older a damn sight faster than you are by the looks of it—but we're not kids. I'd like to make it official. I'd like to marry you."

Norry was about to open her mouth, but it was full of tiramisu, so Bud bought himself another moment.

"I know you're going to say it's too soon. And you'll probably say *Why bother?* We already know what we know and feel how we feel. But I'll tell you what—I want more than that. I want to be your husband—or your spouse or your married partner or whatever jargon you like best—because I'm a kind of old-fashioned guy and I just can't think of another thing on earth that would make me as happy as knowing I had you on my team for life."

Norry had finished the tiramisu. "Bud, I'll always be on your team."

"I know. But I want it to be official."

"We've both been married before. We know that making it official doesn't make it permanent."

"It would for me. It would for us. That's the kind of people we are. I know that."

Norry leaned back in her chair. She had expected some kind of declaration, but she had not expected a proposal. She hadn't even contemplated it. She wasn't prepared. She had no rehearsed script. She felt this weird sense of exhilaration, as if this was some kind of emergency—and funny at the same time—like when a bear broke into one of her cabins. She struggled for something sensible to say.

"We're very different," she pointed out.

"We are. But we're alike in all the ways that matter."

Norry looked at Bud. He was as serious as a heart attack. She thought about how long she'd known him. When he was younger, he was considered kind of a player. His two wives had been young and pretty. He drove a fast car when he wasn't in his pickup. Everyone thought Bud Gustafson could do and have whatever he wanted in life.

But Norry had known him better than that, even then. His wives had been young, but they had also been damsels in distress, and that was something Bud could not resist. They both had big problems, and Bud had to pick up the pieces many times before the marriages eventually fell apart for good. She thought of her own marriage and realized she had played a similar role, always a steady and reliable contrast to the emotional drama her husband required every day, the drama he needed to convince himself his life was worth something.

Norry wondered what it had been like for Bud in those two tumultuous marriages. He never spoke much about them. He never said a negative word about the two ex-wives, and to this day, he could not speak of the child he lost in the second marriage without getting choked up.

But here he was, ready for a third time at bat, thinking Norry should be on his team. It was nuts. It was exactly like a bear breaking into a cabin, and she knew she needed to stop it right now. She needed to bang on a pot and scare him off. The problem was, she wasn't sure what she could use to scare Bud off. The bigger problem was, she wasn't sure she wanted to. But he was sitting there, expecting her to say something—and there was no more tiramisu.

"But we're very different in our day-to-day life," Norry finally managed.

He remained silent.

"We like different things. I hate to fish. You hate classical music."

"I don't hate classical music. I made a contribution to Minnesota Public Radio."

"You donated to Minnesota Public Radio?"

"I became a sustaining member."

"You did not."

Bud fished out his wallet and slapped his Minnesota Public Radio membership card on the table. Norry picked it up.

Is this what love looks like?

Being on Bud's team would mean having his strong and loyal presence by her side every day and his warm and gentle body by her side every night. Bud might not know much about the books she read, but he knew things about the outdoors she would never know. And Bud was kind. He was deeply, instinctively kind. He was kind when he didn't need to be, kind when no one asked. He was kind to people he didn't know, and kinder yet to his friends. He was grateful for his life, and his face lit up whenever he set eyes on Norry.

That was the most important thing. She knew how happy it made him just to see her. And she felt the same way every time she saw Bud.

Bud was sitting quietly. Fishing taught a guy to be patient. You never caught anything if you were always fussing with the line. He picked up his fork—then saw all the tiramisu had been eaten.

"I think I'd like to marry you, Bud Gustafson," Norry said.

Bud looked up, and Norry was startled to realize he had honestly not known what she was going to say. His eyes watered for a moment, then he stood up, walked around the table to her, and kissed her, right in front of everyone.

The server was standing nearby, looking slightly ill at ease.

"Hey!" Bud said to him. "We're getting married. We're gonna need some more tiramisu!"

The diners at the other two tables on the deck applauded.

Bud seemed to notice the other customers for the first time. "Tiramisu for everyone!" he declared.

"Right away, sir," the server said.

~

Wendell almost turned around and went home.

This was the stupidest thing he'd ever done in his life, he was sure of that. Although, as Wendell thought about it, he hadn't done all that many stupid things. Most of the stupidity in his life had been things he had not done. That is what he was discovering, as he wrote in his unicorn notebook. Most of the really dumb stuff had been what had happened from inertia.

His life had been ruled by inertia. Inertia wasn't a thing he slipped into from time to time, only to pull himself out and get on with his life. No. Inertia was his operating principle. "When in doubt, do nothing" had been Wendell's motto. And Wendell had lived in a constant state of doubt as long as he could remember.

Wendell had a lot of great ideas, but he was much better at finding fault with his ideas than he was at putting them into action. He'd thought he could probably have gotten a better job than the one he had at the tool and die. But then he'd thought of all the things that could go wrong at a new job, and he'd never applied. When they'd closed up shop, Wendell had no idea what to do, so he'd taken a temporary gig as a maintenance man at the mobile home park—just as a stopgap measure. He'd stayed until the day he turned sixty-two. And even then, Wendell had imagined he was going to do something—something more than the next to nothing he had done. He never referred to himself as retired, even though he was collecting social security. He was "self-employed." Although, if pressed, Wendell would have had a hard time telling you what this employment was. At the end of the day, Wendell did very little. In fact, he did nothing at all.

It was with this in mind that he got in his car this morning and drove to Lucille Munson's house in Loon Point.

This is dumb, he said to himself as he drove. *This is really dumb.*

He kept driving. The effort of getting himself into the car and headed to Lucille's house had taken all his energy. He now had momentum in his favor. Whether he liked it or not, he was going to Lucille's.

He pulled onto the street where he used to live. He wasn't going to look, but of course, he had to. The lot where his house had once stood was scraped clean, as Lucille described. There was a **For Sale** sign on the lot. Wendell figured, if he was lucky (and when had that ever happened?) he might get enough from the sale of the lot to cover the demolition costs of his house. Wendell could not believe he was required to pay to have his own house hauled to the dump, but it was the truth.

He felt the familiar anger rising.

But then Wendell remembered being in that house. It had been very dark. He remembered that. It was very full of stuff. Now the house was gone, his stuff was gone, and he was driving to Lucille Munson's house because he'd forgotten to tell her something important. He owed it to her.

Maybe she wouldn't be home. That would be nice. If she wasn't home, he could tell himself he made the effort and fate got in the way. And Lucille was out a lot. She was always off pestering people. She kept busier pestering people more than anyone else he knew—other than possibly Bud Gustafson. Bud had taken pestering to a professional level.

Damn. Her car was in the driveway.

Wendell took a deep breath. He was surprised at how deep a breath he was able to take. He was kind of nervous, and in the past, he'd have needed his inhaler by now. But he'd seen the doctor for a checkup last week and his asthma was a lot better. The doctor seemed to think Wendell had been suffering from "environmental factors." Doctors. They thought they knew everything. Oh well. It was nice not to need the inhaler all the time.

Okay, here we go.

Wendell hauled himself out of the car and hitched up his pants. He had noticed the pants he'd gotten from Earl Söderberg had gotten baggy lately. Wendell figured they were stretching out, but maybe he was shrinking. At any rate, he was finding it a little easier to get around these days. He looked at Lucille's house. This was the dumbest thing he'd ever done. But here he was.

Wendell walked to the front door—stalling a few times under the guise of admiring her flowers—and pushed the doorbell. He heard it ringing through the screen door. Maybe she was on one of her endless phone conversations. Maybe she wouldn't hear it. But soon he heard steps headed toward the door. *Damn.*

Lucille was wearing a muumuu, as usual, but this one might have been a robe. It was hard to tell. She was wearing slippers. They were pink and furry. She had a dish towel in her hand and had come from the kitchen.

"Wendell! Isn't this a nice surprise? Come on in."

Lucille opened the front door, and Wendell entered her predictably clean and cluttered home. She had knickknacks hanging from every inch of wall space, as near as he could tell. Hanging in a frame near the door was a cross-stitch that read **Gratitude Sweetens Even the Smallest Moments.**

Wendell took a deep breath.

"Lucille, I came over here to tell you something I forgot in the heat of the moment. It's been on my mind and so I thought I should come on over before any more time passed." Wendell had that part rehearsed. So far, so good.

"Goodness! What is it, Wendell?" Lucille looked concerned.

"You called the fire department."

Lucille looked confused.

"The night my house collapsed, you called the fire department. In the middle of that big snowstorm. I don't think anyone would have noticed before morning. The rest of the house came down that night."

Lucille was still standing there with a towel in her hand, a perplexed look on her face.

"I have to assume you saved my life."

"Oh! Wendell . . ."

"And I never thanked you. Thank you, Lucille."

There. Done. And it hadn't even been as hard as he'd thought it would be.

~

The days set into a routine. Lizzie had finally gotten Mom to take her to the library. She didn't have a permanent address, but the librarian was nice, and they let her use Laura's library card.

"You just update us when you get your own place," the librarian told Lizzie. Lizzie promised she would.

Lizzie signed out as many books as she could carry and brought them back to the big apartment building. She didn't bother trying to play with the girls in the playground. They were as mean as Jodie Johansson, and they used worse language. Cindy wasn't any company. She just watched TV all day. Lizzie wasn't allowed away from the building, and she didn't know where she'd go even if she was. The neighborhood was all apartments and bigger houses that had been cut into apartments. There was a tattoo parlor and the KFC and a gas station. No tall buildings in sight. It wasn't what Lizzie expected from the Twin Cities. She thought there would be skyscrapers.

The store where Mom worked was short of cashiers, so she was working a double shift almost every day. Lizzie hardly saw her, and when she did, Mom's eyes were red and had dark circles under them like a raccoon's.

"What did you do today?" Mom asked as she watched television with Laura before going to bed.

"I didn't do anything. There's nothing to do here. I just read a book."

"I wish I had time to read."

Then Lizzie felt guilty. But she didn't know what else she could do. She helped wash the dishes at Laura's. She made her bed every morning and made her mom's bed, too, since she had to leave so early. She offered to help with dinner, but Laura didn't usually cook dinner. They had food delivered, or they heated things up in containers in the microwave. Lizzie set the table, but usually Mom and Laura took their dinners to the living room and watched TV while they ate. Then Mom went to bed.

Sometimes, before she went to sleep, Mom would tell Lizzie about how things were going to be. "With the money I'm making now, by fall we'll be able to make a security deposit and the first two months' rent and have enough left over to get it furnished," Mom said. "We might even qualify for a mortgage. How would you like that? To own our very own place?"

Lizzie didn't know what to think. It would be nice, she supposed. Maybe Mr. Benson could come live with them then.

"We'll have a little yard. It'll have a deck or a patio. We'll sit outside in the evening."

"Where will it be? I don't like it here."

"I don't know, Lizzie! We don't have it yet." Mom sounded annoyed. Lizzie waited to hear more about this place they were going to live, but after a couple of minutes she heard her mom breathing more slowly and knew she had fallen asleep.

Lizzie stared up at the ceiling and pretended she was in Norry's cabin. That was her way of going to sleep. She pretended the walls were made of logs and Mr. Benson was lying beside her, and sometimes she even imagined she heard loons calling. The baby loons would be hatched by now. They'd probably be riding around on their parents' backs. Later, in the fall, the parents would fly away and leave the loon kids all alone. The parents would migrate to somewhere warm, sometimes a thousand miles away, and the kids would watch them fly off because they weren't strong enough to make the flight yet. It would get colder, Lizzie imagined. The days would get shorter, and those loon kids would have to know it was time to leave. How did they do it? Weren't they scared?

"How did they know where to go without following their parents?" Lizzie had asked Mr. Benson (her teacher). Mr. Benson didn't know. He said the loons just knew. They just knew some things right from the time they came out of the egg. It was a mystery.

Lizzie wondered if there was anything she knew that she hadn't learned in a book or from a teacher. She wondered if there were things she knew from the time she was born. She wanted to ask Mom about this, but Mom was sleeping, and Mom probably wouldn't know. Lizzie wished she could ask her teacher, Mr. Benson. Or Norry. Norry might know.

Lizzie heard a siren outside and saw red and blue flashing lights. She remembered the night Sheriff Calvin had come and her mom had almost died. It seemed like a long time ago. Then she remembered her deal with God. Mom had gotten better, and Lizzie wasn't sure if she'd kept her side of the bargain. She decided to give God an update.

"Thank you, God," Lizzie began. "I'm really glad Mom is better." She thought for a moment. "And I'm grateful I got to go to the library, and that Mr. Benson has a good home—even though he isn't with me."

She thought a little longer. "Please take care of Norry and Bud and Wendell and Mr. Benson. I'm going to try to be happier and not complain so much. Amen."

Then one day, Laura came home without Mom.

"Did you have a fun day?" she asked.

Lizzie didn't know how to answer that. She had read another book. "Yeah, I guess so."

"You spent the day with your mom, didn't you?"

"No."

Laura gave Lizzie a funny look. "Oh. Okay."

Lizzie waited for Mom to get back. She didn't want to ask Laura why she thought Mom was with her today. She didn't want to know the answer. She wanted Mom to walk in the door complaining about how she'd ended up working a second shift after all. But why wouldn't Laura know that? Lizzie knew. She didn't want to know. But she knew.

Laura and Lizzie had dinner alone. Lizzie heard Laura call Mom when she was in the bathroom, but she didn't say anything, so Mom's phone must not have picked up. Lizzie didn't like the frozen dinner that Laura had made, and so she threw the rest away when Laura wasn't looking.

"I'm going to bed," Laura announced later that night.

"Is it bedtime?"

"It is for me." Laura looked like she was going to say something more. "I hope your mom gets home safe." She looked tired, and she looked a little mad.

Lizzie washed the dishes. Then she dried them. Then she went to bed. She heard more sirens. *Please, God, please don't let Mom die. Please, God, please. Amen.*

She put on her *Little House in the Big Woods* nightgown. She brushed her teeth. Mom would get back soon. She was sure. She turned off the lights in the kitchen and went into their bedroom, leaving the bedroom door open behind her. She lay down on her bed. She heard another siren. An ambulance and a police car parked outside the apartment building. Lizzie stood on the bed to get a better look out the window.

She watched as two police officers left their car. Red and blue lights flashed against the walls. She waited. The police came back. No one got in the ambulance. In a couple of minutes, the police car and the ambulance drove away.

Please, God, please don't let Mom die. Please, God, please. Amen.

Chapter Twenty-Two

Mom came home late. Lizzie was still wide awake in bed. She heard the key in the lock and felt a wave of relief wash over her. Then the keys hit the floor, and her mother swore. Through their open bedroom door, Lizzie saw her mom stumble into the bathroom. There was the sound of coughing, and the toilet flushed. Mom came into the bedroom. She stood in the doorway and swayed.

"Lizzie?"

Lizzie decided to pretend she was asleep. Mom was high. She could tell. Lizzie was glad she was home, but she was frightened and didn't want to talk to her when she was like this. Mom came over to her bed. She didn't take off her clothes or even her shoes. She collapsed onto the mattress and fell asleep in a moment.

Lizzie listened to her mom's breathing. She wondered what would happen next. Would Mom lose her job? Go back to rehab? Stay in bed? She listened to the noise on the street outside and tried to imagine it was the sound of loons calling. Sometime that night, she finally fell asleep.

The next morning, Laura knocked on the wall outside their bedroom door. "Cat, it's almost eight!" she yelled.

"I'm not . . . I'm not going in today."

Laura stood at the door, silent. Lizzie was awake, watching Laura, watching her mom.

"Cat, I got you this job. You can't just . . ."

"Look, I've been working doubles nonstop. I need a break, okay? I'm wiped out."

Laura was still standing in the doorframe. "I'll tell them you're sick. Just for today. That's it, Cat."

"Oh, for fuck's sake, Laura. Do you have to be such a hard-ass? I've been working my tail off every day . . ."

But Laura was gone. Lizzie stayed where she was until she heard the apartment door close behind her.

"Mom?" Mom's eyes were closed, but she was awake. Lizzie could tell from her breathing. "Mom?"

"What?"

"If you're not going to work, do you think we could go to the library today?" Mom didn't answer. "I mean, not right away, but later?"

"Lizzie, I need to sleep. Do you not get it? I need to rest."

Mom's eyes were still closed. Lizzie got up and changed into her Last Resort T-shirt and shorts. Then she went into the bathroom and brushed her teeth. Mom was still in bed. Mom wasn't going to work.

It doesn't mean anything, Lizzie reminded herself. Mom had been working really hard. She deserved to have a day off.

Lizzie closed the bedroom door. She had read all her books. She decided to read one over again. It didn't matter. Everything was okay. Lizzie bit her lip. Everything was going to be okay.

It wasn't until late that afternoon that the bedroom door opened. Mom went into the bathroom, and Lizzie heard water running. When Mom came out of the bathroom, Lizzie noticed she was wearing different clothes, but she still looked tired.

"I'm going to go out and get some things."

"Can I come with you? Can we go to the library?"

"No."

Lizzie looked hard at her mom. Mom kept her eyes down, staring at the floor.

"Why not?"

"Lizzie . . ."

"Don't leave. I'll go with you."

"I told you, no."

"Please?"

Mom didn't answer. She went into the bedroom, and Lizzie heard her swear as she picked up her purse and keys. Then she was gone. The door slammed behind her. Lizzie thought she should run outside and get in the car. She almost did. But then she heard the car start up in front of the apartment. She could tell it was Mom's car because the muffler didn't work. She heard it pull away.

Night came. Lizzie read the same book all over. She finished the book before Laura came home.

"Where's your mom?"

For a moment, Lizzie thought she should make up a story—tell her Mom had just left and was getting some groceries. But Laura would know.

"She left."

Laura didn't say anything. She called Lizzie's mom's number and left a message. It was very short.

Lizzie and Laura had dinner alone again that night. Lizzie went to bed. In the morning, Mom was not there. Laura called her mom again and left another message.

"Should we call the sheriff?" Lizzie asked.

Laura shook her head. "No. I'm not getting the cops involved. Not yet."

Laura went to work, and Lizzie didn't know what to do. She couldn't read anymore without knowing where Mom was. She kept reading the same sentence over and over, wondering where Mom could be. She gave up and went outside. The same mean girls were in the playground.

"Is that the only shirt you have?" the older one asked.

"It's a different one. It's a different color."

The mean girl laughed. Lizzie went back inside. She tried to read another book that she'd already read, but she couldn't get past the first page.

That evening, the door opened, and Lizzie's heart jumped. Finally.

It was just Laura. No Mom. It was evening, but it was still light. Tomorrow was the solstice. It would be the longest day of the year. Mr. Benson—her teacher—had told them all about it.

"Look," Laura said. "I got ahold of your mom."

Lizzie let out a sigh of relief.

"She says she's coming home later, but . . ."

"She's doing drugs, isn't she?" Lizzie said. Her stomach tightened again.

"Well . . . yeah. I'm guessing that's it. Listen, I can't have you here if your mom isn't going to be around," Laura said.

"Maybe she'll be home tonight."

"Maybe."

They didn't say any more about Mom that night. Laura and Lizzie had dinner alone for the third night in a row. Lizzie went to bed early, even though it was still light. She listened to the sounds outside, but no matter how hard she tried, she couldn't imagine the loons calling.

Everything is okay. Everything is going to be okay.

~

Wendell heard the news at the diner.

He had gone to the diner to have his morning coffee. The coffee maker in his apartment was on the fritz. First, Wendell swore. Then he drove to the diner to get a cup of coffee. He brought his unicorn notebook, just for the heck of it. It was kind of nice. He didn't feel like an old guy sitting by himself drinking coffee, because he had a project to work on, although truthfully, most of the time he wasn't writing. He was listening. The diner was a hub of activity. Wendell decided it was not as unpleasant as he'd expected.

The next day, Wendell decided to go to the diner, even though he'd bought a new coffee maker the previous afternoon. Again, he brought his notebook. But before he left, he realized the diner was just four blocks away. Honestly, there was nothing in Big Pine more than four blocks away from Sleepy Pines except the sweet corn stand out on County Road 6. It was an easy walk. It was a nice day. Wendell decided to walk.

"Good morning, Wendell!" a waitress hollered at him as he walked in the door. Wendell was startled. He didn't know how she knew his name. He couldn't remember her name. He knew he wasn't supposed to call her a *waitress*. He was supposed to call her a *server*. Wendell didn't think he'd ever remember that.

"Good morning," Wendell replied.

"Sit anywhere you like. You want coffee again?"

Wendell wasn't quite sure how he'd managed to become a regular in one day, but it appeared he had.

"Um, sure."

"Cream and sugar, right?"

"Um, yeah."

Wendell sat down at the same booth he'd been in yesterday. It looked out over Main Street. Big Pine was a busy place in the summer. And it was almost officially summer. Tomorrow was the solstice.

"Can I get you something besides coffee?" the chatty waitress asked, bringing him a menu.

"Oh. I don't know."

Wendell never knew.

Going to a restaurant was an excruciating experience because Wendell was always overwhelmed by the choices. There were too many. He could never decide. He would feel the tension building as the waitress (server) came by again—and then again, asking him if he hadn't made up his mind already. (They never actually said that, but Wendell was sure that was what they were thinking.) So he'd panic and order the first thing he saw on the menu, and as soon as they wrote it down on their pad, he was sure he'd made a terrible mistake.

The food would come, and Wendell would be filled with regret, thinking of all the things he could have ordered and didn't. Restaurants were always a disappointment. He should stick to coffee.

But then Wendell had an idea.

"What do you recommend?"

Wendell felt fancy, all of a sudden, asking for advice from an insider. This waitress would have the straight skinny. She'd know things he would never guess.

The waitress considered for a moment and then said, "The farmer's omelet is good."

"I'll take it." Wendell handed back his menu without opening it. He felt an enormous burden lifted. Maybe he'd like the farmer's omelet, maybe not. But the decision was made. No looking back. Wendell had asked for advice and taken it. He tried to remember if he'd ever done that before. He didn't think so. No, he was quite certain he had not.

The omelet arrived. It looked good. Wendell tasted it. It was probably the best omelet he'd ever had. This server knew her business, no doubt about it.

"Are you new here?" she asked, refilling Wendell's cup.

"Um . . . yes. I mean, I used to live in Loon Point. Now I live at Sleepy Pines."

"Oh, that's a nice place. Where did you live in Loon Point?"

Wendell wondered whether he had to tell this virtual stranger the story of his house and its collapse and subsequent removal to the county dump. He decided he did not.

"I was staying at the Last Resort."

"Oh! With Norry. Then you've probably heard the news."

Wendell's heart sank. Something awful had happened. Maybe a bear had been to the resort and killed someone. It didn't happen often, but it happened. Or maybe the resort had burned to the ground. That was more likely. Wendell had wondered about the wiring. He had wondered if it was original. Wendell waited, a forkful of farmer's omelet halfway to his mouth.

"No," he said. "What news?"

"Norry's getting married!"

Wendell felt a rush of relief. Then he wondered why he had not been by the resort to see Norry. He'd missed her. Yet he had not been by because he was not a person who did things like that. But he did, he realized. He'd been over to Lucille Munson's house just the other day. Anything was possible.

"And you'll never guess who she's marrying," the server said, leaning in a little closer.

"Bud Gustafson," Wendell said.

The server looked surprised. "You're right!"

Wendell felt the satisfying and unusual pleasure of being in the know. But then, he was an excellent judge of character. He always had been. He knew there was something going on between Bud and Norry ever since he saw that big red truck parked overnight at the resort. Nothing got by Wendell. At first, he'd wondered why someone as independent as Norry would want that big doofus hanging around, but Wendell now conceded that Bud was helpful, in his way, and Norry deserved to have someone give her a hand.

"Yup," the server went on, "Bud was in here telling everyone in earshot that he and Norry were engaged. I couldn't believe it. They both grew up here. They've known each other forever. Isn't it just wild they've decided to get married after all these years?"

Wendell thought about this for a moment. Now that he was an acknowledged expert in interpersonal relations, he wanted to get it right.

"I think . . . I think they are well suited."

"Well, you would know, having lived there and everything."

Wendell was pleased. He was a person who knew things. He knew things about people.

"How's that omelet, by the way?" she asked.

"The omelet is very fine."

"Let me know if you need anything else."

"Umm, yes. One thing . . . What is your name?"

"Shelby."

"Shelby. Thank you. Thank you, Shelby, for the excellent recommendation."

"Oh, you're welcome, Wendell! Thanks for coming in."

Shelby left, and Wendell noticed she was smiling. He might be getting the hang of this.

~

Virgie's reaction was predictable.

Norry and Benson came into her shop to break the news of her engagement, and Virgie's reaction was a full two seconds of stunned silence.

"I said you should sleep with him. I never said you should marry him!" she said. Virgie was outraged that her best friend, who never changed outfits and rarely changed her routine, would suddenly jump at the first proposal that came her way after more than a decade of living happily as a single person. "You haven't thought this over, obviously." Virgie was arranging a jewelry display and—although this was far from Norry's specialty—Norry didn't think she was doing a very good job of it. She was too riled up. "You don't know anything about a person unless you've known them for at least a year," she continued.

"I've known Bud Gustafson for almost thirty years."

"I was using *known* in the biblical sense, obviously."

Since this was the second time Virgie had said *obviously* in the space of five minutes, Norry decided there must be something more obvious to her than there was to Norry.

What was obvious to Norry, when she woke up this morning next to Bud, was that keeping him in her life was the best decision she'd ever made—after her decision to return to Loon Point. Waking up, with his large comforting presence snoring away beside her, filled her with joy. She realized, as good as she had been at filling vacancies in the seven other cabins, she had neglected the one she lived in. There had been a vacancy in her cabin, one she had not recognized until Lizzie showed up. And Bud had stepped in, as if on cue, to fill it.

Virgie might see it as desperate or impulsive—and Norry could see how it would appear that way. But Norry knew otherwise. It was more like inevitable. Norry had spent a long time becoming the new person she now was, and that new person wanted Bud. Resisting the force of Bud would be like denying the coming of spring or the first snowfall. It would do no one any good. It was an immutable fact. It was the change Norry had been preparing for without knowing it.

"I suppose I don't need to remind you he's been divorced twice already," Virgie added. Virgie hadn't lived here during either of Bud's marriages, but everyone knew everything about everybody in Loon Point.

"I don't have a stellar record in the marriage department, either, if you recall."

"Everyone is entitled to one mistake. Two just shows bad judgment."

"Virgie! That's not fair."

"Maybe not." Virgie stopped fiddling with a strand of turquoise beads. She seemed to realize she was making a hash of her necklace display and sighed in frustration. "I guess I'm just thinking of myself. I was with Verne for seven years, if you recall—he was still in the picture when I moved to Loon Point—and he turned into such a raging asshole."

"But he was always kind of an asshole, wasn't he?"

"Yes. But not a raging one."

"I see."

"Oh. I don't know. Obviously, I'm not the one to be offering relationship advice," Virgie continued. But Norry knew she would still offer it—obviously.

"I don't mind your advice, Virgie. I just don't think you're going to change my mind. I know it sounds peculiar to just up and decide so quickly, but I want him in my life."

"So, have him in your life, have him in your bed, have him anyplace you want him. Just don't marry him! At least not right away."

"We haven't set a date."

"Well, don't rush it!" Virgie finally had her necklaces more or less corralled on the display. Norry was surprised to see the final result was nice. Then Virgie looked at Norry. She shook her head. "But if you do set a date, you damned well better make it when I can attend. I expect to be your maid of honor."

Then she grabbed Norry and gave her a fierce hug. This hugging thing was becoming routine, Norry realized, and she didn't mind.

"I just want the best for you. You know that," Virgie said.

"I do."

Virgie took another look at Norry, her hands still on Norry's shoulders, and shook her head again. "You and Bud Gustafson. Well. I guess I can see it. I actually can. As a matter of fact, I think I was the one who suggested it."

"You told me to give him a squeeze. You see what that led to?"

"I am obviously going to have to be more careful with my advice in the future."

Norry smiled. Virgie wasn't mad.

"Okay. I gotta go. Come on, Benson." She gave a light tug on Benson's leash. "I've got more guests arriving any minute. I just wanted you to know before the gossip mill started. I'm sure Bud has told someone. News will be all over Loon Point—and probably Big Pine—by the end of today."

"Bud Gustafson and Norry Last are tying the knot? I should think so!"

Norry headed out of Virgie's shop feeling strangely lightheaded. She had wanted Virgie to be the first to know, and now that she knew, it felt as if it was a done deal, as if they were already married. She wasn't sure they even needed a ceremony if Virgie knew.

The thought of a ceremony made Norry frown. She didn't attend the Methodist church in town. Her father had, but she hadn't been there in ages. Her first wedding had been a pretty formal affair. She remembered she'd worn a long white dress and her father had paid for a lovely reception. There were flowers and music and a lot of froufrou. Norry didn't think she was up to all that again. She wondered if they could elope. She'd have to ask Bud. She was afraid Bud would want at least half of his ten thousand friends to be there. Just thinking about it made Norry dizzy.

Later. There would be time to worry about it later.

Norry pulled into the Last Resort, and Benson jumped out to resume his duties. Norry was relieved she had arrived before her next guests. She never used to leave the resort when campers were expected. She felt slightly ashamed—and a little exhilarated.

Then Norry checked her phone, to see if the guests had sent word of their expected arrival time, and the feeling evaporated. She'd missed a call. There was a short message.

This is Laura. I'm a friend of Cat's. Lizzie says you know her. Please call as soon as you get this.

~

That morning, Mom still hadn't returned to the apartment.

"I'm going to have to make some calls," Laura said.

Lizzie hadn't liked the way Laura said *some calls*. Lizzie didn't know who you called in the Twin Cities when your mom didn't come home. She wasn't sure she wanted to find out. "You're going to call the sheriff?"

"I'm not sure who I'm going to call. She can't leave you alone like this. I can't be responsible for you. Do you have some family I could call?" Laura didn't look mad anymore. But she was frowning as she stared at her phone. She was just sad and disappointed, Lizzie figured.

"I don't have any family here. I have family in North Dakota, but I don't know where they are."

"I see."

Laura had called Lizzie's mom again. Lizzie could hear Mom's recorded voice saying "Hi! This is Cat. Sorry I missed your call. Leave a message." Laura hung up.

"I could go to the Last Resort," Lizzie suggested.

"The what?"

"The Last Resort."

"What is the last resort?"

"It's a place with cabins. I stayed there with my dog when Mom was in rehab." Lizzie pointed to her T-shirt.

"It sounds like an animal shelter."

"No, it's a regular resort."

"A resort? I don't think you can afford to stay at a resort right now."

"No . . . I mean, I just stayed there. I stayed there with Norry." Lizzie could see that Laura was confused. "I went there in a snowstorm when there wasn't any heat in our trailer and my mom wasn't home yet, and Norry—she's the owner—she let me stay."

Laura didn't look like she believed Lizzie. But she got on her phone and scrolled. "Okay. In Loon Point. That's where you used to live, isn't it?"

"Yeah. First in the trailer. Then at the Last Resort."

"Okay. I'll call them. But by tomorrow, you've got to go somewhere. I can't have you here any longer."

"Not until my mom gets back."

"No. I can't have your mom here either. Not anymore."

"Oh. Okay."

Lizzie watched as Laura called. Lizzie could hear the phone ringing in the background. Then the ringing stopped. She heard Norry's recorded voice followed by a beep. "This is Laura. I'm a friend of Cat's. Lizzie says you know her. Please call as soon as you get this."

Laura hung up, then she made a face that was almost a smile and shook her head. "The Last Resort. I guess that makes sense." She looked directly at Lizzie for the first time. "I'm sorry."

"It's okay."

Lizzie went to her bedroom. She'd wanted to say a prayer, but she wasn't sure what to pray for. Mom's stuff was still all over the room. There was a bra and a T-shirt still lying on the floor from the night she came back late. There was a packet of information the grocery store had given her the day she started work. There was a pair of jeans on the bed. Mom's cowboy boots were still in the closet. It didn't look like Mom had thought she was leaving. Not for two days. She had just stepped out the door and disappeared.

Lizzie gathered up the things that belonged to her—her *Little House in the Big Woods* nightgown, her two extra Last Resort T-shirts, Norry's copy of *Little House on the Prairie*, and the book about Minnesota animals. Lizzie gathered her belongings, piece by piece, and put them in the duffel Norry had given her. When she was finished, she sat on the bed with her bag, and she waited.

Chapter Twenty-Three

Norry and Bud drove until it was almost dark.

It was the solstice, so the day lasted longer than usual. But the day grew shorter as they drove south, and the sun dropped lower, and by the time they reached the first ring suburb, where Lizzie was staying, the sun was almost down.

Bud was driving the Last Resort Jeep, and Norry was happy to have him behind the wheel. She hadn't driven to the Cities in a few years and was surprised to see how far the suburbs had spread. Little towns that used to have a lot of space between them had now merged and fused into one more or less unending development. She felt claustrophobic and impatient. They were hitting the end of rush hour—which lasted for several hours these days—and there was a lot of traffic. Fortunately, most of it was headed in the opposite direction at this time of day.

She had left three messages on Cat's phone after letting Laura know they were on their way. Laura had heard nothing from Cat all day. Norry was dialing Cat's number again.

"You might want to just let it be, for now," Bud said. "She'll see all the messages. If it gets to be too many, she might freak out and not listen to any of them."

Norry knew he was right. Bud was an expert at dealing with people in trouble. Right now, he was dealing with an erratic driver on the freeway, careening between lanes. They were in a hurry, but Bud slowed to let the sports car fly between them and the car in the other lane.

"You didn't have to come, you know," she told him.

"Your boyfriend didn't have to. Your fiancé did."

The sports car was now tailgating the car ahead of them. It finally maneuvered its way in front, the impatient driver giving the finger as they passed.

"People have all kinds of problems, don't they?" Norry said.

"They do."

"I mean, problems they never let on to."

"I guess everyone has some kind of problem at some time or another," Bud agreed. "I wonder if we ever really know what's going on with anyone."

"I told Cat she could stay. I offered her the guest room to just . . . heal and get her shit together. But she had to take off—right away. I don't get it."

"It's hard to ask for help, and a lot of folks get mad if you suggest they need it."

"But you do that all the time."

"Do what?"

"Help people who need help, whether they know it or not."

"I think most people appreciate help, most of the time." Bud smiled. "Even if it takes them a while to realize it."

"It can't be very satisfying . . . helping someone who's cursing you out."

"Well, no. It's not. I've helped buddies who were in trouble, and they got pissed off with me when I did, and never thanked me after the fact. But I suspect they'll pass it on when the time comes."

"You think so?"

"I do."

"You're a good guy, you know that?"

"I don't know about that," Bud said, squeezing Norry's hand. "I just know I'm damned lucky."

Norry's phone rang, and she jumped. It was a camper wondering if they could take a canoe out after dark.

"Go for it," Norry said. "I think that's a great way to celebrate the solstice. Uh-huh, it is. Yup, today." Norry hung up. "I've never left the resort for this long with a full house. Can you imagine, when my father started the resort, he didn't have a cell phone? If he was away, there was no way for anyone to be in touch." Norry remembered thinking her father never wanted to leave the resort. She now realized that, for years, he couldn't have left even if he'd wanted to.

Bud was scanning the street signs as they passed. He had the directions on his phone, but being Bud, he was not going to drive somewhere with no idea where he was going.

They pulled up in front of a nondescript three-story apartment building in an older neighborhood. The KFC next door was doing a brisk business.

"You hungry?" he asked.

"No."

"Me neither."

They walked up to the building and found the front door was locked. There was no button outside to summon residents.

"I guess everyone has a cell phone these days," Bud noted as Norry dialed. A moment later, a tired-looking woman opened the door.

"Hey, Laura? I'm Norry."

Laura nodded. "Thanks for coming."

"Any word?"

"Not a thing."

"Did she give you any idea where she might be?"

"She said she was with some old friends. Other than that, I have no idea."

Norry shook her head, then wondered if Laura was going to invite them in. "This is Bud. My friend. My fiancé." Norry hadn't said that before. Bud took Norry's hand.

"Come on in," Laura finally said. "Lizzie's waiting for you."

Norry and Bud entered the small, plain apartment. Lizzie was sitting on the couch. The duffel Norry had given her was packed and waiting beside her.

"Norry!" She ran across the room and hugged her. "I told Laura you would come."

Norry looked directly at Laura. "Thanks for calling. It was the right thing to do. Cat may be pissed off when she finds out. She probably will be. But we'll deal with that when the time comes. I'm happy to take care of Lizzie—"

Norry wanted to say *forever*, but that would sound like a kidnapping for sure. "For as long as it takes."

"I called the rehab place in Big Pine," Bud said. "They can probably get her in if she could hang tight for a little while. I don't know how hard it would be to find help here in the Cities . . ."

"Impossible," Laura said. "I made a few calls. Without insurance and on short notice, it's just about impossible unless she commits a crime or threatens to harm herself."

Lizzie frowned at the mention of her mom harming herself. Norry squeezed her shoulder.

"It's getting dark," Bud said. "We better hit the road."

"You got everything?" Norry asked.

Lizzie looked worried. "I have library books signed out with your card, Laura, that have to be returned. I promised I'd have them back by the due date."

"I'll get them back," Laura said. She shook her head. "You're a good kid, Lizzie. I'm sorry about your mom. I hope everything works out for you."

"Thank you. Thanks for dinner and everything."

"You're welcome. You better get going. You've got a long drive ahead."

Bud picked up Lizzie's duffel, and Norry looked gratefully at Laura. "Thank you for calling and taking care of her. I know this can't be easy for you."

Laura shook her head and looked at the floor. "Shit happens. Cat was trying."

Bud and Lizzie and Norry headed out of the apartment building. The door clicked shut behind them, and Norry felt as if some new chapter had started but was too frightened to contemplate what would happen next. She opened up the back door of the Jeep and heard Lizzie scream.

"Mr. Benson!"

Norry had questioned whether it made sense to bring the dog along, but Bud reminded her it would be cool enough—almost night—by the time they got there and they could leave the window open for him. As usual, he had known the right thing to do.

Lizzie piled in the back seat with her duffel and Mr. Benson, who leaped all over her, kissing her face and jumping up and down before finally settling onto the seat, his face on her lap.

After that, they drove in silence for a while. Norry wondered if her phone would ring with a furious Cat on the other end, demanding they return her child. The last time this happened, she had threatened to call the police. Calling up Deputy Calvin Webb at the sheriff's office in Big Pine didn't sound like a big deal. Calling up the Minneapolis Police Department and reporting a child kidnapping sounded a lot more serious. She'd call Calvin right away to let him know she had Lizzie.

Norry looked over at Bud, who was concentrating on the road. The sky was still light, although the sun was down. She was lost in her thoughts when she heard Lizzie in the back seat.

"It's the solstice today."

"It is," Norry said.

"That means the days are longer, the further north we go."

"Yup."

"Do you think if we drove fast enough, it would never get dark?"

"Probably. But then Bud would get a ticket, and that would slow us down."

It was quiet in the back seat for a while. Norry felt she should say something, but she didn't know what to say. Maybe, as Virgie often told her, she didn't need to do or say anything. After a few minutes of silence, Lizzie spoke again.

"My mom . . . she doesn't mean to be like this."

"I know that. We know that."

"It's hard to kick those drugs," Bud said. "I've had a couple of buddies who've been fighting them for years. It's not easy once they get ahold of you. Your mom doesn't want to do what she's doing, that's for sure."

"I know." Lizzie sighed. Then Mr. Benson sighed, as if imitating her.

"Oh, look!" Lizzie said, pointing out the window. "A star! Mr. Benson said that star is Venus."

"Your dog has an impressive grasp of astronomy," Bud said.

Lizzie giggled. It was the first time she'd laughed since they'd picked her up. "Not this Mr. Benson! My old teacher Mr. Benson."

"Oh!" Bud said. "It gets confusing. There are so many Mr. Bensons."

Norry listened to Bud and Lizzie talk all the way home. She watched Venus get brighter and more stars appear. She watched the traffic thin, and the trees grow more dense. She watched the lights at the side of the highway become fewer until they turned off the interstate onto a smaller county road, and it finally got dark.

At last, Norry and Bud and Lizzie and Mr. Benson pulled into the Last Resort. Most of the lights were on in the cabins. Someone had made a fire down by the beach. The wind was coming off the lake, and the air was cool. Benson jumped out of the car and waited for Lizzie. Lizzie got out with her duffel, and just as she did, a loon called from the lake.

"Well, I guess we're home," Bud said.

Norry wasn't sure he should have said it, but she knew it was what they were all thinking.

~

Lizzie was back in her room with the log walls around her.

On the way home, Bud had told her the good news. He and Norry were getting married.

"Hurray!" Lizzie had cheered, and Mr. Benson had barked. "Maybe Mr. Benson can be the ring bearer," Lizzie suggested.

Norry helped her unpack. They put all her clothes in the closet or the dresser in her room. Norry took the duffel and put it up high on the closet shelf. She didn't say anything, but Lizzie knew what that meant. That meant Lizzie could stay as long as she needed to.

"Wake me up," Lizzie said as Norry put her to bed, "if there's news. Wake me up if we hear from Mom, okay?"

Norry nodded. She looked serious. "How are you, honey?"

"I'm okay. I don't think my mom is, though."

Mom was gone and probably in trouble. Lizzie tried to remember what her mom was like before she was in trouble, but it was hard. Last year, maybe. But even last summer, she was sleeping all day and then up all night and missing work. When Lizzie remembered her mom putting her artwork on the fridge or looking over her tests, she wasn't remembering third grade. She wasn't even remembering second grade, most of the time. Lizzie was remembering first grade, when Mom had snacks with her after school and asked what she had learned. It had been a long time since Mom had been okay. But she hadn't been like this. She hadn't been gone for days.

Lizzie slept through the night, and in the morning when she got up, Bud was in the kitchen eating blueberry pancakes.

"You are up in the nick of time," he winked at her. "I almost got the last one."

Lizzie sat at the table, and Norry gave her a plate of pancakes, and before she had time to ask, Norry said, "No news." Maybe it wasn't right, but Lizzie was relieved. No news wasn't bad news.

The day was sunny and warm, and Lizzie was surprised to see all the campers. There were people on the dock and in canoes and taking out the pontoon boat. It was like a playground except there were grownups too. And the people were nice. Lizzie was picking up shiny rocks on the beach when a boy named Kirby joined her. He lived in Florida.

"Which cabin are you in?" Kirby asked. Lizzie pointed to Norry's cabin.

"You live here all the time?"

"Not all the time. Just when my mom is missing."

"Is that often?"

"Fairly often."

"What's it like in the winter?"

"There's nobody here. And the lake is frozen over."

"No way."

"And the snow comes up to here." Lizzie gestured to her waist.

"No way."

Just then, a familiar car pulled in.

"Wendell!" Lizzie said.

"Who's that?" Kirby asked.

"He's my adopted grandpa," Lizzie said, running over to the car. Lizzie didn't have a grandpa—and she wasn't sure if it was possible to adopt one—but if it was, she hoped Wendell wouldn't mind.

Wendell looked a little different. He wasn't wearing his thick glasses, and he seemed skinnier. He was also smiling, and Lizzie didn't remember him doing much of that before. Lizzie ran up to him and gave him a hug.

"You're back," he said.

"My mom is on drugs again."

"I'm sorry to hear that."

"Yeah. Norry and Bud picked me up last night."

"Where were you?"

"In the Twin Cities."

"Have you heard the news?" he asked.

"What news?"

"Norry and Bud are getting married." Wendell seemed excited—for Wendell.

"Yeah, Bud told me," Lizzie said. "I hope I'm invited."

"Me too."

Wendell was looking off toward the cabin. "Is Norry around?"

"Yeah, she's fixing a toilet, I think."

Lizzie heard someone in a cabin say their toilet was clogged, and she'd seen Norry head off with a plunger and something she'd called a snake.

"I can find her for you," Lizzie offered. Wendell followed Lizzie to the Moose Cabin. "Norry! Wendell's here."

"I'm in the bathroom."

Lizzie led Wendell to the bathroom and found Norry running the snake down the toilet.

"Good to see you, Wendell," Norry said as she wound the snake up. She flushed the toilet. Everything seemed to be working now.

"Yes. I wanted . . . I mean, I forgot . . ."

"You forgot something?" Norry asked, pulling off her gloves. "Did you leave something in the Chickadee Cabin?"

"No. No. I just forgot to tell you something I meant to tell you."

Lizzie and Norry waited. Norry was still on her knees in the bathroom.

"I just . . . it was very nice, the way you took me in when you did. In the Chickadee Cabin. It was a very nice thing to do, and I never thanked you."

"Oh, Wendell, I loved having you. It was nice to have the company this spring."

"No, I know it was . . . inconvenient. And you invited me to dinners. And bonfires. And made a moose pie. You didn't charge me much for rent and you did all that shopping for me . . ." Wendell's voice trailed off. "I just realized I never thanked you . . . I meant to thank you. Thank you."

Just then, Norry's phone rang. She dug it out of her back pocket. "This is Norry," she said.

Then her smile faded. "Oh. When? Oh. I see. Okay. Call me when you know more, okay? Yes. Yes, I understand. Okay. Thank you." Norry looked terribly serious all of a sudden. Lizzie's stomach tightened.

"What's wrong?" Lizzie asked. *Please, God, oh please. Please, God . . .*

"That was Laura, honey. They . . . they found your mom."

"What happened? What's wrong?"

"I'm so sorry, Lizzie. Your mom . . . she had an overdose."

"Is she in the hospital?"

"No, honey. I'm afraid she's not."

Lizzie heard Wendell's sharp intake of breath. "Oh . . . no."

"She's dead," Lizzie said. The cabin started spinning, taking Lizzie with it.

"I'm so sorry," Norry said, reaching for Lizzie. "I'm so, so sorry."

The log walls kept spinning, faster and faster around her, and Lizzie felt herself coming loose and falling into pieces, with nothing but Norry's strong arms holding her together.

~

The details were sketchy, but Norry learned Cat had met a guy she knew from a couple of years earlier when she was working at the grocery store in Big Pine. They'd gone out for a drink. She had overdosed in his apartment two nights later.

Lizzie had very little family, it turned out, and none in the area. There was no father on record. Cat's aunt Esther lived in Devils Lake, North Dakota, and appeared to be the next of kin.

"I can't take care of her" was what the great-aunt told Norry, before Norry had even asked. "I've got a husband with Alzheimer's, and my kids . . . well, they've got problems of their own. I can't take on a seven-year-old at this point in my life. I'm sorry. I just can't."

Norry wanted to say that Lizzie was eight—about to turn nine. But she decided this wasn't important.

Then there were appointments and there were papers to sign, but things went much more smoothly than Norry had ever imagined they could, under the circumstances. With Esther's consent, Norry was appointed Lizzie's temporary guardian.

"What would you like done with the ashes?" Norry asked Esther.

"No point in sending them to Devils Lake," Esther said. "She never spent much time here."

"She has friends in Big Pine. If we had a service up there, could you make it?"

Esther sighed. "I sure would try."

A small memorial service was held at the Loon Point Methodist Church the following week. Bud got the word out around town, and a surprising number of Cat's old friends from the grocery store and around Big Pine turned out. A couple of counselors from the rehab center came. Esther drove up from Devils Lake for it. Wendell was there. And, of course, Lizzie.

The minister who gave the eulogy had never met Cat, but a couple of Cat's friends and coworkers stood up and said a few words about her. They said she had a great sense of humor and had always been fun to be with. They said she had been a caring friend. Norry had never seen any of this. She wished she had.

Lizzie sat motionless and dry eyed next to Norry throughout the service. She was wearing a new dress they'd picked out in Big Pine. The dress was black with just a little trim in white.

"You don't have to wear black, you know," Norry had told her.

"No, I know. I just like it."

Norry thought how much older and taller and more grown up she looked, sitting perfectly still in the pew.

Lucille Munson organized a luncheon in the church basement afterward. Esther thanked Norry after the service. "It was very nice," she said. "You were a good friend to her."

Norry didn't think she had been a good friend to Cat. They'd only known each other because Lizzie had knocked on Norry's back door in the middle of a snowstorm. Norry had never seriously tried to befriend Cat.

Esther looked like an older, plumper version of Cat, with the same sharp nose and chin. Norry glanced across the room at Lizzie, her wild dark hair tamed into submission, wearing that somber dress, and wondered where her gentle features had come from. Wendell was introducing Lizzie to Lucille Munson. He'd been keeping a close eye on Lizzie since her mother's death, bringing her chocolates from the candy shop in Big Pine and playing Uno with her by the lake.

"Cat had so many troubles, as I'm sure you know," Esther said.

Norry didn't know. She wondered why she didn't.

"She wasn't much older than Lizzie when her mother—my sister—died. You know, Cat was there when she had an aneurysm and died, right there in front of her. That was so hard. It seemed like she was just lost after that. Then she was in that terrible relationship. He ended up in prison. Then she got pregnant with Lizzie, and I don't think anyone knew who the dad was. She just had such a hard time of it."

Norry hadn't known. She had known nothing about Cat. She wished she had. She'd made a lot of assumptions, and most of them had not been kind.

"She was such a bright little girl," Esther continued. "It was so sad to see her get mixed up in drugs."

"I promise we'll take good care of Lizzie."

"Oh, I know you will. You and your husband are such nice people. You've been a blessing to Lizzie." Norry decided not to tell Esther that Bud was not yet her husband.

Just then, Lizzie crossed the room to stand by Norry.

"I can't tell you how much you look like your mother today," Esther said, suddenly teary. "I swear, she wore nothing but black for five years, and she was a tall, skinny thing, just like you." Esther reached out and took Lizzie in her strong arms and gave her an enormous hug. Lizzie looked as if she was trying to escape, and Norry was about to rescue her when Esther let her go.

"I need to be getting back," Esther said. "It's a long drive to Devils Lake, and Ralph doesn't do well when I'm not there."

Norry escorted Esther out of the church and watched her get into her old car.

"We'd like to bring Lizzie to visit you in Devils Lake," Norry said.

"Oh, that would be nice," Esther said vaguely. Norry could tell she was working out the logistics of having guests. Esther's life was full. Norry waited while Esther got the old car running and headed out of the church parking lot and back to Devils Lake.

When Norry returned to the church basement, she didn't see Lizzie. The women from the church circle were cleaning up the kitchen. Wendell was chatting with Lucille Munson. Bud was thanking the folks from the rehab center for coming. They were taking the flowers from the funeral to the in-house patients. Norry wondered if those flowers would provide comfort or serve as a stark warning—and decided it probably didn't matter. After the rehab counselors headed out to the parking lot, Norry asked Bud, "Where's Lizzie?"

Bud looked around the hall. "I don't see her."

"Would she have gone back upstairs?"

Bud and Norry went up the stairs to the sanctuary. Cat's ashes were still on the altar, lonely without the flowers beside them. Bud picked up the urn. "I guess we can ask Lizzie later what she'd like to do with them."

"But where is she?" Norry asked again. She felt panic rising. It was now late afternoon. "Where would she go?"

Bud and Norry rushed down the aisle of the church and out the front door. Loon Point Methodist stood on a slight hill on what passed for the main street of Loon Point. Cutting across the main street was County Road 6. The turnoff to the Last Resort was only half a mile farther down the road.

Norry and Bud piled into his pickup. Norry was peering through the window as they made the turn off County Road 6, past the old sign her father had posted so many years ago. It needed paint, she noticed. She was watching the road ahead for a little girl in a black dress, and so she almost didn't see the old trailer, buried in the woods.

"Bud, stop!"

"Here?"

"You never know."

Bud pulled the pickup into the gravel beside the trailer. The door to the trailer was open. Norry wondered if Cat had left it that way.

"Lizzie?"

Norry stepped into the trailer. It smelled like mold. She'd forgotten how bad it was. The ceiling was stained. The carpet was bunched up and filthy. There were still dishes in the sink. And there was a little girl, dressed in black, sitting on the couch.

"Oh, Lizzie."

Norry sat beside her on the dirty plaid couch, and Lizzie pulled away.

"I am not just like her!"

"Like who, honey?" But Norry knew that was a stupid question.

"I am not like her at all!" Lizzie's voice was loud. "I don't lie. She lied when she said she was going to work, and she lied about things getting better, and she lied when she said she was coming home, and when she said I could keep Mr. Benson and get a library card. She lied all the time! She never told the truth, and I am not like her!"

Norry opened her mouth and closed it again. Instead, she put her arm around Lizzie's thin shoulders and sat silently. Nothing in life had prepared Norry for this. Lizzie was staring down at the ugly plaid sofa as if her eyes could burn holes through it. Norry looked up at Bud and saw his face was crumpled with concern.

"No, honey, you are a different person," Norry said. "You are honest and smart and kind. But your mom did the best she could. And she loved you very much."

Lizzie stared at the couch for a moment longer. Then she looked up at Norry, and for the first time that day, looked like the not-quite-nine-year-old she was. Then she threw herself into Norry's lap and finally cried—great, jagged sobs that sounded like they would never end.

The sun slowly lowered over the beat-up little trailer in the woods. Norry held Lizzie tight, and her vision blurred as she tried to focus on the white piping around the collar of this slim little girl dressed in black, who had been asked to take on so much, so early, and had done so well through all of it.

Norry wiped her eyes, and she felt Bud lay his gentle hand on the back of her neck. And they stayed right there, the three of them, just as they were, for a very long time.

Chapter Twenty-Four

The summer passed, as it always did, as they always had. But this one was different for Norry.

By midsummer, Norry could no longer remember what it felt like to come home—after a day of cleaning cabins and starting pontoon motors and signing out fishing equipment and raking out firepits and restocking toilet paper and distributing moose-pie makers—to her small cabin with the maple syrup–colored walls and an evening spent without Bud and Lizzie.

And one day, Norry saw the first loons migrating overhead, heading south, their children left behind to float on the lake for another full month or more. The season was winding down and so Norry and Bud decided it was time to tie the knot.

"Do you think it's too soon for Lizzie?" Bud had asked.

"No . . . no, I don't," Norry said. "I think it will be a good memory in a year that's had too many bad ones."

"We're getting married in the middle of September," Norry told Virgie, and she was immediately engulfed in an enormous hug. They seemed to do a lot of hugging these days, and Norry had decided that wasn't a bad thing.

Virgie insisted she be put in charge of what Norry would wear, and Norry expected she'd be wearing a sixteen-color patchwork dress with a fruit basket on her head. Instead, Virgie had her try on a simple pale-saffron-colored dress with a full skirt and sleeves and a fitted waist that complemented Norry's trim figure.

"I've had this for ages. It doesn't fit me anymore, but I couldn't bear to part with it. Now it's yours."

Then she loaned Norry a silver turquoise necklace. "A rich lover in Santa Fe gave me this," she explained. "And now I've covered three of your four requirements."

"Requirements?"

"Something old, something borrowed, and something blue. If Bud shows up with a new ring, you're all set."

Norry was happy to delegate her wardrobe choice to Virgie, but they had a harder time figuring out who should marry them and where they should be married. Bud assumed it would be in the Loon Point Methodist Church.

"But you never go there," Norry pointed out.

"So? They're always happy to get the business."

"Wasn't your last wedding there?"

"Both my previous weddings were there."

"That settles it. It's time for a new venue."

"How about just getting married at the resort?" Bud suggested.

"At the Last Resort?"

"Why not? Isn't that appropriate?"

Norry waited for the inevitable joke. It didn't come. "Okay," she said, "It wasn't my first choice, but . . ."

"But the Last choice is always the best choice," Bud finished, and he kissed her for a long time.

They decided to have the wedding on the beach, and Norry figured they could fit everyone in the Bald Eagle Cabin if the weather turned out to be less cooperative than Bud was sure it would be.

But then, they needed someone to officiate.

Virgie couldn't do it. She'd already decided she was going to be the maid of honor and wedding planner. Lizzie had been designated the flower girl and Benson was the ring bearer—but only if Lizzie promised he'd fulfill his duties and not run off after a gull and lose the rings in the lake.

"He'll be perfect. I promise," Lizzie said. "Won't you, Mr. Benson?" Benson looked up with what Norry was sure was mischief in his eyes.

Bud suggested one of his fishing buddies could officiate. "He knows a lot of jokes," Bud said, as if this was the primary qualification.

"I don't want someone to make a lot of jokes about how long we've taken to get married after knowing one another for thirty years. We'll get enough of that at the reception."

"That's true," Bud agreed.

"And I don't want someone who is going to drone on forever," Norry added. "Who do we know who talks the least?"

Norry and Bud realized that, for a couple of relatively introverted people, they had a lot of talkative friends.

"Wendell!" Bud and Norry said at the same moment.

"Why not?" Bud asked.

"I'm not sure he'd say anything at all," Norry said. "He'd just ask us if we wanted to get married."

"Is there anything wrong with that?"

"No. Not really. That would be perfect."

"I'll ask him," Bud said. "I already invited him, and he said he was coming. I'll stop by his place and see if he'll officiate."

"Settled."

~

Wendell could not say he was surprised.

He'd never actually told Bud or Norry about his writing and speaking talents, but he imagined it must be self-evident. Bud was not the most perceptive person, but even Bud must have recognized Wendell's innate oratory abilities, because he came over last week and asked if Wendell would officiate at their wedding. Wendell readily agreed. He had the application filled out in no time flat and was now a registered marriage officiant in the state of Minnesota.

And he had been glad to see Bud because Bud was the last person on his list he needed to talk to. He'd been harboring a grudge against Bud. Wendell knew it was more than likely he'd be dead if Lucille hadn't called the Big Pine Volunteer Fire Department and if Bud hadn't gotten there as quickly as he had. Bud got there before the roof collapsed, and he'd climbed right through the roof while it was falling. It was, Wendell had to acknowledge, a rather brave thing to do.

Bud had hauled him out of his house and to safety, and he'd put him up in his home that night. As Wendell reviewed the events of the evening, he realized a volunteer firefighter was not actually obliged to provide shelter to everyone they rescued. Bud had no reason to do that. But he had. Then he'd come up with the idea of Wendell staying at Norry's until there was an apartment available at Sleepy Pines. Bud was responsible for all that. Bud was a terrible nuisance, but Wendell felt he really ought to thank him.

"I've been meaning to thank you," Wendell said.

"For what?"

"For saving my life when my house collapsed. And all the other stuff."

"Oh, anyone would have done the same," Bud said, which Wendell knew was a lie. But now he'd done it. He'd fulfilled his obligations and wouldn't have to thank anyone for anything else.

Except, Wendell was discovering new things every day that deserved a little thanks.

His lot in Loon Point, where the house had once been, had finally sold, and he ended up with some extra money after his bill for the demolition was paid off. Sleepy Pines was subsidized by the county, and so Wendell's social security check easily covered the rent with enough to spare. He had plenty of furniture in his new place and he wasn't putting many miles on the car, so he decided to splurge and get his teeth fixed. Now, when he caught his reflection, he saw the smile he'd always imagined he had. Wendell stopped and smiled at himself every time he passed a mirror. He had a great smile. He had a Hollywood smile. So, Wendell was grateful for the little windfall and grateful for his new teeth.

Then there was Lulu, who cleaned Sleepy Pines. She was really something. She was a widow, Wendell learned from the manager of Sleepy Pines (who was a bit of a gossip, Wendell thought). She had been hired to clean the public areas in the senior apartments, and the old people who lived there made a terrible mess in the rec room, he noticed. (Wendell had always been rather fastidious.) This little Mexican lady, Lulu, she was there cleaning up after everyone. Wendell found out that she came from Guanajuato state, which Wendell had to look up on a map. Her English wasn't perfect, but her Spanish was, and so now Wendell was learning a new phrase a day just so he could talk to her.

"¡Buenos días!" Wendell said one morning. Wendell could see she was impressed, so the next day he asked her, "¿Cómo estás?"

She said she was doing well. Now Wendell had started attending the Spanish classes held twice a week at the Big Pine Community Center so he would have something new to say to Lulu. But no matter what else he said to her, he always said "Gracias" because she worked so hard, cleaning up after everyone. And she wasn't terribly young. She seemed to be about Wendell's age, although it was hard to know for sure because she was a beautiful woman. Wendell wondered if she'd ever want to have dinner with him sometime. He'd like to ask her. But he figured he should ask her in Spanish if he did, so Wendell had redoubled his efforts.

Now Wendell was busy. He had his Spanish lessons so he could impress Lulu (and possibly ask her on a date), and he had this sermon to write for Norry and Bud's wedding. Then, he still had his unfinished project in the unicorn notebook.

That project, he noticed, had shifted in focus considerably.

He had planned to write his treatise on the unfairness of the world—and he still believed the world was a terribly unfair place—but Wendell was no longer sure the world had been unfair to him. When

Wendell thought about that little Lizzie girl, losing her mother the way she had, and Lulu, losing her husband and having to work so hard at this point in her life, Wendell was no longer sure he really had it any worse than anyone else.

It was a new thought.

Instead of cataloging the many ways in which the world fell short of Wendell's expectations, he found himself recording things that surprised him. He wrote about how nice Shelby, his server at the diner, had been when he told her he was officiating at Norry and Bud's wedding.

"You'll be perfect!" Shelby said. "They're so lucky to have you."

That had touched Wendell. It really had.

Wendell looked out his window at the park, and he felt as if he had started a brand-new life here at Sleepy Pines. And, yes, he knew it was a seniors' home, and he probably didn't have a whole lot of time left, but his doctor had been impressed at his last checkup. His asthma was all but gone lately. And Wendell had lost thirty pounds. It was all the walking, Wendell figured. He spent his days walking all over town.

And everywhere he went, Wendell met new people, and he said hello, and he found himself talking more than he ever had in his life. At first, this was kind of hard. But Wendell soon learned he didn't have to say much about himself. People liked to talk about where they came from and what they were doing, and Wendell (probably because he was such an excellent judge of character) found these revelations fascinating. People were pretty darned interesting. That was what Wendell was learning. And, by and large, they were very kind.

So now the unicorn notebook was filled with interesting observations about the people he met every day. He wrote down stories he thought were funny and stories he thought were moving, and Wendell decided maybe he didn't need to set anyone straight. Maybe he didn't need to tell anyone how wrong they were about anything. Maybe he could just listen and write down stories and learn something interesting every day.

~

The day of the wedding finally arrived. Norry knew Lizzie was excited about the wedding, but there were still days when she seemed very withdrawn, very far away, since her mother's funeral. Sometimes Norry would see her sitting alone at the end of the dock, and Norry would go out and sit there with her. Usually, Lizzie didn't say much. Sometimes she had questions.

"What do you think it feels like to overdose?" she'd asked Norry one day. Norry had no idea.

"I think maybe you just fall asleep and never wake up," Norry had guessed.

Lizzie nodded, and Norry again felt that she was woefully unprepared for this task she had taken on. So, most of the time, Norry just listened and watched and tried to be there when she was needed—even if she wasn't sure what to do or say.

They'd begun the process of filing adoption papers, and Norry knew it could be a long road. But the truth was, no one else was fighting for custody of the now-nine-year-old girl, which Norry found unbelievable, and Lizzie had told the social worker her preference was to stay with Norry and Bud. Norry felt sure the paperwork would be sorted out soon. And it didn't matter, because they were already a family.

Lizzie had started school and seemed happy to be back. She loved her teacher, Ms. Hart. And Benson had resumed his previous routine of following his near-perfect dog sense and trotting down the road just in time to meet the arriving bus every afternoon.

But today was Saturday and Norry was getting married.

Bud had spent the night at his old place after going out with some buddies. Norry stretched and enjoyed the full bed, without his large presence taking up more than half the space. *Enjoy it while it lasts,* she told herself.

But Norry did not want it to last. She was eager to cede two-thirds of the bed to her happy, furry, kind, and loving man. And, just as she thought this, she heard Bud's truck pull up.

"Rise and shine!" Norry hollered into Lizzie's bedroom. "People are getting married today and we've got work to do!"

Lizzie appeared at her bedroom door with Benson behind her. She was wearing her *Little House in the Big Woods* nightgown, and Norry noticed the hem was not nearly as close to the floor as it had been. She'd needed all new clothes to start school and, the way things were going, would need more before the year was half over. Her black curly hair was in wild disarray and her eyes were still half closed, but she was smiling.

"Who's getting married?" Bud asked, coming into the kitchen.

"I dunno. I thought I would," Norry said. "I've been thinking I needed to do something different, so I've decided to marry someone."

"Who're you gonna marry?" Lizzie asked, smiling.

"I dunno. Who would you suggest?"

Lizzie pretended to think. "I think . . . I think maybe you should marry Bud Gustafson."

"Bud Gustafson! Isn't he that funny guy who's always wearing a hat? Why would I marry Bud Gustafson, of all people?"

Lizzie thought for a moment. "Because I love him a lot. And you do too."

Bud smiled and turned pinker than usual.

"You're pretty smart first thing in the morning," Norry said.

"Are we having pancakes?" Lizzie asked.

Bud looked at her expectantly. Benson looked up too.

"How could anyone possibly get married without pancakes?"

Norry saw Virgie's car pull up, and she invited her in for pancakes as well. Then the folks bringing the chairs and tables for the wedding arrived and started unloading the truck. Norry thought she should go out there and direct them in the setup, but she knew Virgie would do a better job than she ever could. The flowers wouldn't arrive for another hour. There was plenty of time for pancakes.

"Benson, can I get you a pancake?" Norry asked, and Benson got the first one.

Then they all ate pancakes together. It was exactly how it had always been. And completely different.

~

Lizzie was excited.

Today was more exciting than her ninth birthday—which had been the best birthday ever—so that was saying a lot. Norry and Bud had taken her to a restaurant in Bemidji for her birthday. It was like a giant log cabin, but the logs were dark brown instead of the color of maple syrup, and they told her she could order anything she wanted off the adult menu, which was a terribly hard choice.

Lizzie had ordered walleye because she loved it. And Bud said, "That walleye probably came from Canada!" And Norry said, "Hush! She can order whatever she wants." But the walleye came with shrimp, which Lizzie had never had, and garlic mashed potatoes. And when it was all done, three servers came out carrying a little chocolate cake with a sparkler on top and sang "Happy Birthday," and everyone in the restaurant joined in. Lizzie thought it was probably the best day of her life.

But today was better. Today Norry and Bud were getting married.

Lizzie had a new dress. She was going to carry flowers and Mr. Benson was going to be the ring bearer. Lizzie was afraid she would have to wear the same dress she wore to her mom's funeral, because that was the only dress she had, and she never wanted to wear that dress again. But Norry said she needed a new one for the wedding, and so she'd gotten a yellow dress and yellow sandals to match, and they found a yellow bow tie for Mr. Benson and a matching yellow dog vest with a pocket (which was perfect for the wedding rings), and he was the handsomest thing ever—except maybe for Bud, who looked really good too.

Bud was wearing a white shirt, without a jacket or tie, and dress pants and shiny boots, and Lizzie thought he looked like a movie star.

There were a lot of people at the wedding. Lizzie hadn't believed they would fill all the chairs, but every one was taken. They had waited to have the wedding until September because the resort usually didn't have many guests, but there was a nice couple staying in the Beaver Cabin and Norry had invited them, and so they were sitting with everyone else, all dressed up, and Lizzie thought they seemed happy to go to a wedding as part of their vacation.

And now there was music playing. A woman with a violin was standing in front, right at the edge of the lake, and Lizzie knew she was playing something by Chopin because Norry said Chopin was Bud's favorite music. Lizzie could understand why. It was beautiful.

Then Norry came walking out to the beach in an orange dress as bright as the sun, and now she and Bud were standing with Lizzie and Mr. Benson in front of Wendell, who was wearing a black suit and a red tie. He had a microphone on a stand in front of him, and he looked a little nervous.

The music finished.

Wendell cleared his throat. The microphone made a bad squeaking noise, and Wendell jumped back. But then he adjusted the microphone and spoke right into it, and his voice was loud and clear.

"Life is full of disappointments," Wendell began.

Lizzie saw Norry shoot Bud a surprised look. Bud raised his eyebrows. Wendell continued.

"Things don't turn out the way we expect, and we feel as if life has let us down. Whatever it was we thought was going to happen didn't happen. Whatever we thought we were going to do, we never did. Whoever we thought we were going to be, we didn't become. And that disappointment can make us feel lost and angry and ashamed.

"But here's the thing: Disappointment is an opportunity. Only when we have the experience of being disappointed about important things—about our hopes, our future, ourselves—only then are we allowed to discover there is another way to live, a different life, another choice, a new perspective. Disappointment allows us to set aside what we imagine to be true about ourselves and our life. We have a chance to make new friends, forge new relationships, find new communities, and make the friendships and relationships and communities we already have stronger and more meaningful. Disappointment frees us to discover the people we were meant to be and the lives that are waiting for us—lives we could never have imagined, lives too rich to hope for, before disappointment.

"Norry and Bud and Lizzie have all been disappointed. Yet they are here today because they've decided to become stronger and happier as individuals by becoming a family. A change like this requires courage—which I know, from personal experience, all three have in surplus. But it also requires them to love more, accept more, change and grow together. Becoming a family is an act of imagination and an act of faith. Creating a loving family is tangible proof that dreams can come true, and disappointments can be overcome.

"Norry and Bud and Lizzie, I won't wish you good luck, because you have made your good fortune and will continue to do so. So I will simply say—congratulations."

After Wendell finished, Lizzie had to run and track down Mr. Benson because he had wandered off with the rings. She found him sitting with the nice couple from the Beaver Cabin, who had given him a new chew toy. But once they got the rings back, Norry and Bud exchanged vows, and the violin started to play again, and Bud grabbed Norry and gave her a huge kiss.

"I saved the best for Last!" Bud said. And everyone clapped and cheered, and Mr. Benson barked and jumped up on Norry and Bud and Lizzie and Wendell. Then everyone had lunch at the resort.

It was a perfect day. And Lizzie had a new thought. She realized that this day was not her first perfect day and probably it would not be her last perfect day, and even if bad things happened, she would always have this day on the beach to keep in her mind—this day with Norry and Bud and Mr. Benson and Wendell. This day was a treasure she got to keep forever.

~

The last of the wedding guests were pulling out of the drive. Norry waved goodbye to each of them, watching as the taillights faded down the dirt road, headed to County Road 6. As the sun set over the lake, Virgie gathered up the flowers and put them in Wendell's car. He'd offered to take them to Sleepy Pines for the residents to enjoy. Bud and Lizzie were throwing the new chew toy to Benson and laughing as he chased it along the beach. As Norry walked over to join them, she heard a loon call from overhead. Another loon headed south. It still felt like summer, but the loons knew that this would soon change.

Norry had thought about changing her name—now that she had the chance. She could be Norry Gustafson. She could rename the resort as well, once and for all. It wouldn't hurt business any. But Norry knew she wouldn't.

She knew a lot of things had changed, and she knew things were always changing, and would never stop changing. But she would always be Norry Last. And this place she loved would always be the Last Resort, now and forever—or for as long as forever lasts.

Acknowledgments

I would like to thank my agent, Annie Romano, who called me up and asked me to write this book, and my friend Wally for the inspiration he provided beforehand and the good humor he exhibited after the fact. I'd like to thank Chantelle Osman for taking a chance on me, and Nancy Holmes for her belief in *Loon Point* when the book needed a champion. I'd like to thank retired police chief David H. Miller for his valuable expertise, editors Krista Stroever and Jen Bentham for making the book better in so many ways, and Emily Anderson for her brilliant cover art: www.emilyandersonartwork.com. I'd like to thank my husband, Peter, who makes my writing life possible. And, most of all, I'd like to thank my readers. Thanks for coming along for the ride.

Book Club Questions

1. How did the book make you feel? What were some of your favorite scenes from the book? Why did they stand out to you? Did they make you laugh, cry, or cringe?
2. Which character did you find the most complex or intriguing and why?
3. The character of Wendell is based on a real person. How would you feel if a character in a book was based on you? Do you have anyone like Wendell in your life?
4. What were some of the major themes and conflicts in the book? What contemporary problems were central to the story?
5. This book was told from three points of view: Norry's, Lizzie's, and Wendell's. Would the story have been different if it was told by an impartial narrator? Were there other characters you would have like to have heard from?
6. Did the setting of northern Minnesota affect your enjoyment of the story? Was the location important to the narrative?
7. How would you adapt this book into a movie? Who would you cast in the leading roles?

8. What connections does this book have to your life? Did it evoke any memories?
9. What do you think Norry, Lizzie, and Wendell have in common?
10. What do you think happens to the characters after the novel concludes?

About The Author

Photo © Ian Gough

Carrie Classon is a performer and nationally syndicated columnist with Andrews McMeel Universal. She was born in Minnesota and had a fourteen-year career in the theater, performing in dozens of shows from Oregon to Maine. After founding and running a professional Equity theater for seven years, she got her MBA and worked in international business. She has an MFA in creative nonfiction from the University of New Mexico and has written a memoir, several plays, and more than six hundred columns.

In her weekly column, the Postscript, Carrie writes about the transformative power of optimism and how to find the extraordinary in the ordinary. She champions the idea that it is never too late to reinvent our lives in unexpected and fulfilling ways. She performs a live show featuring material from her writing—and lots of sequins.

Carrie and her husband, Peter, and former street cat, Felix, split their time between St. Paul, Minnesota, and San Miguel de Allende, Mexico. *Loon Point* is her debut novel.

For updates, check Carrie's website at www.CarrieClasson.com or join her friends and family mailing list: https://subscribe.carrieclasson.com.